To Su...

Terror

A Silver ...

Morgan St. James

Morgan St. James
Phyllice Bradner

MARINA

Welcome to
Silver Sisters
Mysteries.

Marina Publishing Group
Las Vegas NV 89141

www.marinapublishinggroup.com

Terror in a Teapot

They all turned around as the door flew open again, making the bell jingle furiously. A whale of a woman with bright red hair, wearing a caftan covered in red and gold swirls, huffed and puffed as she lumbered into the crowded antique shop.

Belle Pepper was three hundred and seventeen pounds of pure drama. She plucked a crumpled hankie from her purse and mopped her damp forehead. "I just came from the Russian church." She gulped, trying to catch her breath as her multicolored bosom heaved up and down. "He's dead! The priest is dead!"

Nora and Dora chorused, "Father Innocent? Dead?"

Belle shook her head wildly. "Not Father Innocent. Father Augustine! He's been murdered. Right there in the church."

With that, Belle collapsed on one of the antique settees in the middle of the store, and Goldie held her breath, praying it would support her mother-in-law's weight.

MORE SILVER SISTERS MYSTERIES
A Corpse in the Soup
Vanishing Act in Vegas
Diamonds in the Dumpster
OTHER BOOKS BY MORGAN ST. JAMES
Betrayed
Confessions of a Cougar
The Mafia Funeral and Other Short Stories
Eight Surefire Signs of a Jewish Mother
Writers Tricks of the Trade
Ripoff (co-author Caroline Rowe)
Bumping Off Fat Vinny (co-author Dennis N. Griffin)
La Bella Mafia:True Story of Bella Capo (Co-Author Dennis N. Griffin)
Incest, Murder and a Miracle: The True Story Behind the Cheryl Pierson Murder-For-Hire Headlines (Cheryl and Robert Cuccio with Morgan St. James)
Can We Come In and Laugh, Too? (Rosetta Schwartz with Morgan St. James)

Copyright © 2014 by
Morgan St. James and Phyllice Bradner

Special paperback edition pricing for quantity purchases by book clubs.
Email request to marinapublishing@gmail.com
Second edition
ISBN-13: 9781496155238
ISBN-10: 1496155238

Library of Congress Control No: 2014904444

Cover and interior design: Joan Hudson

Reviews

Great Fireside Mystery! Morgan and Phyllice manage to incorporate just the right mix of tension and humor to keep it lively and interesting page after page. If you like the warm, friendly amateur detective mystery then this is one you should get and read right away. Don't miss it!!
  ~Sid Weaver, Mainly Mystery reviews

My Cup of Tea. Despite what seems an obvious connection between samovars and the unusual crime spree, the police are not convinced and arrest an innocent local drunk who was simply in the wrong place at the wrong time. What follows is a clever and very funny adventure, from Alaska to Seattle to Los Angeles, as Goldie, Godiva, their eighty-one year-old mother and uncle, Flossie and Sterling, former vaudeville magicians, attempt to save an innocent man and warn the remaining customers (including Caesar Romano) who have no idea of the danger they face—not to mention picking up Flossie's husband's lifetime achievement award and meeting Godiva's column deadlines.

What I really like about this book is the long list of zany characters who we meet along the way, a recurring motif about doubles and twins, and the fact that no one, on the surface, is who they seem to be. Look for surprises right down to the very end.
  ~Mystery Reader

Snappy dialogue, hilarious names, fun mystery fiction! The second book in the Silver Sisters Crime Caper series moves the action from Beverly Hills to Juneau, Alaska, where Goldie, the more practical of the twins, runs an antique shop for tourists. The trouble begins when a delayed shipment of Russian tea urns finally arrives. Goldie quickly realizes the rare Samovars she unpacks are not the cheapies she ordered. But hey, that's business.
  Devilishly clever plots, outlandish names for adorable, well-

developed characters, and hilarious alliterative narration are all part of what makes the Silver Sisters mysteries a hoot to read. And in this particular audio edition, the reader's sense of drama and comic voice characterization add to the enjoyment.

~ Jackie Houchin, Reviews by Jackie

Well-written, fast-paced, full of laughs.　...loved the wacky, cheeky characters in the 1st Silver Sisters book, "A Corpse in the Soup"...tried this 2nd entry to see if it was just as good...was not disappointed...in fact, it is even better...mismatched twins, frumpy Goldie Silver & glitzy Godiva Olivia DuBois (G.O.D.), are still witty, clever and persistent as ever...their nosy, wanna-be elders, mother, Flossie & uncle, Sterling are a riot as retired vaudevillians up to their meddling tricks once again...Goldie's mother-in-law, the hilarious & notorious Belle Pepper, a politically well-connected former cathouse madam, has a larger role in this episode...the villains, the Dumkovsky brothers, like the classic "Gang that couldn't shoot straight"—menacing and bumbling.

..never been to Alaska, but the scenes there convey an authentic sense of the exaggerated spirit I would expect to find in our largest, wildest state...this book is well-written, fast-paced, full of laughs and builds to a great final twist...whether a summer beach day or winter fire night, this is the fun read for any comical, cozy mystery buff!

~Reviews by Messr. E.A. Poe

SAMOVAR. A large metal urn traditionally used in Russia to heat water for tea. The container has a faucet near the bottom and a metal pipe running vertically through the middle which is filled with solid fuel to heat the water. Many samovars have an attachment on the lid to hold a small teapot used to brew the *zavarka*, a strong concentrate of tea. The Russian expression "to have a sit by samovar" means to have a leisurely talk while drinking tea.

Dedication

To our dear late mother and all our fun-loving relatives and friends (in this world and beyond), who have given us a wealth of subject matter to draw upon. And to our loyal readers who tell us how much they love our quirky characters, wacky names and ploys that backfire. We appreciate your constant encouragement and requests for more Silver Sisters escapades.

Thank you to those who appreciate the feistiness of the twins' octogenarian sidekicks, former vaudeville magicians Flossie and Sterling Silver, their mother and uncle respectively. It proves that snow on the roof doesn't mean there isn't fire in the fireplace!

Acknowledgments

Sincere thanks to our first readers for their suggestions, praise, and brutally honest critiques. We are especially grateful to Judy Deutsch for her keen eye and helpful comments. A special thanks goes to Stan Arend for his inspiration for the ending. Kudos to Hugh Kottlove, for constantly cheering us on and for being our consulting physician when we have medical questions.

We are so grateful to Henderson Writers' Group for critiques and help, Sisters in Crime/LA and all of the many people we may not have mentioned by name who are there when we need them.

Chapter 1

Goldie Silver slammed down the phone. *Can't trust anyone these days. Late again. I've had it!* She stomped over to the stairs at the back of the Silver Spoon Antique Shoppe and yelled, "Rudy, get down here."

A balding beanpole in his mid-sixties flew through the open door and ran down the stairs. He tripped over an inert ball of black fur at the bottom and caught hold of the stair rail for support. The fat cat stretched, blinked and slinked toward his favorite perch in the front window. Rudy Valentino turned his back on the finicky feline.

With his shirt sleeves rolled up, orange fluorescent bowtie askew and purple suspenders, Goldie's assistant was an odd looking duck.

"What's up, boss? Need something fixed?" He looked at her expectantly.

She squinted to see the notes on her pad. "Yeah! See if you can fix my problem with the D-C-C-R-M-F-R-R!"

Rudy looked heavenward. "The what?"

"The Russian customs department. All their agencies have names a mile long so I'm just giving you the initials, the English ones anyway. Better yet, maybe you could just call that darn Pistov Forwarders and see if you can get them to track our shipment of Russian antiques. I swear, Juneau has to be the hardest place in the world to get freight delivered. I'll never get those samovars here in time for the church ladies."

"Don't get your britches in a bunch, Goldie, it ain't so bad. There's plenty of places worse'n this."

"Like the moon?"

"Nope, Smarty Pants, right here in Alaska. Hey, take Sitka, for instance. That church waited a whole year for a stained glass window from some fancy Eyetalian glass-makers. They sent it to Stuttgart instead of Sitka. When it finally arrived, they open-ed the crate and it was a Jewish Star o' David. They went ahead and put the darned thing up anyway, didn't they? What the heck? It's a window, ain't it?"

A little smile played on Goldie's lips. "That's not a very comforting story, Rudy."

"Well, yeah, but it's a big point of interest now. Gives the tourists something to talk about. So see, things work out."

She reached for a dusty pleated skirt in McGregor tartan and waved it in his face. "Okay, so, if the church in Sitka doesn't mind having a Jewish star in their window, maybe the Sister-hood of St. Nicholas would be willing to give Father Innocent a nice Scottish kilt instead of an antique Russian tea urn."

"Calm down boss. Our boys in Vladivostok probably just sent the order out a little late."

Goldie Silver plopped down in her chair trying to control her anger. Rudy was right, it could be worse. So far the shipment of samovars was only two weeks late. The door banged open and two plump women in cheerfully flowered dresses marched purposefully to the back of the shop.

Nora, the taller one, smiled. "Okay, Goldie. Let's see what you've got to choose from. Father Innocent will be so surprised when he opens his retirement gift and sees a genuine Russian samovar. We've even collected a little extra money from everyone."

The shorter lady broke in, "You know, in case one of them is really special, but it's more expensive." She grinned, exposing a chipped front tooth.

Goldie winced. Every morning for the last two weeks, the tenacious Russian Orthodox women appeared as soon as she opened. The dear old priest would be leaving them soon, and she understood their excitement at the prospect of giving their beloved Father Innocent such a wonderful gift. His replacement, Father Augustine, had already arrived. Time *was* running out.

"I'm sorry ladies, the shipment still isn't here. I've got Rudy checking on it right now. I don't..."

The two women glowered at her. Nora loomed angry and menacing. Dora shuffled back and forth as though she had to go to the bathroom.

"You said the shipment would be here two weeks ago and you still have nothing to show us," Nora huffed.

Goldie shot Rudy a desperate glance. "Anything on the samovars, Rudy? These ladies—"

Nora pushed up her sleeves like Popeye getting ready for a fight. "These ladies are going to bust some chops if that shipment doesn't get here before Father Innocent leaves."

Dora was more diplomatic. "We can't wait much longer, you know. That nice young Father Augustine has already come to take his place. Nora thinks he's too young, wet behind the ears, you know," she tried to stifle a giggle, "but I think he's real handsome. Clever, too."

Rudy leaned over the counter and patted Dora's arm. "Now don't you ladies get your blood pressure up, we'll get them samovars in time."

They all turned around as the door flew open again, making the bell jingle furiously. A whale of a woman with bright red hair, wearing a caftan covered in red and gold swirls, huffed and puffed as she lumbered into the crowded antique shop.

Belle Pepper was three hundred and seventeen pounds of pure drama. She plucked a crumpled hankie from her purse and mopped her damp forehead. "I just came from the Russian church." She gulped, trying to catch her breath as her multicolored bosom heaved up and down. "He's dead! The priest is dead!"

Nora and Dora chorused, "Father Innocent? Dead?"

Belle shook her head wildly. "Not Father Innocent. Father Augustine! He's been murdered. Right there in the church."

With that, Belle collapsed on one of the antique settees in the middle of the store, and Goldie held her breath, praying it would support her mother-in-law's weight.

Chapter 2

It took three cups of chamomile tea for Goldie's mother-in-law to fill her in on all the gossip surrounding the young priest's murder. "Your friend, Ollie Oliver, is the most worthless Chief of Police I've ever seen. He doesn't even know where to begin. No motive, no clue."

Goldie sighed. "Yeah, I know he seems pretty clueless sometimes, but he tries hard."

Belle harrumphed, gathered up her tote bags and headed for the door. As she was leaving, she called over her shoulder, "Thanks for the tea, Goldie, I'm off to order the balloons for my salmon bake. See ya."

The moment the door slammed shut, Goldie broke out in a cold sweat.

Rudy looked up. "What's got hold of you?"

"You mean besides the missing samovar shipment and Father Augustine's murder?"

"Yes'm, you look like your evil twin sister put the mojo on you."

"Well sort of, but it's really more about Belle. When she mentioned the salmon bake, I remembered I was supposed to invite Godiva to her seventy-fifth birthday bash. I completely forgot."

A swift glance at the calendar confirmed the worst. Belle's big salmon bake was less than two weeks away.

"How are you gonna hornswoggle that stuck up sister of yours into comin' two thousand miles to sing Happy Birthday to someone she don't even like?"

"Ohhh, I don't have a clue. And, that isn't all of it. Belle wants Mom and Uncle Sterling to come, too. I think she's got the hots for poor Unk, and she even wants Godiva's boyfriend

> come."

100 hoo," Rudy swung an invisible lasso with his right
i'm glad I'm not in yer Uncle Sterling's boots!"

1st do me a favor. Try calling Pistov Forwarders again,
and if the church ladies phone, tell them I've gone to Russia to
get their samovar."

Goldie took a deep breath and ducked into the back room.
First she needed to call her daughter Chili, who worked for
Godiva's boyfriend, the famous chef Caesar Romano. Then,
when she got up the nerve, she would have to bite the bullet
and dial her sister's number.

Angel Batista waved a letter in the air to get her boss'
attention. "Wait till you hear this one. You're gonna love it."

Goldie's identical twin, Godiva Olivia DuBois, looked up
from writing an answer for her syndicated advice column, *Ask
G.O.D.* With an all-knowing Mae West look, she fluffed her
mane of silver hair. "Okay, Toots, let's have it, and it better be
good."

Angel giggled. "You put me in the dirt when you do that
Mae West imitation. I'm so glad I left the L.A. Times when you
offered me this job. Besides, it's way nicer working in a Beverly
Hills mansion than a six-by-six cubicle in downtown Los Angeles." She cleared her throat. "Okay, here it is."

> *Dear G.O.D.,*
>
> *I work in an insurance agency and yesterday a client
> came in with her grandson. While she was signing papers
> the little boy pointed to a photo of my husband Jack and
> our dog Bozo and said, "Look Grandma, she knows my
> daddy and his friend's doggie, Bozo!" The little boy looked
> just like him, and the woman gushed about her wonderful
> son-in-law Jack. My husband does spend a lot of time away
> on business trips. Do you think he could be a bigamist?*
> *~Doubtful in Duluth*

Godiva gave a thumbs up. "You're right, Angel. It's a

winner. Answer it like this…"

Dear Doubtful,
Looks like your dog isn't the only Bozo in the family. Tell your hubby you'd like to invite your client's son-in-law over to meet his "double." Be sure to have the video camera running. You might win a prize on America's Funniest Videos. And keep his life insurance paid up. No telling what his other wife might do when she finds out.
~G.O.D

Angel pushed her huge glasses a little higher on her tiny nose. "Good call, Boss. You always come up with such great answers."

"Now it's your turn to answer," Godiva said. "Pick up the phone. It's Goldie."

Angel had gotten used to the E.S.P. Godiva shared with her identical twin. She reached for the receiver just as it began to ring. "G.O.D.'s little Angel speaking, may I help you?" Her stock greeting drew Goldie's delighted laughter.

"Hi Angel, I'll bet Godiva told you I was on the line. Is she standing there looking all superior and smiling like a Cheshire cat?"

"Actually, she is. It blows me away every time she does that. Good thing it's only with you, otherwise it would really freak me out. I'll transfer you to her line." She nodded to Godiva.

After a little warm up chat, Goldie sucked in her breath and blurted out, "Belle's seventy-fifth birthday is coming up on June seventeenth and she's planning a fabulous salmon bake. Half the town is invited and she insists you come and bring Caesar, Mom and Uncle Sterling. I just talked to Chili and she can't wait to come back up to Juneau to see Grandma Belle."

Godiva snorted. "Whoop de doo. Belle's birthday. How exciting."

"Godiva, if you guys don't come I'll never hear the end of it. You'll have fun, meet interesting people."

"Like Salty Sam and the Bear Man from Pack Creek?"

"Don't be such a snob. Besides, everyone who's anyone in Juneau will be there. The Governor, the Attorney General, judges and legislators. Belle has some pretty influential friends."

Godiva winced, picturing hefty, flamboyant Belle Pepper in some outlandish muumuu. Goldie's overbearing mother-in-law was one of those deceptive Alaskans who appeared to be one step above a bag lady, but owned a few million dollars worth of downtown property. Between the shady origins of her wealth and the spirit and energy of a seventeen year old, Belle was a Juneau legend.

Trying to sound apologetic, she said, "Sorry Goldie, there's no way we can come to the party; we have other fish to fry."

"No way, I'm not letting you off the hook. What could be more important?"

"Look on your calendar, Sis, didn't you mark down the Icons of Illusion Awards Banquet on the twenty-second? In Seattle? Remember? Mom and Uncle Sterling are featured presenters at the Convention. There's a special tribute to the Three Great Harry's of Magic. I'm sure Mom told you. We all have to be there."

"Omigod! I forgot to write it down! Harry Houdini, Harry Blackstone and our dear departed daddy, Harry Silver. I promised Mom. I can't believe I forgot."

"Well, anyway, it's impossible. Mom and Unk have lots of rehearsing to do. They have to polish up those acts they do at the Home for Hollywood Has-Beens, so there's no way they can come to Alaska before the Icon's Convention. Not at their age."

"Well that means you and Caesar will have to come without them."

"Nope, I'll be busy helping Mom. Eat some salmon for me, Sis."

"Look, Godiva, I'll move heaven and earth to go to the banquet, but if you don't come up here for Belle's party, she'll beat me to a pulp and I'll never make it to Seattle. How many times have I gone out of my way for you?"

A tiny twinge of guilt must have tugged at Godiva. "Okay, I guess I owe you that. I'll fly up to Belle's shindig with Chili, and I'll try to talk Caesar into coming with us. I'll just stay in Juneau for a few days and we'll fly to Seattle together for the banquet. Angel can make the reservations today. First class, my treat."

"Oh, I knew you wouldn't let me down. We'll have so much fun!"

Godiva sighed. "Well, I don't know about that, but I guess it will be a relief to get away from all the crime in L.A. and spend a few days in sleepy little Juneau. Caesar would probably enjoy it."

"Um, Godiva, things aren't quite as safe and sleepy as you think. You won't believe what happened today. A young priest was murdered, right there in the Russian Orthodox Church."

"Murdered?"

"Yep. Belle was the first to bring us the news."

"Why am I not surprised?"

"By the afternoon it was all over the front page of the *Juneau Fish Wrapper* and the TV crews from KJNO and AlaskaOne invaded the church and sent old Father Innocent into a tizzy. Took three of the worshipers and his helper, Rimsky, to get him calmed down."

"Sounds like you're all wound up, too. How did you get so busy that you forgot Mom's banquet?"

"Well, the church sisterhood collected donations to buy Father Innocent an antique Russian samovar for his retirement. I have seven on order from Vladivostok, but wouldn't you know it? They're already two weeks late and those nice old women are getting very impatient. We can't reach our Russian antique dealers, Minsky and Pinsky, and the freight forwarder isn't helping."

"So how much time is left until he retires?" Godiva asked.

"It was supposed to be next week, but that's all changed now. That young priest was Father Innocent's replacement, so I guess the only good thing about the murder is that they won't need the retirement gift yet. That gives me a little more time for the samovars to get here."

"Yeah, Sis. Some spot of sunshine. The new priest gets knocked off and you're relieved because that buys you time with the samovar shipment."

"Gee, when you say it like that, it sounds terrible. More like something you would think of."

Godiva changed the subject. "Listen Goldie, I'll see if I can have Angel track your samovars. You know how great she is with that sort of thing. And can you call the Baranof Hotel and make a reservation for Caesar and me? A suite if they have one."

"I would, but every hotel in town is booked solid for weeks. Not only is it tourist season, but there's a big Alaska Native convention coming up. Don't worry, though, we'll figure something out. You may not get a hotel room, but you won't be sleeping in the park."

Godiva frowned. "The park would probably be better than that closet you call a guest room. Only one bathroom for the whole house. When are you going to remodel?"

"Come on, Sis. You've become so spoiled. You would think we live in some little cabin at Tee Harbor with an outhouse. I'll try to make some other arrangement for you, but you know my 'closet' isn't all that bad. Will Caesar stay in Juneau until we go to Seattle?"

Godiva grumped back. "How am I supposed to know? He doesn't even know he's going yet."

Chapter 3

Godiva grumbled as she paced around the room, "You know what, Angel? Goldie's getting craftier in her old age and I don't think I like it. How did she manage to trick me into going to that Godforsaken place? Wait till I spring this on Caesar."

"Oh, come on, Boss. Goldie didn't trick you. She just played on your sympathy a little. It would never enter her mind to manipulate people the way you do."

"Angel, I do not *manipulate* people. I use tactical reasoning and the power of persuasion."

"Well, I don't think you'll need to use much of that on Caesar. Alaska's an exciting place. I bet he'd love to go."

Godiva glared at Angel. "That's only because he's never been to Goldie's house. It's claustrophobic, boring, and there's no escape from Juneau, no road out of there."

"But it's so romantic! He'll get to spend time with you away from the pressures of Hollywood, and you'll get a rest from writing your column. Trust me, it'll be fun."

"Right. We'll both work our butts off to get ahead of our schedules so we can take the trip, and then we'll be stuck in that little attic room of hers, pounced on by her outlandish mother-in-law and all of her goofy friends. Yeah, it'll be a blast."

"Oh, cheer up. Goldie's going to Seattle, and you know how happy that will make Flossie and Sterling. Your sister does so much for everyone, don't make such a big deal about doing something for her."

Godiva shrugged her shoulders. "By the way, sounds like there was quite a bit of excitement up there."

Angel pushed up her glasses. "Well, from what you told me when someone robs a candy store it's front page news. So what happened?"

"Murder. That's what. Someone bumped off the new Russian Orthodox priest."

"Oh, that's awful."

Godiva cleared her throat. "Of course it's awful, but Goldie lucked out. See, the victim was sent to replace the old priest who's retiring. The church ladies wanted an antique samovar as a retirement gift and Goldie ordered some from Russia. The shipment is late and those women have been driving Goldie nuts."

"So now the pressure's off because the new guy's dead and they have to wait for another replacement? Man, some luck!" Angel leaned back in her chair and frowned.

"Okay, I know it seems petty, but Goldie really sounded frazzled. I'd like you to give her a call and get all the details. I offered your help to track that shipment down. There, see? I'm not so selfish. I did two nice things in one day."

Angel smiled. "Sure, Boss, if anyone can find it, I can. Maybe it's sitting on a dock somewhere."

After talking to Goldie, she looked over all of the information and placed an international call. Angel first tried the antique warehouse of Minsky & Pinsky in Vladivostok, but had no luck getting through. "No wonder Goldie couldn't reach them. The number's been disconnected."

Godiva looked confused. "Disconnected? Why don't you go online? Maybe they've moved. Meanwhile, I've got to call Caesar. He said he'd go to the ends of the earth for me. Now's his chance to prove it."

She picked up the phone and dialed Caesar Romano's number while Angel logged on to Google.

After about twenty minutes of pounding keys, Angel let out a low whistle. "Well, I can tell you one thing, Boss. Those guys aren't going to be returning anyone's calls. Take a look at this."

Two sheets of paper fluttered out of the printer. She grabbed them and slapped them down on Godiva's desk with a solid thump.

Godiva picked up the top sheet. "What's this? Something from a Russian newspaper?"

"Yep. The first sheet is. I ran it through a language translation program and the second sheet is sort of a loose translation. The article is two weeks old." She jabbed her index finger halfway down the second sheet and read out loud, "Today nothing left of warehouse of Vladivostok importers/exporters Minsky & Pinsky. Last night fire raced through building. This morning, only ashes. Authorities fear Vladimir Minsky of Pinsk and Uri Pinsky of Minsk and all eight workers perished in flames."

Godiva's eyes widened. "Wow. Look at that photo. It sure is a mess. Goldie's going to flip when you send her this. The place is a total loss."

Angel nodded. "It looks like even scavengers won't be able to find anything. A little farther down the page it says that arson is suspected. Guess you'll have to call Goldie and tell her the bad news. Maybe I can find her some samovars on eBay just to get the church ladies off her back."

Godiva shook her head. "I hate delivering bad news. Why don't you call her for me? But first check with that forwarding company. She said Rudy had no luck with them, but Rudy only speaks Texan. Sometimes I can't even understand him."

Angel thought for a moment and then brightened. "Yeah, these shipments take a long time in transit. I'll bet the samovars were sent before the fire. Let me see what I can find out before I call Goldie. By the way, what did Caesar say?"

Godiva held up her hands, palms out. "You were right. No snide comments please. He actually jumped at the chance to go to Juneau and the salmon bake. They have to film two shows ahead anyway, because Chili asked for time off to go up to Juneau for her grandmother's party."

It was clear that Angel loved the idea of being right for once.

"He really likes Goldie." Godiva made a show of clearing her throat. "He said he's always wanted the adventure of seeing Alaska. He'll get an adventure, all right."

"Of course it will be an adventure."

"Ah, Angel, that's not what I meant. Wait until he sees

Goldie's guest room. A double bed in a little loft. You bump your head on the ceiling when you get up. And the narrow stairs are only a little better than a ladder. One bathroom for everyone. Wow. I can hardly wait."

"It can't be that bad."

"Yes it can! Just keep checking all the hotels to see if you can find a cancellation. Hmmmph. You practically need a Sherpa just to get up to the house. There must be a gazillion stairs."

Chapter 4

"So, what's that big smile about, Goldie? Did ya talk yer high falutin' sister into comin' to Belle's shindig?"

"You bet. She reminded me that I told Mom and Unk I'd go to Seattle for the Icons banquet. Of course I would have done that anyway. I wouldn't disappoint the old folks for anything, but now she's picking up the tab." Rudy gave her a victory sign, hitched up his striped pants and started toward the back of the shop to continue his tinkering.

"Hey, Rudy," Goldie called out, "maybe things are looking up. When I told Godiva about our samovar problem, she even offered to have Angel track them down. That girl is really a whiz."

He turned around before disappearing through the beaded curtain. "How 'bout that fancy chef of hers? Is Belle gonna have her Hollywood celebrity at the party?"

"If I know my sister, she'll get him to come. You know how she likes to show off."

Rudy jabbed his thumb against his thin chest. "Bet my buddies can teach him a thing or two 'bout how an Alaskan cooks a salmon."

Goldie chuckled as she pictured one of the grizzled fishermen giving advice to the slick Italian chef. "I wish Mom and Uncle Sterling could come too, but I guess all that traveling really would be too much for them. At least Red's ship is in port that night. His mother would never forgive him if he missed her big day."

"Oh, ya know Belle. She'd have called out the Coast Guard to bring him back to port."

"You got that one right! The best part is I'll have my husband with me for a whole day."

"Let's hope that Angel gal finds them samovars," Rudy called over his shoulder.

Midnight the cat padded over and rubbed against Goldie's leg. A moment later the huge feline jumped into her lap, snuggled up and let out a few enormous puffs of tuna fish breath.

"Ooooh, Midnight, we need to do something about your breath. Belle's friend Molly brushes her cat's teeth with chicken flavored tooth paste—would you like that?"

Midnight narrowed his eyes and stuck out his little pink tongue. "Mrrrroowww," he said and jumped down. He headed for his favorite footstool in the shop window and never looked back.

The old-fashioned phone on the sales counter rang twice. "Silver Spoon Antiques. Goldie speaking."

"Oh, Goldie," Angel said, "I had to call you right away. You're not going to like this. I'm afraid your samovars may be toast."

An involuntary shudder ran through Goldie's body. "Toast?"

"Yep, as in burned to a crisp. I found an article online from the Vladivostok newspaper that said Minsky & Pinsky's warehouse burned to the ground two weeks ago."

Goldie let out a gasp.

"It gets worse. It looks like your importers died in the fire along with all their employees. A real tragedy. They think it was arson. Everything was a total loss. I'm so sorry to have to tell you this."

It took Goldie a moment to compose herself before she said, "Oh, no! Poor Uri and Vladimir! I never expected anything like that."

When Angel spoke again, her voice brightened a little, "Goldie, there is one glimmer of hope. Maybe the samovars were sent out before the fire. I sweet-talked the guys at Pistov Forwarders and they agreed to at least check and see if they received that shipment. I figured, maybe we'll get lucky. Anyway, you're supposed to call a Mr. Slackanov. He's the one going through the bills of lading. Let me know what happens."

Goldie looked up the number for Pistov, while mumbling to herself about the moon being on Mars and other astrological portends of disaster.

After several rings she heard a barrage of Russian on the other end. "English, please," she shouted into the phone.

"Okay. Okay. Slackanov here. What you want?"

"Mr. Slackanov, this is Goldie Silver from Silver Spoon Antiques in Juneau, Alaska. Angel Batista called you this morning about my problem with the missing shipment of samovars. She said you were checking to see if you ever received them from Minsky & Pinsky in Vladivostok. Did you find anything?"

"Oh, yeah, yeah. I talk two times to some guy in your shop. I tell him I can't find. He yell at me and I hang up. But now your little Angel call, and she very nice, so I look up."

There was a silence on the other end of the line.

For a moment Goldie thought they had been disconnected. "Well, did you find the shipment?"

"No, no. No shipment. But maybe you didn't hear about Minsky & Pinsky? Whole place up in smoke. Poof! Like burnt shish kabob. Only thing we are sending to Alaska, week and a half, maybe two, is shipment of Siberian parkas to Anchorage. Handmade, very good quality. No samovars to Juneau. Sorry."

The next thing Goldie heard was a click. After years of experience, she knew that a high percentage of shipments coming to Alaska, especially from Russia, were subject to some mix-up or another. Armed with the information from Slackanov, she decided to check with customs in Anchorage just in case.

When the customs agent heard her story, he scoffed. "Lady, do you have any idea how many files I have to go through to find out if some fool in Russia mistook a crate of samovars for a crate of parkas?"

Goldie put on her sweetest voice, syrup dripping from every word, as she convinced the reluctant bureaucrat to check through reams of paperwork. When the customs agent came back on the line Goldie let out a whoop of joy. "You did. Thank you. You don't know how much this means to me. I'll make all the arrangements. Thanks again."

She hung up the phone, and dialed a number in Anchorage, which was followed by a call to Alaska Marine Lines. Five minutes later she called out, "Rudy, come over here. You'll never believe what happened."

"Hold yer horses. I'm comin'." He skidded to a stop in front of her. "Okay, what in tarnation happened that's got you so het up?"

"Apparently some idiot at Pistov bundled our crate in with parkas going to Anchorage. The customs office got a call three days ago from Wilderness Wear on Spenard Road. The fellow who called said they received someone else's shipment of samovars and Russian antiques along with their fur coats. Of course, no one bothered to track us down. Apparently our name was misspelled on the packing slip."

"Well, that's just great, Goldilocks. Them church ladies will be plum tickled. How long do you reckon it'll take for those dang teapots to get here?"

Goldie frowned. "That's the hitch, Rudy. The customs guy said there's all kinds of paperwork, and Alaska Marine Lines only loads on Fridays, so they still won't be here for about a week and a half." Goldie threw up her hands in exasperation. "Why can't just one thing be easy?"

Chapter 5

Godiva slumped down in the plush limo seat, clutched her latte vente, and grumbled all the way to LAX. "It's inhuman, getting up so early to catch an eight o'clock flight. What were we thinking? Couldn't we travel at a civilized time, like noon?"

Caesar patted her knee. "There, there my love. Once we get on the plane, you can sleep all the way to Seattle."

Chili looked over her shoulder. "And you can sleep all the way to Juneau, too, Auntie. Glad we didn't get the 'milk run.' That one takes forever with stops at Ketchikan, Wrangell and Sitka. I can't wait to get there and show Caesar my home town."

They crawled along in the security line for over an hour until they finally made their way to the gate, and arrived just in time for boarding.

As they settled into their seats in the second row, Godiva looked around and mused, "Well, at least we're traveling First Class, although there's really nothing very classy about it. Can you imagine being crammed into one of those coach seats? Ugh."

Chili leaned across the aisle. "The coach seats are a little tight, Auntie, but if you think that's bad try flying in a float plane."

"You know, Godiva, I'm pretty excited about seeing Alaska." Caesar patted her arm and gave her a peck on the cheek. "I've been all over the world, but that's one place I've never been."

Godiva smiled up at him. "Well, Caesar, don't be surprised if there's a lot of hoopla at the airport. After all, those small town hicks don't get to see celebrities like us very often."

The plane coasted to the gate, while Caesar gawked at the majestic mountains and scenery showcased by a glorious summer day. For some reason, he expected to see snow in Juneau. There was no snow in sight, not even a characteristic drop of rain. Instead, the intense green of the Northern rainforest took his breath away.

In the terminal, a huge crowd had gathered at the bottom of the escalator, waving banners and cheering. Godiva heard shouts behind them and when she turned to see what the racket was about, saw lots of kids in matching outfits lining the escalator, waving and gleefully shouting. She nudged Caesar. "Must be cheerleaders or something. They should know better than to do all that jumping and shouting on the moving stairs."

"Never mind about those kids, *cara mia*. You better put on your best smile, because that's quite a crowd waiting for us down there. I guess they'll be wanting autographs." He ran his free hand through the silver hair at his temples.

As they reached the bottom of the escalator, none of the adoring fans approached them.

"They must be overwhelmed by us."

Godiva eyes widened when she realized what the crowd was chanting. She tugged at Caesar's sleeve.

"Juneau Jumpers, Juneau Jumpers. You're our champs." Caesar read the lettering on the banners aloud, "Welcome Juneau Jumpers. National Champions."

Chili clasped her hands and let out a cheer. "Wow, this is *sooo* cool! Isn't it great? Our Jumpers won the National Title!"

Godiva huffed. "What, may I ask, are Jumpers?"

"It's a jump rope team. They're really hot!"

Godiva and Caesar squeezed past the cheering mob. How humiliating! No one even glanced at them. When they rounded the corner, Caesar caught a glimpse of what turned out to be their welcoming committee. Holding back a chuckle, he pointed toward the baggage carousel. "Look over there. Some people are really a joke."

On the other side of the room, Belle Pepper, larger than life in a purple muumuu covered with yellow and red flowers, waved wildly. Her broad-brimmed yellow hat, decorated with a stuffed hen nestled in deep purple plumes, set off her flaming red hair.

A short, plump woman in a violet pantsuit hovered near Belle. She wore a luscious lime green derby topped by an orange velvet flowerpot overflowing with silk poppies. Goldie, whose dress might have been made with fabric from discarded draperies, was wedged between them.

Godiva snickered. "Caesar, my dear, that's *our* cheering section." She pouted. "Humph! Imagine that. All those people were here for a silly jump rope team, and no one even noticed us." She waved to the colorful trio as she dragged Caesar toward the baggage carousel with Chili trailing behind.

Amid a wild flapping of her flowered tent dress, Belle wrapped her arms first around Chili and then around the astounded chef and bellowed, "Welcome to Juneau, Chef. This here's my friend Clara." She merely nodded to Godiva, focusing all of her attention on Caesar.

Goldie hugged her twin and stifled a giggle as she whispered, "Guess she's after your boyfriend. Better look out."

Alaskan travelers claimed duffel bags, duct-taped suitcases, insulated fish boxes, and chain saws while matched sets of Samsonite, American Tourister and Ricardo bags were rolled away by the tourists. The luggage carousel was nearly empty; still no sign of Godiva's three Louis Vuitton traveling cases or Caesar's leather valise.

"Don't worry," Clara said. "They lose luggage here all the time. One time they lost a whole suitcase full of *lutefisk* my brother was bringing me from Petersburg. They sent it up to Fairbanks, and from there it went to Memphis. By the time I got it back it smelled pretty bad. But they found it! They'll find your stuff, too. Hope it doesn't have any fish in it!"

Belle and Clara howled with laughter as Caesar and Godiva exchanged bewildered looks.

"What's *lutefisk*?"

Chili pulled Godiva aside. "It's really awful, Auntie. It's a kind of dried fish soaked in lye. The Norwegians love it but it tastes like soap and smells so bad it would gag a goat."

Godiva nodded, "Why am I not surprised?"

"Sorry to rush," Belle said as she took Clara's arm and headed toward the door, "but we promised to meet the Gastineau Gadabouts for a Mad Hatter's fashion show."

"That's why we have our finery on." Clara patted her flowered hat.

"See you back at my house later." Belle chirped over her shoulder. The two women made their way across the parking lot and climbed into Belle's pink Cadillac.

Meanwhile, Godiva raised hell with the baggage handlers, the ticketing agents and the Assistant Manager of the airport, but in the end they had to file a lost baggage report.

Godiva took a handkerchief from her purse and wiped the dusty seat of Goldie's beat-up old Subaru before sliding in.

"So, did you manage to get us a hotel room?"

Goldie cleared her throat. "Um, not exactly. Everything in town is still booked solid, but Belle has offered to have you stay with her. There's always my guest room, or you could grab the one unbooked cabin at the Last Resort B&B."

"I knew you'd find us something, Sis. Tell me about the Bed and Breakfast place."

Trying to keep a straight face, Goldie answered, "It's a charming group of cabins on Thunder Mountain Road. You'll really like my old friends Moonbeam and Stoney who own the place. Of course it is pretty rustic."

Godiva didn't sound as sure as she had a moment before. "And, rustic means..."

"A private outhouse for every cabin. I'm sure you'd be more comfortable there than in my little 'closet of a guest room'."

Caesar broke in, "Surely you don't mean one of those little houses with the half moon on the door and a hole in the floor."

"Oh no, Caesar, they're much more modern than that. Last year they replaced the lanterns with electric lights and put padded toilet seats over the holes in the plank benches."

Caesar's voice sounded strained as he said, "And your mother-in-law's accommodations?"

Goldie hopped right on it. "She's in the heart of downtown so you can walk around on Franklin Street. You can do some tourist things on your own, without having to trudge up and down my hill."

Godiva threw up her arms in protest. "Oh, no you don't. You're not going to get away with that. I'll take the closet before I take Belle. That woman is unbearable."

Caesar chuckled. "Oh I don't know, my love. Maybe it's just because you're jealous. She gave me such a warm welcome. Shouldn't we take a look?"

Godiva chose to ignore the last suggestion and changed the subject. "What happens if they don't find our luggage? Maybe we should go shopping for something to wear to the party. After all, Caesar and I have to keep up our images. Do you have any decent stores here yet? Nordstrom's? Saks?"

"'Fraid not, Sis. Your choice is Fred Meyers, Gottschalk's, or the Nugget Outfitter. We could try some of the little stores downtown, but by the time we get there, they'll probably be ready to close for the night."

"You could try Mom's favorite place, the Salvation Army Thrift Shop," Chili offered. "And I like this really cool shop in the Nugget Mall." She looked at her aunt and hesitated, then added, "No, forget that, they only go up to size ten."

"Those are the choices? Nothing else?" Godiva groaned.

"Nope. Don't worry, you can borrow something from me, and Red can lend Caesar some clothes. Might be a little big, but no one will notice."

Caesar made no comment. Godiva sighed. "Maybe the luggage will show up in the morning."

Avoiding more discussion about Belle's guest room, Godiva said, "So, Goldie, Angel said you found the samovars after all. What happened?"

"She's the best! She got me through to the right guy, but they couldn't find the records. Rudy was ready to throw in the towel but I called customs and discovered that my samovars wound up in Anchorage with a crate of Siberian parkas. They'll be delivered sometime tomorrow. Good thing, too, because the women in the Sisterhood of St. Nicholas were ready to tear me limb-from-limb."

"Did they find out anything more about that young priest's murder? Who would have expected something like that to happen in sleepy little Juneau? I was shocked when you told me. "

Goldie shook her head. "Nothing yet. The police are stymied. Everyone says that Father Augustine was so nice. Why would anyone want to kill him? Now poor old Father Innocent is waiting for another replacement. He's really been going downhill, you know." She tapped her forehead to indicate mental decline. "According to Nora, one of the church ladies, his assistant does almost everything around the church now. I hope another priest gets here soon."

After giving Caesar a little tour of the area, Goldie drove downtown and parked in front of a four-story building. The Grizzly Bear Gift Shop and the Hitching Post Saloon occupied the entire ground level with offices on the middle floors.

"What are we doing here?"

"Please Godiva, just look at Belle's guest room. You can make up some excuse why you can't stay there, but I don't want her to feel like she's been snubbed. We need to keep peace in the family, after all."

"All right, I'll look. But I'm relying on Caesar to save us from this fate." She squeezed his hand. "You're the actor, darling—break a leg."

They rode the elevator to the top floor and Belle met them at the door. "Still no luggage?" she boomed. "Well, don't worry, I've got lots of extra clothes."

Godiva looked at Belle's huge shocking orange tunic covered with hot pink flamingos, and bit her tongue.

Goldie's mother-in-law showed them around her flat, which spanned the entire fourth floor of the building, one of five she owned in town. She ushered them into a huge living room and dining room decorated in more crystal and gold leaf than an imperial palace. Statues and doodads adorned every available surface.

She led them down the hall and they peeked into her bedroom. Godiva tried not to gasp as she surveyed the huge room decorated entirely in red and black velvet, complete with a quilted spread, tufted headboard, flocked wallpaper and a genuine velvet painting of Elvis.

When Belle flung open the door to the guest room, Caesar's jaw dropped in amazement. A gold leafed, bejeweled four poster bed sat atop a broad platform in the center of the room. The metallic gold bedspread, highlighted by rhinestone-studded side curtains, glinted in the light of the crystal chandeliers sparkling over the ornate nightstands. The entire place reeked of a heavy musk scent.

"My goodness, Belle," Godiva said. "Where did you ever find this bedroom set? It's like something out of a movie." Then she thought, *porno movie!*

"When I retired, this furniture is the only thing I kept from my place of business," Belle answered.

Caesar smiled, "It must have been quite the showcase."

"Oh yes! Every room had a fantasy theme, and my girls had costumes to match." Belle's eyes twinkled. "All the customers loved it."

"Hmmm..." Godiva mused, "I'm sure they did."

Suddenly, Caesar began to sniffle and cough slowly escalating to a believable sneezing fit. He pulled out a handkerchief and held it in front of his face, alternately hacking and sneezing. "Belle, my dear," he said, "it is so sweet of you to offer this wonderful room to us, but I must be allergic to your delightful perfume. It's such a beautiful room. Godiva, I'm so sorry to disappoint you darling, but my allergies—"

They made a graceful exit before the aroma of musk asphyxiated them all.

Chapter 6

On the day of Belle's party, a light drizzle hung in the air. Red maneuvered Goldie's 1987 Subaru station wagon into a parking space only steps from the entrance to the Thane Ore House. A hand lettered placard, "Closed for Private Party", covered the Gold Rush style lettering "Salmon, Halibut, Ribs," on the wooden signboard. They all piled out of the car like five circus clowns emerging from a gaily painted Volkswagen.

Godiva shook her head. "I can't believe you're still driving this thing. It looks like it has a serious case of mange."

"Yeah, I guess it does have a 'Juneau body'," Goldie said apologetically as she smoothed down a piece of duct tape on the left front fender. "A little rust here and there, but it still runs good."

"Yes indeed," Red added, "trusty Old Paint makes it up the hill every time. No need to get anything fancy in this town."

Godiva wobbled around the gravel parking lot in her Italian high-heeled boots. She plucked at the sleeves of Goldie's peasant blouse. "Speaking of fancy, I sure do feel *fancy* in these rags of yours. Boy, it's a good thing nobody knows me around here." Her borrowed skirt and vest looked like remnants of a patchwork bedspread.

"I think you look positively charming, my dear." Caesar put his arm around her shoulder and pecked her cheek. "Unfortunately, I can't say the same for myself," he continued, trying to tuck Red's extra large plaid shirt into oversized Levis cinched at the waist with his own gold-buckled Gucci belt.

Chili turned her face toward the sky and tiny droplets settled on her nose. "Wow, it's not raining! What a great day for Grandma's party."

"Not raining? What do you call this?" Caesar held out his

damp sleeve.

Red laughed heartily. "Just a heavy mist, old boy. Certainly doesn't qualify as rain." He gave the wussy Californian a manly slap on the back.

As they started down the trail toward the Ore House, a tour bus pulled up behind them with a banner taped to the side that said, "Belle's Salmon Bake, Climb Aboard". Goldie whispered to her sister, "Belle wanted to make sure all the folks she invited from the Glory Hole Soup Kitchen had a way to get here."

Godiva surveyed the passengers as they got off the bus, then said sarcastically, "I guess I'm dressed just right for this crowd."

A huge man—or maybe it was a woman—wearing floppy red high-tops and a Mohawk hairdo stumbled off the bus followed by a scruffy fellow in a threadbare gray halibut jacket. A Lincoln Town Car with Alaska license plate Number One zipped in and parked beside the bus.

"Hey, cool. It's Governor Pickle and his wife, Emily." Chili waved to them.

The governor was all smiles. He even shook the hands of folks who probably didn't vote. His wife caught sight of the Peppers and extended her arms.

"Goldie, Red, how good to see you!" She turned and did a double take. "And you must be the sister who writes that entertaining column." She clasped Godiva's hand.

She called out, "Chili dear!" and took a few steps toward Goldie's daughter, then gave her a big bear hug. "I can't believe it! A television star. Is this your fabulous Chef Romano?"

"You certainly made a good choice for your assistant, Chef Romano." She held out her hand for a polite shake.

The Governor joined his wife. "Chili's quite the little chef herself, you know. She helped our kitchen staff make thousands of hors d'oeuvres for the Christmas open house. Everybody raved about them."

He put his arm around Chili's shoulder. "Saw you on TV, young lady, and you looked damn good! Never thought you'd catch ol' Willy Pickle watching a cooking show, but your grandma made me promise. And you know, if Belle says do it, you do it."

A crusty old fellow walked up the path from the beach below the Ore House, his knee-high rubber boots turned down to his ankles, Brillo pad hair bristling out from under a cap with a "Salty Dawg Charters" logo. "Well, if it ain't the Pickles and the Peppers! All you guys need fer a perfect appetizer's a little Herring, and here I is!" He turned to Caesar and held out a sandpaper hand. "Name's Herring, the wife calls me Stanley, but everyone else calls me Salty. Salty Herring, get it?" He pumped Caesar's hand.

"Ah, yes, Salty Herring, very catchy. Call me Caesar." He smiled broadly and gestured toward Godiva. "And allow me to introduce you to this lovely lady."

Goldie and Godiva were standing next to each other, and Salty looked intently at one, then the other.

"Well, one of 'em's Goldie, but now ya got me goin'." He stared a little longer, eyed Godiva's high-heeled boots and pointed to her. "I 'spect this one here must be that twin from Californie. Belle tol' me all about ya." He tipped his hat. "Good ta meetcha, Missy."

Godiva reluctantly took his outstretched hand.

They all headed to the Ore House to look for the birthday girl. They found her behind the big barn of a building, presiding over the bank of outdoor grills where fresh salmon and halibut sent out luscious aromas. Caesar headed straight for the barbeques. Within minutes he was engaged in lively conversation with the chefs, checking out what the locals were doing at the grills and asking questions about the sauces and seasonings.

Belle bounded toward them like an oversized St. Bernard puppy swathed in a bright red dress with dazzling marine life swimming across her bosom and bottom. "Darlings! Isn't it a fabulous day?" she sung out in a booming alto. "Willy, Emily, I'm so glad you could come." She bussed their cheeks. "Godiva, looks like you already lost your beau to the lure of the salmon." She nodded in Caesar's direction.

"Salty, you old scumbag, now don't you try flirting with these beautiful women. Your wife's over there by the lemonade—got her eye on you." She scurried around like a hen gathering her chicks. "Come on, come on, grab some plates, fill 'em up. Mingle." And in a twinkling, she was gone, dragging the Pickles with her.

Godiva felt the presence of someone close at her elbow and turned to find herself level with a set of confused eyes. The meek little woman wore four threadbare coats, one on top of the other. She looked from twin to twin. "Are you both Goldie? I see double lots of times, ya know…"

"It's all right, Ella, you're not seeing things. This is my twin sister Godiva. We look alike." Goldie turned the Coat Lady around and pointed to the tables full of food. "Go find a plate and fill it up. Get a nice big piece of cake, too." As Ella drifted away, Goldie explained how this bewildered little street person wore the coats summer and winter, carrying her closet on her back.

"Belle sure does know some oddballs—" Godiva began, but Goldie cut her off.

"Everybody's odd in one way or another, Sis. If they were rich, most of the Glory Hole folks would be called eccentric. Given enough money, they might even be in politics or something." She sighed. "But people like the Coat Lady, and Red Shoes, and Jack, over there, just don't have that luxury."

Godiva followed her glance across two tables to Jack and his bedraggled dog. Jack wore a cape made of plastic bags over his clothes. The dog, an Australian Shepherd crossed with something, sat on the bench beside his master, delicately sharing a plate of salmon and potato salad.

Red led the twins over to a group of raucous fishermen who were debating the fate of the salmon industry. A burly fellow with unruly blond hair shouted to Red, "Hey, Cap'n, I hope you don't serve any of that farmed salmon on your ship. If ya do, I might have to shoot ya!"

He shook the man's hand as they came face to face. "Tell you what, Tommy, the Empress Line tried to put that crap on the menu, but I told 'em I wouldn't sail the ship to Alaska unless they let me serve the real thing."

"Cap'n, my Cap'n," an old salt with four missing teeth and three missing fingers chimed in, "you are truly a fisherman's friend. And you have a lovely wife to boot, or maybe it's two wives you have now." He looked from Goldie to Godiva.

"Haw, haw." A big guy with a face like cottonwood bark slapped his leg, and some of the dried fish scales covering his overalls flew into the air like little silver snowflakes. He said to his mates, "See, the Cap'n here has it all figgered out. Ya get yerself two wimmin what looks alike, an' ya never have to remember which is which. Ya jus' calls 'em both Honey."

Goldie shook her head. "Andy, you're going to give my sister a bad impression of Alaska fishermen." She scanned the group. "Listen up, gentlemen, this is Godiva, she's very influential. Her boyfriend is that famous TV Chef over there." She gestured toward the barbeques. "So behave yourselves and maybe you'll get a plug for wild salmon on his next show."

A clean-shaven member of the rag tag gathering held up his hand, pinkie in the air, "*Saumon Sauvage*, is what he'll call it. He's the guy from *Flirting with Food*, isn't he? I saw your daughter on his show, Goldie. I couldn't believe it. A couple of years ago Chili was in my marine biology class at J-D High. She was one of my best students."

A quiet man in a frayed green slicker got off the bench beside the fishermen and presented himself to Godiva. "Say, I know who you are." A beer bottle dangled from his hand. "You're that gal that writes the newspaper column, I saw your picture in the *Fish-wrapper*. You give people advice, don't you?"

"You've seen my column?" Godiva seemed surprised that he could read.

"Rudy told me Goldie's sister was coming to town. You two really look alike, but you didn't have me fooled."

"Oh?"

He pointed to her feet. "Goldie would never wear damn fool shoes like that to a salmon bake." The other fishermen guffawed and pointed at the inappropriate footwear.

The quiet man looked down at his own beat up rubber boots, took Godiva's arm and gently pulled her away from the cluster of rowdy men. He had a pronounced limp. "Um, ya know, Miss G.O.D., I was actually thinkin' of writin' you a letter." He looked over his shoulder to see if the others were listening, but they were complaining to Red and Goldie about the low salmon prices this year.

"Are you having trouble with a lost lover, Mr., um...?"

"Taku, everybody jus' calls me Taku." He looked at his boots again. "Nope, it ain't exactly a lost love, more like a lost boat. I suppose you could say I lost everything I love, though, since I lost the boat. Busted up my leg so I can't fish, lost the boat so I got no place to live. Lucky for me I got some nice friends. Rudy buys me a drink or two, Belle finds me a bit o' work to do now and then and pays me way too much to do it, this angel named Mimi lets me sleep in her storeroom, and the folks at the Glory Hole feed me real good."

"So, what were you going to write me about?"

"Y'see, I feel like my life is over."

Godiva judged him to be forty-five at the most. "I wonder if it makes sense to go back to Bellingham and try to find my family. Maybe my Mom's still alive, or my Aunt Bea...

"Maybe my sister would take me in. Is it a stupid idea? To want to die where you were born? Maybe they'd just be pissed at me for not contacting them. I reckon it's been twenty years."

Godiva fought the urge to give the poor soul a hug. "Taku, you know what I think? I think you need to sober up and stop feeling sorry for yourself. So what if you can't fish anymore? Your mind still works, your hands still work, and your legs seem to get you around. There are a hundred things you can do to feel useful. Go over there." She pointed toward the bright glow of Belle's red dress. "Give Belle a big hug and ask her to help you find a steady job."

Taku responded to the suggestion by swigging down the rest of his beer. He mumbled something unintelligible as he left Godiva and headed for the ice chest to get another.

31

The drizzle was quickly turning to rain. Godiva dragged Goldie inside where the Crabgrass Revival Band belted out a bluegrass tune. She heaved a sigh of relief when Emily Pickle waved to her and introduced her around to a group of the social elite. The hot topics of conversation were the Juneau Jumpers' Championship and the young priest's murder.

Chapter 7

Rudy closed the Silver Spoon at eight o'clock and hurried to the party. He found the Silver sisters working on their third helpings of grilled salmon while they joked with a distinguished judge in a red plaid shirt.

He pulled Goldie aside. "Well Goldilocks, all yer troubles are over. Them wayward samovars finally arrived at about six o'clock. Got the crate in the storeroom and we can open it tomorrow."

When the Alaskan sun set at midnight, Belle's salmon bake was still in full swing. By two in the morning, the last of the revelers headed home and Red's ship pulled out of the harbor.

The next morning, while the others slept off the effects of the party, Goldie sat at her hundred-year-old oak table sipping a cup of ginkgo biloba tea. Feeling a bit groggy from less than four hours sleep, she took a few more sips hoping the blend would sharpen her mind. It wasn't working.

She definitely didn't feel up to unpacking the crate of Russian antiques this morning, but she had agreed to meet Rudy at seven to inventory the items before opening the shop.

As she looked out the window at the boats in Gastineau Channel, she pictured Rudy, in his little apartment above the Silver Spoon, buttoning on his suspenders and straightening his bow tie. He would head down the back stairs and over to the City Café for a cup of java and the breakfast special just as he did every morning. That gave her about forty-five minutes to get her butt in gear.

Goldie stumbled through the door as Rudy was attacking

the crate with hammer and crowbar. The tiny bells on the fringes of her Balinese vest tinkled softly as she hurried into the storeroom.

"Hard at work already? Looks like you're having a little trouble opening that crate."

"Yes'm, two things them Ruskies know how to do—make vodka and build crates." Rudy handed her the customs papers, waybills and packing slips that were attached to the shipment. Flamboyant headings in English and Cyrillic proclaimed the shippers as MINSKY & PINSKY, Importer/Exporter—Moscow, Vladivostok, Minsk, and Pinsk.

She sighed. "Poor Uri and Vladimir. It breaks my heart to think about what happened to them and all their wonderful antiques. Rudy, do you realize this must be the last thing they sent out before the big fire?"

"Yup. When ya think about it, it's kinda like shipping off the Tsar's crown jewels while the Commies is bustin' down the back door."

"Well, I hadn't meant it quite like that, but it does feel kind of creepy knowing this is all that's left of Minsky and Pinsky."

Midnight the cat strolled by, rubbed against Goldie's legs and let out a little growl. Goldie tried to nudge him away and he rewarded her with a puff of fish breath accompanied by a loud meow. She went to the front counter and dropped a handful of Nature Nuggets Kitty Kibble into the antique silver bowl she kept beside the wrapping paper.

By the time she returned to the storeroom, Rudy had the huge crate open. The worktable and floor were covered with Russian artifacts and seven bubble wrapped samovars, each about the size of a medium coffee urn.

Goldie's face lit up. "Lucky for us they didn't send us the crate that was full of Siberian parkas. That would have been the final straw. I'll be glad to get those church women off my back."

Rudy wiped his damp forehead against his pinstriped sleeve. "If you ask me, I think ya bought too damn many of these fancy teapots." He unwrapped one and held up the elaborate samovar by its ivory handles.

"Oh, don't be such an old grump. I'm giving one to Belle as a birthday gift. Mimi down at the teashop wants at least one for her samovar collection, and, of course, there's the one for Father Innocent. That only leaves four, and we have three ships in port today. One of the Mad Hatters from Belle's group says if I have one left after tourist season, she'll buy it at my 'locals' discount."

Goldie started to inventory the smaller items, writing down each of the nesting Matrushka dolls, religious icons, military paraphernalia and a beautiful clockwork automaton in her ledger.

Rudy pulled the wrapping off the rest of the samovars. "Will ya lookit that?" He whistled. "These samovars musta come outta some Ruskie palace or somethin'."

Each one was more ornate than the one before.

"Wow. These are incredible." Goldie swung around and brushed a strand of silver hair from her eyes. She picked up one that was particularly beautiful and inspected it closely. "They are not the ones I ordered from their inventory catalog. They're way more elaborate. I've never seen such fabulous pieces."

"You ain't complainin', are ya?"

"No way! I just wish I'd ordered more."

At eight o'clock she phoned Mimi Mendoza. Belle's group was meeting at her teashop that afternoon, and Goldie knew Mimi would want to show off a new samovar.

"Hey, Mimi, are you up and dressed? We just unpacked the samovars, and if you hurry over you can have first pick before the tourists have at them. Trust me. You've never seen anything like these."

Mimi lived above her shop, Tea & Sympathy, on South Franklin Street. The cozy little Russian tearoom with its lace curtains, crisp white tablecloths and glass pastry case was a popular gathering place for some of the groups in town. Every day four different types of tea were dispensed from antique samovars on the marble counter. A gilded shelf along the back wall displayed the rest of Mimi's collection.

Goldie looked out the front door as Mimi, a spry, no-nonsense woman with shiny black hair and a copper complexion, bounced down the street toward the Silver Spoon. The thing Goldie liked best about Mimi, was the perpetual twinkle in her eye.

"Hey Goldie! Hi Rudy! Isn't it a beautiful day? The forecast says partly cloudy but you know what that means? The other half is partly sunny."

As she looked over the exquisite assortment lined up for her inspection, Mimi's twinkle became a laser beam. "Goldie, where did you get these? They make the rest of my collection seem so ordinary." She picked up the one with the ivory handles. "How much?"

The wholesale price Goldie had paid, even with shipping and handling was just a fraction of what they were probably worth. Goldie thought for a moment, before quoting a price that was much lower than what she could have asked. After all, Mimi was a friend and a good customer.

Mimi said without hesitation, "I'll take it." Then she pointed to the one with fluted panels and lion paw feet. "And that one too, if the price is as good." After sharing some local gossip, Mimi headed out the door with the ivory handled samovar in her arms. Rudy trailed behind, balancing the beautiful vessel with lion paw feet.

By nine o'clock, when Dora and Nora bustled into the shop, Goldie had entered the remaining five samovars in the inventory book and slapped some heavy price tags on the new additions. The church ladies headed right for the counter, and picked exactly the one they wanted for Father Innocent without wavering. Goldie gave them the fifteen percent discount she reserved for certain locals and put the gift in a big box covered in royal blue paper with silver spoons and swirls on it.

"Father Innocent will be so excited when he sees this," Nora said, grinning from ear to ear. "Poor old dear, he's been beside himself since Father Augustine's murder."

"Yes," sighed Dora, "now Rimsky has had to do everything but give the Sunday sermon. He's really a vile man, you know, but what can you do? He is a big help."

"Any news on the investigation?" asked Goldie.

Dora shrugged. "Nothing. That young priest was the nicest person you would ever meet. And so smart, too. According to gossip in the church, the police don't even have a clue why he was killed. Who would want to murder him?"

All three women shook their heads in dismay. Nora picked up the box and the two ladies bustled out, their flowered dresses disappearing into a cluster of tourists on South Franklin Street.

At noon, Belle blasted into the shop in a flurry of magenta and purple. She gave Goldie a hug. "Wasn't the party fun? I just love that handsome devil your sister's got hold of. And did you see that dress Emily Pickle had on? Were you there when that windbag, Senator Smiley made a pass at me?"

"The party was a great success, Mama Belle, you really out-did yourself. Did you come to get your birthday gift?"

"Yes, dearie. What have you got for me? I love surprises."

Her eyes opened wide as Goldie led her to the counter with the four remaining samovars. She swept the expanse of the display with her right hand. "There you go, Mama, choose any one."

"Are you serious? What a wonderful gift!"

As Goldie expected, Belle chose the most ornate one and hustled out with it under her arm.

At two o'clock a small group of tourists came into the shop. An impeccably dressed woman with hair the color of mango sorbet zeroed in on the remaining samovars. She examined each piece carefully and settled on the one with floral ornaments and a rich coppery patina. "These are exquisite!" she said. "I never thought I would make such a find out here in the sticks. I'm surprised you have anything of this quality so far from civilization."

"Well, we aren't as isolated as most people think." Goldie

answered politely, while secretly gritting her teeth. "Where would you like us to ship this?"

"Oh, I'll take it with me. I live in Seattle, so I won't have far to go when I end my cruise."

She handed over her platinum credit card and wrote down her address information for Goldie's ledger book. All but one of her cruise ship companions had moved on, and she sweet-talked the remaining old duffer into carrying the bulky package back to the ship for her.

At quarter past three, Godiva breezed in with Caesar and Chili in tow. She was wearing a beautiful mauve pantsuit accessorized with a flowing silk scarf. Caesar was dressed in a casual, but expensive, suit. It was obvious that the luggage finally showed up and the Hollywood fashion plates were able to dress in their own clothes. They had come by the shop on their way to the airport. Godiva had flatly refused to let Goldie drive Caesar and Chili there in the rusted old Subaru and was driving an expensive rental car.

Caesar smiled warmly "I want to bid you farewell, Goldie dear. We've had a lovely time. I would have loved to stay longer but *Flirting with Food* calls. Unfortunately we must head back to L.A. on the next Alaska Airlines flight,"

"Bye, Mom, I really hate to leave so soon." Chili gave her mother a big kiss. "But we really do have to be back at the studio first thing in the morning. The show must go on, you know."

Godiva fidgeted with her scarf. "I'll drive the car up to your house when I get back from the airport, see you after you close the shop."

While mother and daughter exchanged hugs, Caesar caught sight of the two samovars still on display. "So these are the notorious samovars, eh?" He ran his fingers along the bronze fluted edge of one. "Goldie, these are magnificent. I would love to buy one and send it to my dear mother for her birthday next week. She collects antiques and I know she will adore this."

A few minutes later Caesar headed out the door with a

package, expertly wrapped by Rudy to withstand the rigors of air travel.

"That will fit right in the overhead," Rudy assured him. "Don't you go checkin' it now, 'cause it might wind up back in Russia."

At closing time, Goldie looked wistfully at the last remaining samovar from the Minsky & Pinsky shipment. "There, you see, Rudy? This morning we had seven of those 'fancy teapots' and now there's only one. Let's take it off the counter. I've decided to keep it for myself. Somehow I just can't bear to part with the last one."

Rudy was carrying it to the back room when two burly men in ill-fitting suits pushed their way into the shop and nearly knocked over a departing customer. The men looked menacing as they walked toward Goldie and Rudy.

"These guys don't look much like antique buyers," Rudy whispered in his boss's ear.

One pointed to the samovar Rudy held. "You got more samovars like that? Maybe have seven?" he growled.

"Sorry, gentlemen, I had quite a few this morning, but it's been a busy day. I sold the ones I had, and this one's not for sale." She smiled sweetly, displaying her dimples and pearly teeth.

"You got wrong shipment, lady. We look for precious antiques, not like your other junk." He waved his beefy hand to dismiss her entire stock. Then he lunged at Rudy as the little man nimbly fled to the back room. "You must give back to us this one and telling us who is buying other six." His beady eyes flashed.

"Or else!" the other goon chimed in.

Goldie looked from one to the other. By now she was shaking. "Really, gentlemen, you must be kidding. I bought those samovars from a reputable dealer." She held up the invoice and customs papers. In the back room she heard Rudy dialing the police.

They advanced a step closer. "You *will* give samovar and names!"

"Or else!"

"How dare you threaten me? I'm sorry, I have no more samovars for sale and my customer information is confidential."

Both men fixed her with evil stares as they exchanged angry conversation in Russian. The smaller of the two giants said, "You be sorry, lady. Boris and Igor Dumkovsky no play games. You must—"

Just then Goldie heard the siren coming down Franklin Street, and felt a little braver. She cut them off in mid-sentence. "Gentlemen, the police are coming, I must ask you to leave now or they will escort you out."

Both of them quickly stormed out of the shop. The larger man shouted over his shoulder, "We be back!"

As the cruiser pulled up to the curb, Goldie tried to regain her composure and keep her lunch down.

Chapter 8

Goldie had her key in the lock when the phone rang. Still rattled from her encounter with the Russians, she tried to ignore it, lock up the shop and hurry home, but curiosity won out. Unlike her sister, who could turn her back and walk away from a ringing phone, Goldie could never resist answering. "Good evening, Silver Spoon Antiques, Goldie Silver speaking."

"Thank goodness I caught you." Mimi Mendoza's voice was strained. "Can you stop by the teashop in the morning before you open up? I want to show you something really weird about those samovars."

Goldie thought of all the things she had to do the next day and groaned. "Can it wait until later, Mimi? Maybe I could stop by with Godiva tomorrow afternoon. What do you say?"

After a brief silence, Mimi said, "I know how busy you are, but I really want to you to see these. If you come by early I'll fix you a cup of my special blend with some of those poppy seed cakes you love so much. It'll only take a few minutes to show you what I found."

Goldie thought about the pastries and gave in. "Okay Mimi, I'll be there around quarter to eight."

As she locked up, she regretted answering the phone. It was like the samovars were cursed from the time they left the warehouse. Starting with the demise of Minsky and Pinsky, then all the shipping mix-ups, those horrible thugs, and now Mimi found something strange. What next?

Goldie walked up Franklin Street. When she turned on Sixth and headed toward her little house on Starr Hill, she looked over her shoulder. She had the vague feeling she was being followed, but all she saw were some neighborhood children playing ball in the Chicken Yard playground.

A light morning fog hung over Gastineau Channel and little droplets of mist settled on Goldie's rain jacket as she headed down the hill toward downtown. Before she reached Mimi's shop, she heard a siren. Her eyes swung across the street and focused on a police car parked in front of Tea & Sympathy. She craned her neck to get a better look as a second cruiser came around the corner and skidded to a halt.

Juneau's Police Chief, Ollie Oliver, jumped out of the second car and was busy directing his officers by the time Goldie reached the teashop.

She ran over to him. "Good Lord, Ollie. What's going on? Where's Mimi?" Not waiting for an answer, she headed for the front door.

Ollie reached out and placed a hand on her shoulder. "Ummm, I can't let you go in there right now. I got a crime scene here, and I'm gonna have to clear the sidewalk."

Goldie huffed at him, "Wait a minute, I'm supposed to meet Mimi for breakfast. If something's happened here she might need my help."

Ollie clamped his hand down on her shoulder as she edged toward the door. The color drained out of his face and his expression softened. "Goldie, honey, I'm not sure how to tell you this, but your friend Mimi is dead."

The mist had turned into a light rain that trickled down Goldie's forehead and mixed with the tears welling in her eyes. She felt like she had been punched in the gut. "D-d-dead? I don't understand. She was fixing me tea, Ollie, and poppy seed cakes. She had something to show me. She can't be dead. Let me go in, I have to see her." Once again Goldie tried to push past the burly police chief.

"It's not a pretty sight. My boys just got here and it looks like Mimi's been murdered. Hit over the head a couple times with something heavy. Could have been robbery. The place is pretty busted up. For some reason the killer smashed all those Russian teapots she loved so much. My guys are just starting to check things out now."

Goldie persisted. "Please, let me just go in for a minute. I won't disturb anything, I promise. Mimi said something about the samovars last night. That's why I came to see her this morning." Without waiting, she pushed past Ollie.

Stifling a sob, she carefully stepped through the mess on the floor. Goldie recognized every bashed up samovar in her friend's collection, but the two new ones were not among them. Poor Mimi was sprawled in a pool of blood at the foot of the stairs leading up to her apartment. She wore a fuzzy pink robe over her flannel nightgown. One of her silly bunny slippers lay under a chair, the other dangled from her left toe. Goldie stared at the gruesome scene with the sudden realization that she would never see Mimi's smiling eyes again.

Ollie tried to hustle her out but she stood her ground. "I'm not leaving until I know more. When did this happen? Who found her?"

Goldie was famous around Juneau for never giving up until she got all the facts, so Ollie shrugged. "The Doc's on his way over, but just offhand I'd say it happened sometime around midnight, two a.m. maybe. Something must have woken her up and she probably came downstairs to check it out. A guy from the Silverbow Bakery came by to deliver some tea cakes this morning, saw the mess and gave us a call."

One of the officers rushed through the fancy curtain separating the storeroom from the shop. "Hey, Ollie! You gotta see this. Got the perp back here, sound asleep. Looks pretty open and shut to me. Got drunk, went berserk, busted up the place, she surprises him and he whacks her in the head. Lookit this. He don't even know we're here."

The Chief rushed to the storeroom, and Goldie followed. In the corner, on a pile of rags, Rudy's friend Taku Ted was passed out and snoring for all he was worth. His clothes were covered in blood. A bloody halibut bat rested on his chest, rising and falling with his snores.

Goldie couldn't believe Taku would ever do anything as brutal as flying into a drunken rage and murdering someone. He seemed to be a good person who lost his way. Rudy wouldn't befriend a murderer—would he?

She became aware that Ollie was asking her a question. "Taku was a fisherman before he got hurt, wasn't he?"

Goldie nodded. "But he can't have done this! Mimi was always kind to him."

Ollie pointed to the bloody bat. "Well, this thing is used for killing halibut once they're hauled into the boat. Maybe he took some kind of drug and thought Mimi was a big fish." He shouted to one of his men, "Wake the bum up. He has some questions to answer."

The storeroom reeked of alcohol and the metallic smell of blood. Goldie felt her stomach rolling, but she wasn't going to leave until they kicked her out the door.

The police officer pulled Taku to a sitting position and Ollie loomed above him, firing questions and demanding answers. The confused fellow blinked in the light and rubbed his eyes, as though trying to figure out where he was. Then he let out a big burp and seemed ready to heave. His rheumy eyes slid over to Goldie and there was a flicker of recognition.

"Whaaas...whaass goin' on? Wheeere's Mimi? She'll tell ya it's okay. I ain't tresss-tres-trespissing. She lets me sleep here."

Ollie screamed, "Mimi can't help you. She's dead and it looks like you did it."

Just then Goldie's cell phone rang. She slipped out of the storeroom to answer it.

Rudy was shouting on the other end. "Goldie, Goldie where are ya? We been robbed. It's a gol awful mess. Everythin' topsy turvy. Are ya on yer way down here?"

His voice kept rising until he sounded like an agitated squirrel. Goldie finally managed to break in, "Slow down Rudy. I'm just up the street at the teashop. Something awful has happened. Mimi Mendoza is dead. Murdered! And it looks like your friend Taku did it."

Chapter 9

Goldie put her phone in her pocket and turned to the Chief. "That was Rudy." She took a breath, hoping her voice didn't sound too shaky. "Someone broke into my shop. I know it's small potatoes compared to Mimi's murder, but if one of your guys could stop by later, I'll need to make out a police report. Who knows? Maybe these two crimes are related somehow."

"Don't you worry, Goldie." Ollie gave her a comforting pat on the shoulder. "I know how shook up you must be. Tell you what, go on over to the Silver Spoon, and I'll check it out on my way back to the station."

She hurried down the street, running for the last few yards. When she burst into the Silver Spoon, Rudy stood at the counter holding his head in his hands. Fresh tears ran down her cheeks as she surveyed the overturned displays and broken china.

"I—I just don't know..." Her voice trailed off, as she wiped her eyes on the sleeve of her dripping rain jacket which only made things worse.

"Forget our mess for a minute, tell me about Taku. There's no way that good ole boy would kill anyone. I've seen him get kinda scrappy when he's drunk, but he ain't no killer. Told me once the worst part 'bout fishin' was that he had to kill livin' things. Damn tarnation, if this ain't a rotten day."

Goldie picked up the overturned coat rack from the floor and hung her jacket on it. She steered Rudy toward an old mohair settee. "Let's sit down and try to make some sense of this." They both plopped on the sofa like a couple of rag dolls.

Midnight jumped into Goldie's lap. She gathered up the huge feline and hugged him like a security blanket. He hissed at her and wiggled away. "Sorry, Midnight, I guess I squeezed you a little too tight."

"Don't pay no mind to that worthless cat," Rudy said, shaking his head, "we got other things to think about, Goldie. Like poor Taku. He would never hurt Mimi. He always talks about how kind she was, lettin' him sleep in the storeroom when it got cold out. Called her a saint and an angel." He slapped his hand on the mahogany table next to the settee, and nearly turned it over. "No sir. Them police got it all wrong. I don't care what it looks like, can't make me believe Taku killed her. Goldilocks, you gotta help him."

"Don't worry Rudy, I'll do what I can. We'll get him a lawyer—we'll figure out what happened." She gave him a reassuring pat on the knee.

"Better get that high-falutin' sister of yours over here, pronto. Long as she's hangin' around for a few days, we might as well put her to work doin' what she does best. Snoopin'.".

Goldie glanced at the old schoolhouse clock hanging on the opposite wall. Nine-thirty. She reached for the phone and dialed her home number. After four rings she heard a clattering sound and guessed the phone must have fallen on the floor. A moment later a very sleepy-sounding Godiva said, "Hello, Goldie's not here."

"Of course I'm not there, Godiva. It's me calling. Listen you've gotta wake up right away. Something terrible has happened. I need you to walk down here as soon as you can."

"Walk? Down that steep hill? In the rain? You've got to be kidding. It's enough that you have forty-seven steps up to your house, but I really don't think I can inch down Starr Hill in my high heel boots. What's so important, anyway?"

"Darn it, Sis. Stop thinking of yourself for once. My friend Mimi's been murdered. And Rudy's friend, Taku Ted has been arrested. Remember, you met him at the salmon bake? On top of that, my shop was broken into last night."

"Huh? What? Murdered? Ted? Who—Oh my God!" Godiva's fuzzy voice reflected a tiny glimmer of understanding.

"So, Madame Pompadour, get dressed and leave your fancy shoes at home. You'll find a slicker and some rubber boots by the front door. Now, get your pampered butt down here. I need you."

"But, the hill..."

"Look, if you walk to the end of the street you can come down the Fourth Street stairs. I know it's more steps, but it's all downhill. I'll send Rudy out to get you a cup of coffee and a pastry at Heritage. We'll have it here by the time you arrive."

Uncharacteristically meek, Godiva said, "Um, yeah. See if they have a lemon Danish. If not, some kind of good muffin. Make the coffee an extra large, and black."

Goldie placed the receiver in the cradle. She figured it would be at least an hour before Godiva dressed, did her make-up and hair and dragged herself down the hill.

"All right, Rudy, let's take a few minutes to survey the shop before the police get here."

They did a visual assessment and noted that, although a lot of things were knocked over, only a few items were broken.

"Strange," Goldie muttered. "Offhand I'd say nothing seems to be missing. I really don't see..." She stopped rummaging on her desk and looked up in confusion. "Rudy, where did you put yesterday's sales slips?"

He motioned toward the cash register. "Them slips should be right on the spindle where they always are."

She shook her head. "Nope. Yesterday's slips are missing. Not on the spindle, not on the desk. They're simply not here."

Rudy sprinted back to the storeroom. He looked at the shelf where he had placed Goldie's last samovar when the ill-tempered Dumkovsky brothers charged into the shop the day before. He shouted through the curtain, "Missin', Goldie. Yer fancy samovar is missin'."

"I should have known something awful would happen. The moon is in Mars this week, but I never guessed it would be this bad." She sagged into the settee again. "Rudy, please do me a favor. Run over to Heritage and get Godiva some black coffee, the largest size they have. She wants a lemon Danish, but if they don't have one get her a sweet, gooey muffin. Something for me too, and a chai tea. We're going to need the sugar rush."

A few minutes later, Ollie Oliver sauntered into the shop, notepad in hand, looking frazzled from the morning's activities. His eyes opened wide when he saw the awful mess. "Now, Goldie, don't you worry. Taku is safely on his way to the station. My Lord, do you suppose he did this, too?"

Goldie combed her fingers through her thick silver hair. "Ollie, you're way off-base. I know it looks bad for Taku, but I don't think he did it, and neither does Rudy. He's not a murderer or a thief, just a scruffy guy who's down on his luck."

Ollie threw up his hands. "Okay, okay. Don't go gettin' all upset. You've got to admit when you find a suspect at the scene all covered in blood, holding the murder weapon, it's pretty damned incriminating. You got a better explanation?"

"Not exactly, but I do have some idea of what happened here in my shop. I got this shipment of antique samovars from Russia on Saturday. They were so incredible that I only had one left by closing time on Sunday."

Ollie raised an eyebrow. "Boy, they must have been something to sell that fast."

"They sure were. But here's the thing. At the end of the day, these two big Russian guys came in. They insisted those samovars belonged to them and demanded I give them the last one and the names and addresses of everyone else who got one."

Ollie chuckled. "Knowing you, Goldie, that was the wrong thing for them to do."

She smiled. "You bet. When they began to threaten me, Rudy called the police. They heard the siren and ran out of the shop, swearing they'd come back. I think they're the ones who did all this." She blinked back tears.

Ollie nodded. "Sounds like you got that one figured out. But what about Mimi?"

"Oh! Don't you see? She bought two of those samovars, and when I looked around the teashop this morning, they weren't there. That shipment was cursed. I should never have sold them to her. I should have known there would be trouble, the moon and stars pointed to disaster yesterday," she sobbed. "It's all my fault she's dead!"

Ollie huffed. "Don't be so dramatic, Goldie. I'll buy your theory about the angry Russians breaking into your shop, but nobody would kill someone just for a couple of teapots. Nope. My money's on Taku for the killer. The evidence was right there. I'll bet when he sobers up he'll confess."

Just then Rudy came in, cardboard coffee caddy in hand, and a bag of goodies in the crook of his arm. "Oh no you don't. You ain't railroadin' ol' Taku into no forced confession. Goldie's getting him a lawyer. He ain't talkin' to you without a legal mouthpiece in the room."

Ollie looked a little startled at Rudy's outburst. "Now Rudy, don't get so upset. Anyone can see it's an open and shut case."

"Oh no it ain't! Someone's set that ole boy up. You know as well as I do that he's an easy mark. I'm goin' down to the station myself if I have to, and make sure you don't abuse his rights." Rudy was inches from the police chief's face and his nose and cheeks were flushed.

"Okay, okay, we'll put Taku in a cell to sober up until his lawyer gets there. Goldie, if you're going to help him you'd better find a really hot one."

She nodded.

"Meanwhile, we'll look into the break-in here at the Silver Spoon. See if we can find those Russians. But I'll tell you right now. I don't think those missing samovars had a thing to do with Mimi's murder. Just a coincidence."

Goldie was heating up with anger, but she decided not to blow up. She needed Ollie's cooperation. Five minutes after he left, the bell on the front door tinkled and a bedraggled Godiva clomped in wearing floppy brown BF Goodrich boots and a yellow hat and rain slicker. In a weak voice she said, "Coffee. Where is my coffee? Why can't you live on flat land?"

Rudy grabbed a china platter off the back shelf and arranged three varieties of muffins on it. He removed the lid from her coffee and poured part of it into a delicate Meissen Blue teacup. "Here you are, yer Highness," he said with a flourish, and handed her the cup, now balanced on a matching saucer. "Can't have visiting royalty drinkin' out of a paper cup, can we now?"

They sat on the mohair settee while Goldie quickly explained the morning's shocking events. Godiva's lethargy evaporated, bolstered by her java jolt.

For the first time since she came in, she actually looked around. "Geez Sis, this is really a mess."

"Yes, that's what I was trying to tell you. This has been a horrible morning."

Godiva nodded. "I need more information. Why don't you start from the beginning?" She sat on the edge of the sofa, listening to every gruesome detail. In the end she said, "You are so right, Goldie. It must have something to do with the missing samovars. Obviously your friend Ollie thinks he has his man, and doesn't want to even consider murderous Russians."

Goldie produced a yellow-lined pad, and they started to brainstorm, but after a few minutes Rudy interrupted. "I hate to break up the tea party, ladies, but we gotta get a lawyer for Taku. You said you'd call someone Goldie. What about that friend of yours who has an office above the bank? You always say he's the best."

"Oh, Rudy, what was I thinking? It'll cost a fortune to hire a hotshot like Perry Pinkwater."

A shadow crossed Rudy's face. He mumbled, "We can't just throw Taku to the wolves."

Godiva held up her hand. "Stop! Call this guy Perry Pinkelheimer, or whatever his name is, and get him over there ASAP. I did feel sort of sorry for Taku when I talked to him at the party. If I pay part of the bill, maybe this Perry character will agree to do the rest pro bono. Then both of us can figure out how to write it off."

Rudy executed a proper English bow. "Many thanks, yer Majesty. Turns out you ain't so bad after all. I take back every nasty thing I said about you."

Godiva fixed him with a cold stare. "Nasty things? Watch it, Rudy, I could still change my mind."

By the time they broke for lunch, the first page of Goldie's legal pad was full. They walked across the street to the Twisted

Fish restaurant, then continued to brainstorm as they ate. Godiva oohed and aahed over the delicious salmon, cooked and seasoned to perfection. Goldie smiled, finally hearing something positive from her sister.

After wiping crumbs off her designer jeans, and donning the unfashionable slicker she'd borrowed from Goldie, Godiva was ready to slosh back across the street.

They walked into the shop and Goldie let out a low whistle. Rudy rushed to the front, all in a dither. "Rudy, you're incredible. I can't believe you cleaned up the mess so fast."

"Forget the clean up, Goldilocks. You won't believe what's happened now. There's a flippin' crime wave right here in Juneau, Boss."

When Goldie finally calmed him down, Rudy said, "The heck with what Ollie says. I do believe you're right—them samovars is cursed." He took a deep breath, snapped his suspenders and continued.

"I just got a call from Dora. She said they gave Father Innocent his gift. My! Did he love it!"

"So, that's good news," Godiva chimed in, "what's the crime wave you're bellowing about?"

Rudy threw her a venomous look. "The crime wave, Miss Fancy Pants, is that he ain't got it no more. No sir. According to Dora, two strange Russians came into the church. Father Innocent bein' such a nice old guy, welcomed them in, and how did they thank him? They turned on the pore ol' priest, beat him up, and wouldn't ya know it, made off with—"

"The samovar?" the twins said in unison.

"Yup!"

Goldie sighed. "Where was his assistant Rimsky when all of that was happening? Isn't he usually by Father Innocent's side now that the Father's slipping a bit?"

"Rimsky told Dora he was fixin' some lunch. Came back in the church lookin' for Father Innocent, and there he is, a-layin' on the floor with a lump the size of a goose egg on his head. Dora said when she walked in, her friend Nora and that worthless Rimsky were fussin' over the poor ol' priest. He was a-bleedin' and mumblin' something about not letting those hoodlums get away with his samovar. They loaded the ol' duffer into Nora's car and took him to the emergency room."

"This is too much! Attacking a helpless old priest! What else did Dora say?"

"Dora wanted to know if you could get them another samovar." Rudy shook his head. "First that nice young priest—dead as a doornail, then Mimi beaten to death and now this business with Father Innocent. Does yer friend Ollie have any ideas about who kilt Father Augustine yet?"

Goldie looked at her twin and raised an eyebrow. "No. At least nothing I've heard about. Belle says he's clueless, I'm beginning to think she's right."

Godiva's eyes suddenly widened. "Oh no Sis, we forgot about Belle! She's got one of the samovars, too! I'm afraid your big boisterous birthday girl might be in real danger."

Chapter 10

"So Goldilocks, what do you want me to tell that pesky Dora?"

"Tell her I've decided never to sell another samovar. Maybe her twelve-year-old nephew can help find one on eBay."

Just at that moment the phone began to ring. Goldie went to the desk and lifted the old fashioned receiver. "Silver Spoon Antiques, may I help you?"

Exasperation flitted across her face, rapidly turning to astonishment and then fear. "What? You're what? Oh no, I can't believe it. Calm down, we'll be right over."

Goldie stood there stunned, while Godiva and Rudy threw her questioning looks.

"Who was that, Goldie? What happened?" Godiva said, "More bad news?"

She swallowed hard, brushed a wayward strand of silver hair from her eyes and choked out, "I'm afraid that's exactly what it is, Sis. They've already gotten to Belle. Her flat was broken into and her samovar was stolen. Geez, this is starting to feel like the plot of some Russian crime novel."

"Yeah, did Tolstoy ever write a book called 'The Seven Deadly Samovars'?"

Rudy had no patience for academic questions. "Well, what else did Belle say? Is the ole gal okay?"

"I didn't get the whole story, she sounded pretty shook up. You know it takes a lot to freak Belle out. I think she might be injured."

Rudy threw his hands in the air. "See there, this just goes to show it can't be Taku what killed Mimi. It's them Ruskies! Fancy teapots disappearin', people gettin' robbed and killed and what all. I tell ya, there's more here than meets the eye. You gals better get over there pronto, I'll watch the shop." He hustled the twins out the door.

When Goldie and Godiva got off the elevator on the fourth floor, they saw Belle's door wide open. She called out, "Come on in, girls. I think I sprained my darn ankle."

Belle was propped up on the sofa, her foot elevated on a yellow silk ottoman and wrapped in ice. She seemed to be holding back a sob as she fanned her face with a jewel-encrusted hand, her chubby arm flapping like a bird's wing. With a dramatic sigh, her massive bosom heaving, Belle said, "My beautiful things. My beautiful, beautiful things. Look what they've done." Her teary eyes swept the room.

Godiva took in the gaudy artifacts and doodads scattered all over the pink and orange area rug. A lamp had crashed against a carved, gold-leafed credenza, leaving a huge gouge right in the middle of one door. Crystals, knocked off a chandelier, glittered around the room. It looked like a herd of elephants had stampeded through Belle's living room.

"Well, girls, I may look like a fragile flower right now, but I want you to know I gave those goons a run for their money."

Godiva sent her sister the silent message—fragile flower? More like a Venus Flytrap.

"Now, Mama Belle," Goldie said in a soothing voice, "Godiva will fix you some tea and you can tell us what happened." She shot Godiva a look.

Her sister raised an eyebrow. "Tea? Me, fix—oh, yes, of course. You just rest there, Belle, and I'll get you something." She headed for the kitchen.

Belle called out, "First cabinet on the right, Godiva, dearie." She settled back into the poofy cushions and fanned herself dramatically.

Godiva came back into the room with three fancy cups on a gaudy silver tray. She offered tea to Belle and Goldie, and then sat in the chair nearest the window.

After taking a sip of the tea, Belle said, "Now let me tell you what happened. I was taking a little nap, when I heard some heavy clodhoppers stomping up the back stairs. Those stairs come up right beside my bedroom, you know. At first I thought I was dreaming, but the noise got louder. Then I heard some jiggly sounds and a huge thunk. Lordy! That really woke me up. It sounded like someone was in my living room speaking in some strange language."

"Could it have been Russian?" Goldie asked.

"Yeah, it might have been. Swearing is more what it sounded like to me. Good thing I'm no shrinking violet. I've shot a few bears in my day. Did Red ever tell you about the time his Mama saved him from a grizzly sow with twin cubs?"

Goldie rolled her eyes. *Oh no, not again!*

Godiva jumped in, "Tell us about the Russians."

"Well, I was loaded for bear this time! I got my shotgun out of the closet, and threw open my bedroom door. I stood there in my nightgown looking down the barrel at two ugly bullies, and I screamed like a banshee. Honey, I think I scared the bejesus right out of them."

"Mama Belle, those guys are dangerous."

"Not as dangerous as ol' Belle Pepper." She thumped her chest. "They were arguing about something in what I guess mighta been Russian, and I yelled 'You get the hell out of here or I'll blow your damn heads off!' They began to back up."

Goldie gave Belle a big hug. "Mama Belle you shouldn't take chances like that. Your visitors were the Dumkovsky brothers, and they're crazy. You should have just let them take what they wanted and clear out." She glanced at Belle's swollen, ice-wrapped foot.

"Hmmmph. Listen here, Babycakes, I wasn't about to let them hoodlums just break in and take my stuff without standing my ground. Wanna know what happened next?"

Godiva leaned forward. "I can't wait."

Now that Belle had her audience's attention, she took a deep breath, pulled a hankie from her bosom and wiped her face. "The bigger one grabbed my samovar and they both made for the door. Knocked over all my beautiful things trying to get out." She dabbed her eyes, "That's when I took aim and winged that bastard. Guess that'll show 'em."

Godiva noticed the empty frame above the dented credenza. Mirror shards all over the top of it reflected the light from the damaged chandelier. "What happened to your mirror and your crystal chandelier? Did they smash those too?"

Looking embarrassed, she said, "Nah. I tripped over my nightgown after that first shot, and the gun went off a couple more times. Too bad. I can fix the light, but I really liked that mirror." She repositioned the ice pack on her bandaged foot. "Twisted my darn ankle and by the time I was able to get back on my feet they were gone. So was my beautiful birthday gift— gone! I'm sorry."

"What are you sorry for?" Goldie asked. "That samovar almost got you killed. I'm the one who should be sorry—"

"Belle," Godiva broke in, "maybe you don't realize what a close call you had. Did you hear about Mimi Mendoza's murder this morning?"

Belle's bravado melted away and tears filled her eyes. "Yes, dearie, I'm afraid the news is all over town. My friend Molly was walking her cat down on Franklin St. this morning, and spotted the police cars."

"Speaking of police, did you call them and report this break in yet?"

Belle shook her head.

Goldie picked up the phone and handed it to her mother-in-law. "Mama, you call Ollie Oliver right now, and tell him to come over here himself. I know how much he respects you. Maybe you can convince him that those Russians are connected to Mimi's murder. He's sure it was Taku Ted. He is so dense sometimes."

"I don't know. Molly told me they found Taku asleep with the bloody murder weapon in his hand, and it was his own halibut bat."

"Well, that's true Mama, but you know he couldn't have done it."

"Honey, I've seen stranger things in my seventy-five years. But then again, those ruffians looked like they could do anything. I'll talk to Ollie, but you know that boy's about as smart as a box of rocks."

Goldie turned to Godiva. "I'll bet you money Ollie won't do any more than he has to. I guess it's up to us to find out what's going on."

"Well, Belle definitely injured one of those Russians, so it should make them easier to track." Godiva pointed to the trail of blood leading from the living room to the back door.

Goldie looked surprised at her sister's enthusiasm for the hunt. "So you think we should lend Ollie a hand?"

"There are still two more of those jinxed samovars out there," Godiva gulped, "and my Caesar has one of them. Count me in." She gave her sister the thumbs up.

Chapter 11

After leaving Belle in the capable hands of her friend Clara, who happened by to get the latest gossip, Goldie and Godiva navigated the crowded little downtown streets. Clara assured the twins she would help Belle clean the mess as soon as the police had a chance to survey the devastation.

"If we're going to track these Dumkovsky guys, the first thing we need is a sketch or something to show people. Maybe someone has seen them around town."

"I don't know," Godiva said, "a couple of big Russians ought to be pretty easy to spot."

Goldie stopped in front of the Viking Bar and pointed to a sign in the window that read, WELCOME SIBERIAN NATIONAL HOCKEY TEAM. "Then again, maybe not. There's likely to be lots of husky Russians in town this week."

"Great, what's next?" Godiva plodded along beside her sister. Her feet were beginning to sweat in the floppy rubber boots.

"I've got an idea. We'll go over to the docks and find Maurice Flambeau."

"Who?"

"Maurice Flambeau, he's a caricature artist. You know, hangs out at the docks and draws quick sketches of the tourists."

Godiva raised her eyebrows. "Tell me that's not his real name."

"Well, he's actually Marty Feldstein, from the Bronx. But he really plays up the bit with the beret and the French accent. There he is over there." She pointed to a canopy tent that protected the artist and model from the light drizzle. "Don't blow his cover."

Five or six cruise ship passengers wearing clear plastic ponchos over their pastel sweat suits were lined up beside Maurice's tent. The sisters bypassed the queue and ducked into the tent. Maurice looked up. "Ah, Goldie, *ma Cherie*, 'ow lovely to see you." He turned to Godiva, set down his colored pencils and kissed her hand. "And this must be your charming sister, *n'est pas*?"

"Yes Maurice, how did you guess?" She pulled him aside and said in a confidential tone, "We have a very important mission for you and we need your help right away."

Maurice started to turn back to finish the sketch of a geeky looking middle-aged man. "But *Cherie*," he motioned to the line of customers with his chin, "eet is a very beesee day."

Godiva looked at the signboard beside him, noting that his most expensive sketch was forty-five dollars. She opened her purse, slipped three bills out of her wallet and dangled them in front of the artist. She said in a stage whisper, "Here's three hundred dollars. That's more than you would make if you sketched all six of those people."

Maurice magically morphed into Marty Feldstein. He dashed a quick signature on the barely finished sketch and hustled the man out of the tent. Forgetting to use the French accent, he called out to those still waiting, "Sorry folks, something just came up. Go see the museum, or the glacier, or go fishing. Have a nice day."

He brought in his signboard and motioned toward a couple of director's chairs. "Okay, ladies, what's up?"

They explained the situation, described the Dumkovskys, and within fifteen minutes had a reasonably good facsimile of the two thugs.

After several hours of tromping around town without even stopping for dinner, a bedraggled Godiva wailed, "Come on, Sis, we've shown this sketch to everyone. We have to take a break. It's already 10:30 and everything is closed but the bars. I'm getting foot rot from these boots and a serious case of matted hair from this stupid rain hat. I need my beauty rest."

Goldie gave in. It had been a rough day. "I guess I didn't realize how much has happened today," she sighed, "Mimi's murder, Taku's arrest, the shop break in, mayhem at the church, Belle's burglary. Let's walk up the hill and go to bed."

"No way am I walking up that hill." Godiva dug in her heels. Either we take a cab or you carry me."

"But, Godiva, a cab? It's only a few blocks."

"Yeah, straight up. Look, there's the cab company right across the street."

The driver balked at such a small fare until Godiva flashed some folding money at him. His face brightened. "Hop in," he chirped.

They settled in the kitchen and shared a pot of Sleepytime tea and a bag of chocolate chip cookies. Godiva grumbled, "I feel like a drowned rat. I've got to get my hair done before we go to Seattle for the banquet. They probably won't even let me in the way I look. I don't suppose there are any decent hair-dressers in Juneau."

Goldie knew better than to try reasoning with her sister regarding hair, clothes or cosmetics. They were in completely different galaxies when it came to fashion and beauty care. "Tell you what, Godiva, I'll call Ruby first thing in the morning and see if she can squeeze you in tomorrow."

"Ruby? Doesn't sound very classy. Can I trust her?"

"Hey, she's a jewel."

At eight o'clock the next morning, Goldie fired up the rusty Subaru and hustled Godiva into it. The sun had come out and everything sparkled. Windows were flung open in all the funky little houses clinging to the hills. Three massive cruise ships were already in the channel, and by noon there would be four more fighting for space in the harbor.

Goldie parked in the tiny spot carved out of the hill behind the Silver Spoon Antique Shoppe. In the early 1900s, this end of Franklin Street was the red light district. The building that housed Goldie's shop had once been a lively cathouse. Now the only cat in residence was fat old Midnight who sat on a footstool in the window watching the world go by.

They crossed the street, turned down an alley and arrived at the back door of another former bawdyhouse. Godiva read the scarlet letters above the door. "Radical Ruby's? You are taking me to a shop called Radical Ruby's? I don't think so."

Before she could turn and run, a tall, handsome woman beckoned them inside. "Come on in, Goldie." Her eyes moved to Godiva, and she said in a cheerful voice, "And you must be Godiva." Her shiny black hair and chiseled features spoke of her Tlingit Native heritage. "I usually don't open until 9:30, but Goldie said you were desperate." She spun Godiva around in the antique barber chair. "Hmmm, tell you the truth, it really doesn't look that bad."

While Ruby washed and massaged, snipped and fluffed, she eagerly ate up all the gossip about the murder and crime wave sweeping through Juneau. "I know that guy Taku. I don't think he would kill anyone, especially not Mimi."

Goldie nodded. "Yeah, Rudy Valentino, you know the guy who works for me, that's what he says, too."

Ruby stopped fussing with Godiva's hair. "But, you know, my brother's had a couple of nasty run-ins with Taku. I have to tell you, he doesn't have a great reputation."

"Well Ruby," Godiva said. "From what you've told me, the same could be said for your brother."

"Don't I know," Ruby said. "I did have to bail him out of jail last month."

"Listen Ruby, I'm changing the subject now," Goldie said. "This is a sketch of the jerks who beat up Father Innocent, busted up my shop and broke into Belle's. Have you seen them around anywhere?"

Ruby studied the drawing and shook her head. "Nope,

haven't seen them and from what you've said, I hope to heaven I never do." Then she turned the chair around and handed Godiva a hand mirror.

Godiva studied her hairdo and looked surprised. "Ruby, this is fabulous! Your work is every bit as good as Jacques, my Beverly Hills hairdresser. And he doesn't give me that wonderful scalp massage. How much do I owe you?"

"Well, I usually charge twenty-eight dollars, but since I had to come in early I'll add ten percent. So that's thirty dollars and eighty cents."

"You're kidding!"

Ruby hesitated. "Ummm, I guess I could knock off the ten percent if that's too much."

Godiva laughed. "Jacques charges a hundred and eighty five dollars for the same thing you just did, but without the massage. I can't believe your price is so low."

"Well, lots of my clients are strapped for cash, so I like to keep the price down. Besides," she looked around the tiny shop, walls painted with faux texture and plastered with Marilyn Monroe memorabilia, "you can see I don't have much overhead."

Godiva opened her purse, extracted three tens and a hundred from her wallet and tucked them into Ruby's hand. "Well, honey, I stiffed you on the eighty cents so to make up for it here's a tip for a job well done." Ruby smoothed out the bills. When she saw the hundred, she let out a whoop and pumped Godiva's hand. "Wow, I'm usually lucky to get five. Th—thank you."

The twins walked out into the alley leaving a stunned Ruby blinking in the sunny doorway. Goldie and Godiva resumed their quest as they started up Franklin Street, stopping to show the sketch to shopkeepers and pedestrians. When they passed the Glory Hole, Goldie looked through the window and saw several people clustered around something on the counter near the coffee pot. "Godiva, am I seeing things or is that one of the samovars?"

Godiva, who was trying to ignore the homeless men and

women having breakfast at the shelter, forced herself to look inside. There on the table, beside a platter of day-old doughnuts was Belle's birthday gift. It was drawing quite a crowd.

"Come on." Goldie grabbed her sister's arm and dragged her into the big room filled with oilcloth-covered tables.

One of the old timers looked up and saw them come in. "Hey Goldie, lookit here what ol' Jack found in a dumpster." He pointed toward the new acquisition. It had a large dent in the side and the lid was missing.

Goldie zoomed in on Jack, beaming beside his treasure. "Yeah, I was like, dumpster diving behind that big building on Front Street and there's this fancy teapot just layin' there, right on top. I sez to myself, 'Jack, this here teapot would really class up the ol' Glory Hole,' so I brung it in."

"Jack, that's the samovar that was stolen from Belle Pepper yesterday." She ran a finger along some of the dents and saw that it was damaged beyond repair. Jack looked frightened and upset, as if he were being accused of the crime. Goldie patted his arm. "Don't worry about returning it to her. She'll be happy to know you found it and brought it over here."

Goldie pulled out the sketch of the Dumkovskys. "These are the thieves. Have any of you seen them?" She passed the paper around.

"Belle shot one of them in the arm," Godiva added.

"Whooee! Good for Belle!" one of the women shouted.

Everyone gathered around to look at the picture. "I seen these guys," said a man in a bright red jacket. "Y'see I live in my van down in the Harris Harbor parking lot. Well, actually it's an old UPS truck, kinda brown and rusty, and it don't really drive any more. I hope they don't tow me away. There was a notice on the window."

"Get to the point, Simon," someone yelled.

"Oh yeah. Anyhow, I stepped out to go to the can, and there was this trail of blood on the floats. An' I thought maybe a dog got hurt or somethin' but then I saw these two guys climbin' on board the *Custard Pie*. It was gettin' dark but it looked like those guys in your picture."

Godiva cocked her head. "The *Custard Pie*?"

"Yeah, y' know, ol' Cassie Custard's boat. She usually lives on it, but the last couple days she's been in jail. Drunk and disorderly."

"Aw Simon, yer full of it," another wharf rat joined in. He was thin with shaggy, long hair, full beard, bushy eyebrows, and hair coming out of his ears and nose. Godiva moved away from him when she caught a whiff of his clothes that smelled like musty dishrags.

"I was sleepin' in my little boat over there at the harbor. I'm tied up just on the other side of the *Custard Pie*, ya know. Anyway, I seen two big ol' gals gettin' off that boat this morning. One was Cassie and t'other might o'been her sister. They's big gals, and ugly as sin! Cassie ain't no prize but her sister's even worse."

Simon became indignant, "Cassie ain't got no sister, dummy, an' I know for a fact that she is in jail. Should be gettin' out tomorrow. Yer eyes is so bad you took them two men fer wimmen. You don't see nothin since yer glasses got busted."

"They was women. I swear."

"Were not!"

"Were too! They was wearin' dresses."

The twins inched out the door as the bickering continued.

Goldie said, "Hey, Sis, why do you suppose those thugs went through so much to get their hands on that samovar and then they just dumped it?"

"Probably for the same reason it was so bashed up."

Chapter 12

Maurice Flambeau had just set up his canopy tent at the edge of Marine Park when the twins arrived. He looked up and hailed them over. "Thanks for that stack of cash yesterday. Took my lady friend out on the town with some of it."

Godiva looked pleased. "Did you take her to some nice restaurant? The Baranof Hotel, maybe?"

A tourist passed by and Maurice's accent magically appeared. "Ahh, no Madame, I took *ma Cherie* all the way to Gay Parree."

Goldie whispered in her sister's ear, "The Paris Bar at the end of Franklin Street."

Godiva smiled. "Listen Maurice, we have one more assignment for you. And since no one is waiting in line yet, you can consider it part of yesterday's job which I paid five times too much for."

"Ah, *oui*, Madame, you have *beaucoup de credit* in this bank. What do you need?"

Goldie held out his sketch from yesterday, which was now wrinkled and creased. "We want you to draw these same two men with women's clothes on."

"Pardon?"

"Yeah," Goldie said. "Draw some baggy dresses, maybe stripes or polka dots, and put scarves or hats on their heads."

Maurice began a new drawing with the same faces and a different set of clothes. As he put the finishing touches on a shapeless polka dot dress, the young woman selling flight-seeing tours in the booth next to him looked over and gasped.

"Oh my god, Maurice. Did you see those two ugly women this morning, too? I couldn't believe it! They were so gross."

Goldie perked up. She looked at the girl's nametag. "Tell

me, Brittany, where did you spot them?"

Brittany pointed to the little float plane dock behind the Merchant's Wharf. "They were boarding a yellow Cessna. At first I thought those tacky old women were taking an early morning glacier tour, but the plane was unmarked, so it wasn't a regular company."

"Did you recognize the pilot?" Godiva asked.

"Nope. I couldn't even see the pilot. I was too busy staring at those big goofy-looking women." She looked embarrassed, "Geez, my mother taught me not to stare at people who look different, but I couldn't help myself. Besides they were all the way over there, so they didn't know I was watching."

Godiva wasn't finished, "What time was it?"

"Pretty early. My boyfriend drops me off downtown at about 7:30. I don't start work until 9:00, so I was just sitting here in the sun drinking my coffee."

Goldie and Godiva thanked Maurice, and took the new sketch. Their first stop was Capital Copy on Seward Street, where they made a dozen copies of each of the two drawings. From there they went to Heritage Coffee Shop, found a quiet table in the back corner, and began to brainstorm.

Goldie pulled a yellow pad out of her enormous purse made from the remnants of an old Kilim carpet. Godiva handed her a Mont Blanc fountain pen, but her sister had already retrieved a ballpoint from her big handbag. She held it up. "Thanks, Sis, but I've already got one."

Godiva shrugged. "Suit yourself. Where do we start?" She put the expensive pen back in her little Gucci bag and took a sip of her latte.

"Well, I keep going over my last conversation with Mimi, and I really have the feeling it's not the samovars they're after. I think it's whatever she found inside of them. She wanted to show me something, so maybe she took it out and set it aside. I feel like we have to get back into her place to see if we can find anything."

Godiva nodded. "You handle those old teapots all the time, Sis. Tell me, could someone actually hide something inside? Is there a place that wouldn't be noticed, but might be discovered by accident, like if you were cleaning the teapot?"

Goldie gave her thumbs up. "Well, there is a space in the bottom of most of them. I suppose you could fit something small in it." She drew a rough cutaway diagram on her yellow pad, and suddenly snapped her fingers, "I'll bet that's it. They *are* after something hidden in them. That must be why they threw Belle's in the dumpster."

"Of course, that's it. Mimi must have hidden whatever she found. We have to go to her shop first. Do you think we can get in?"

Goldie nodded. "We can sure give it a try." She tapped her ballpoint on the pad. "After we look around Mimi's place, we'll go over to the jail and see if we can talk to Taku. I know he was drunk when they picked him up, but maybe after drying out a little he'll remember something. We just need to ask him the right questions."

Godiva hesitated. "Well, shouldn't that expensive lawyer have asked him all the right questions yesterday?"

"I talked to Perry. He said Taku couldn't remember a thing. Maybe we'll have better luck."

Godiva agreed. "Say, while we're at the jail do you suppose we can get Ollie Oliver's ear for a minute? I want to give him the sketches of our Russians and tell him they left on a floatplane in female disguises. We've got to make Ollie see that your samovars are the key to these crimes."

"You must think this town is like Mayberry, and ol' Sheriff Oliver has the keys to the jail hooked on his belt."

"He doesn't?"

"Sis, this is the big city! Well, big for Alaska. It may interest you to know there's a large correctional institution here run by a staff of real prison personnel. Ollie is the Chief of Police. If we're lucky, we'll find him at the fancy new police station out by Lemon Creek."

"Well, la-dee-dah. *Excuuuse* me. I didn't realize I was in such a booming metropolis. Now that you've set me straight, can we get back to the problem at hand?"

"Okay," Goldie said. "But, I think we should stop at the police station before we go to the jail. We need to ask Ollie to distribute the sketches around to ferry terminals and airports right away. If they wanted to get out of Alaska, maybe they thought the police would only look for them in Juneau, not in some other port. They could take that floatplane to Petersburg or Ketchikan and leave from there. Maybe Ollie can get someone at the FAA to identify that plane, or better yet, give him the flight plan."

The sisters threw around a few more ideas, while Goldie scribbled down the notes. Of course, all of this thinking made them hungry, so they each had a large apple toffee scone before they left. Counting calories wasn't on their agenda today.

When the twins stopped on the sidewalk in front of Tea & Sympathy, Goldie inhaled sharply and wiped away a tear. Then she squared herself up. "Well, the police tape is still in place. We are about to break the law. Still up for it?"

"You bet. We owe it to Mimi. Listen, you know the layout. Is there a way we can sneak in the back, so we aren't breaking and entering in broad daylight on a busy street?" A mischievous spark danced in Godiva's eyes. "What was that you said about crime scene tape?"

Goldie answered, halting while she thought it out. "Yeah. I think we can. The storeroom opens out to the back alley, and Mimi kept a key above the door. Taku used it when he needed a place to sleep. She once told me that no matter how drunk he was, he always put the key back above the door. Let's check it out."

The two silver-haired Mae West look-alikes tried to appear inconspicuous as they crept along a narrow passageway between the two old buildings. Goldie stood on her tiptoes and felt around the top of the back door frame. A smile flitted across her lips. She lifted the key off the dirty ledge. "Got it. Here we go."

She fitted the key in the lock, then placed it back above the door. The sisters stepped into the storeroom, lit only by the weak light filtering in through a dusty window.

Goldie noticed spots of dried blood on the storeroom floor, and on the pile of burlap bags where the police found Taku sleeping. She let out a gasp. For a moment she flashed on the image of poor Mimi, in her nightgown, sprawled at the bottom of the stairs. Tears welled in her eyes again.

Godiva reached toward the shelves to start searching for clues.

"Wait," Goldie whispered, "don't touch anything." She dug around in her carpetbag, and finally pulled out two pairs of gloves. "I knew I had these in there somewhere." She handed a pair to Godiva and they began to poke around.

Taku's backpack rested up against wood shelving filled with supplies, containers of tea and a few tools. They opened the backpack and checked everything inside. His stash consisted of a few tins of tobacco nestled in a rolled up shirt, a hairbrush and a toothbrush, but nothing out of the ordinary. On the shelves, random items were tucked between some boxes of tea, but still nothing suspicious. They moved on.

They had barely set foot into the shop, when Goldie threw out her arm to stop Godiva. She whispered, "Someone is in here. I don't think it's the police."

A loud crash followed by another broke the silence. Afraid to move, they inched back into the storeroom. Then the twins froze and listened, hearts beating like tom-toms. Steps creaked. Someone was coming down the stairs from Mimi's apartment.

Godiva spotted a sudden motion to her right and was almost knocked off her feet as an intruder crashed into her. The back door flew open sending rays of light into the dim store-room.

A stocky figure dressed in black with a ski mask covering his head stood silhouetted in the frame. He paused in the doorway for a moment, then ran out.

Godiva exhaled. "That nails it. Someone else is trying to find whatever was in those samovars. And this time it wasn't the Dumkovskys."

"Well, I don't think the guy who slammed into you found what he was looking for, either. Could it still be here?"

"I don't know." She held up her gloved hands, each knitted finger a different color. "As long as we've got these stylish mittens on we might as well keep looking."

They shuffled through everything in the vandalized shop, then traipsed upstairs to Mimi's apartment. Shards of glass covered the floor below the window next to the fire escape.

"So that's where he came in," mused Goldie, "I wondered at first if he knew about the key, but I guess not." They combed through the cozy little flat, which had been tossed by the fleeing intruder.

At one point Godiva said, "Do we even know what we're looking for?"

Goldie shook her head. "Whatever it is probably got Mimi killed. I guess we'll know it when we see it."

After an hour of fruitless investigation, they gave into defeat, and decided to head over to the police station.

Chapter 13

"What happened to the laid back vacation I was going to have in Juneau?" Godiva sighed, as they settled into Goldie's Subaru. "I might as well be in L.A. with this crime wave sweeping through town."

"At least it's keeping you busy. After one day in Juneau you usually start complaining how bored you are."

"Yeah, I'm busy, alright. I've actually been too busy to check in with Angel. When we're done with Ollie and Taku, I need to go back to your house and get on the computer. I'm running out of the columns I did before I left, and Angel said she'd pick out a few letters for me to answer." She fluffed her hair, shrugged her shoulders, and struck a Hollywood pose. "I still have my public to worry about, you know."

Goldie pursed her lips. "Look, Godiva, we have no idea what we might learn from Taku. Besides, Ollie may have dug up a lead on the Russians. Depending upon what happens, you might not get to that computer until tonight."

"Tonight? What about my beauty sleep?" She pulled down the visor and looked into the mirror Goldie had duct-taped to the back of it. "Ugh. Look at me. Your rural life is doing serious damage to my glamorous image."

"I am looking at you. You look just fine. In fact, you look really healthy. Just like me."

Godiva raised her eyebrows. "Easy for you to say. You don't have to look good for your public."

"That's because the public around here doesn't judge people by the labels on their fancy clothes."

Godiva quickly changed the subject. "Okay, so where do we find the esteemed Chief of Police?"

"It's not far, just up Egan Drive to Lemon Creek. I called

ahead to let him know we're coming. The prison is in the same general area. That's where Taku will be."

When they pulled up in front of the police station, Godiva stared at the glass-fronted modern building. "You said fancy, but I didn't expect it to be this nice."

Goldie shrugged. "We do have some nice buildings, you know."

They found Ollie standing in the lobby waiting for them, a cup of coffee cradled in his big hands.

"Hello, ladies. Before you get started on me, I want to say I think you're absolutely right. It is beginning to look like those samovars of yours set off some kind of crime spree."

They followed him down the hall. He offered some stale coffee, and said, "Okay, tell me what's so urgent. When you said you had to see me right away, you made it sound like a life and death situation."

Goldie gave him a serious look. "It is life and death, Ollie. There are two murderers running amok out there."

The Police Chief narrowed his eyes, made a tent with his fingers, and leaned back in his chair. "Now, ladies, I already told you—"

"Oh I know, you keep insisting Taku killed Mimi and I can see that the odds are certainly against him, but we're sure he's innocent."

Godiva interrupted, "See here, Chief, if you forget about Taku for a minute and look at what's been happening, it's pretty clear those Russians are the real killers."

Ollie opened his mouth to speak but before he could say anything, Goldie said, "For heaven's sake, just hear us out." She pulled two sheets of paper out of her purse, and slapped them down on Ollie's desk. "These are sketches of the guys who stole the samovars. Their names are Boris and Igor Dum-kovsky." She pointed to one paper. "This is what they really look like." Then she jabbed her finger at the other sheet. "We had Maurice draw them wearing these outfits."

"What gave you the bright idea of putting women's clothes on them?"

"We were over at the Glory Hole, and one of the people there saw them climb aboard Cassie Custard's boat. Another guy said he saw Cassie and her sister leaving the boat this morning—"

Godiva broke in. "But the first guy said Cassie was in jail, so we put two and two together and figured they stole Cassie's clothes for disguises."

Ollie said, "I wouldn't put too much faith in those folks at the Glory Hole."

"Well maybe not," said Goldie, "but we figured we'd have Maurice Flambeau do a sketch. When the girl in the stall next to him saw it, she said it looked exactly like two women she saw boarding a yellow Cessna this morning."

Ollie Oliver held both sets of sketches at arm's length. Then he set the first drawing down on his desk, and concentrated on the second one—the one with the men in baggy dresses and babushkas. He laughed out loud. "These guys are even uglier than Cassie. She might have a little mustache, but she sure as heck don't have a beard! Ya know, we did have her locked up for a few days. Another bender, so it was sort of for her own safety."

He scratched his head and furrowed his brow. "Hmmm. But, the old gal was right about something."

"What do you mean, Chief?" Godiva asked.

He spread his hands out on the desk, palms down. "Just before you two got here, Cassie called. She was madder than a wet hen, screaming that she'd been robbed. She said when she got back to her boat, her stuff had been ransacked and some underwear, scarves and her two best dresses were missing. I'm lookin' at the polka dot frock in this sketch and it looks a lot like the one Cassie was bellowing about. I hate to say it, but her dresses really would be big enough to fit these guys."

Ollie started to say something, but Goldie broke in again. "Chief Oliver, two more people could be in danger. A woman from Seattle bought one of the samovars, and my sister's boyfriend Caesar also bought one. I thought you could fax these sketches to the airports and ferry terminals in the area. Maybe they flew to some place they could catch a plane or ferry to Seattle."

He lifted the receiver and punched a button. "Norris, get your tail in here. I need some faxes sent out right away." An officer came in, took the sketches and hurried off down the hall.

Goldie got up and signaled it was time to leave. She said sweetly, "Any problem with us going over to the jail to talk with Taku?"

He walked to the door with them. "For you, Goldie? No problem at all. I'll call over there and get you clearance. Let me know if you find out anything we don't know."

After they stepped into the hall. Goldie turned to him. "And, you'll be sure to call me on the cell if anything turns up at the airports or ferry terminals?"

Ollie nodded and waved as they headed out the door.

Goldie tapped her finger against her chin, lost in thought. "This might sound farfetched, but you don't suppose that Father Augustine's murder is part of this whole thing, do you?"

"Well, maybe. But he was murdered before you started selling those deadly samovars, so it's probably just a coincidence. We'll have to leave that to your friend Ollie to solve."

On the way to the jail, they agreed Cassie's call about the stolen clothes confirmed they were on the right track. Now if only Taku had something to add.

They presented themselves at prison security, emptied their pockets, surrendered their purses and submitted to a pat down by a female guard. They were escorted into a bare visitors' room and moments later an officer brought in a disheveled Taku. He blinked a bit and sat down. He looked at the twins, and mumbled, "That lawyer guy who came to see me said you ladies are payin' part of his bill and he's worked out somethin' with the state for the rest. I wanna thank you for helpin' me. Not sure I'm worth it."

Goldie patted his arm. "Rudy asked us to help you out, and my sister Godiva offered to pay for part of Perry Pinkwater's fee. If anyone can save you, he can. But we need your help here. We don't think you killed Mimi. We think something else happened."

Taku stared blankly at the two women. Goldie said gently, "You need to try really hard to remember what happened the night Mimi was killed. Any little thing could be important."

Taku coughed and squeezed his eyes shut, as though he was trying to picture it. A tear slid down his cheek. He looked from one twin to the other. "How could I have kilt her? She was my angel."

"Think."

Taku scrunched up his face again. As if in a dream he said, "I was in the storeroom, and I hear someone talkin' with a funny accent. I think maybe it's one of them Russian soccer players I seen at the Viking. 'Give it to me', he says. 'Mimi's cryin', but that voice shouts, 'quit stallin'.'"

"What happened next?"

"I don't know," he wailed. "See, I had quite a few and was stumblin' around. At first I think maybe I was just hearin' voices. That happens to me a lot, you know?" He put his head down in his hands.

When he looked up again, tears were streaming down his face. "But then I hear Mimi really screamin' fer help. I remember that I grabbed my halibut bat..." He hesitated a moment before continuing. "I was strikin' out with it, but I wouldn't—just couldn't have hit Mimi with it. Then there's two voices, but now it's all gibberish. Words I don't understand. Uhh, umm, I don't remember anything else."

"Nothing?" said Godiva.

He shrugged his shoulders. "Nope. Next thing I knew the cops were all over me, and the bloody bat was on my chest. I got a lump on my head, too. Right here." He parted his messy hair and revealed a swollen bruise behind his ear.

"Do you think someone hit you?" Goldie asked.

"Yeah, but I dunno, I might of got in a fight over at the Lucky Lady."

Twenty minutes later they headed out of the prison compound.

"I don't know about you," Goldie said, "but I feel pretty bummed out."

Godiva nodded. "Poor Taku Ted. Those thugs must have attacked Mimi for whatever it was she found in the samovars. Then he stumbles in drunk, tries to save her and passes out."

"Or gets hit in the head."

"Yeah, next thing you know the Dumkovskys kill Mimi with Taku's bat, and drop it on his chest as they leave through the back door."

"Maybe they didn't mean to kill her, but hit her too hard. Or maybe Taku aimed for Boris, and hit Mimi by mistake. I hope not."

Goldie chewed on that for a while. "Possibly, but that still doesn't explain the guy we ran into. The samovars were gone after Mimi was killed, and the Dumkovskys were gone, too. So why would someone ransack her flat? She must have taken out whatever she found and hid it. Maybe they sent someone to find it."

Godiva looked over and saw tears running down Goldie's cheek. "I need something sweet. How about a big piece of cherry pie with ice cream on top. What do you say we head back home and get some?"

Chapter 14

Godiva glared at the beat up laptop and tried to make herself comfortable at Goldie's cubbyhole desk. No matter what she did, there was no image on the screen. She called downstairs, "Hey Goldie, is there a trick to getting the screen to light up? This thing could qualify as one of your antiques."

Goldie ran upstairs, trying to stifle a giggle. When the screen went black about a month ago, Rudy had found an old monitor at the Salvation Army Thrift Store for five dollars. He hooked it up to the laptop and it worked perfectly if you pressed F7 each time to fire it up. The ugly old thing was such an affront to Goldie's decorating sense, that she had immediately pushed it to one side, covered it with an antique shawl and placed a potted begonia on top.

She almost felt sorry for Godiva, knowing she had columns to write, but not sorry enough to make it easy for her. Instead, she made a big show of mumbling to herself and fiddling with the old laptop computer while Godiva grew more and more agitated.

When it was clear that Godiva's patience had finally run out, Goldie lifted the shawl and flowerpot. There sat the monitor with its $5 price tag still attached. She pressed F7 and the clunky thrift store screen lit up. Godiva let out a sigh of relief, but her smile turned to a scowl as she realized Goldie had been playing her along just to get her goat. Before Godiva could scold her, the cell phone in Goldie's pocket began to play its tune.

"It's the Chief."

Sounding more optimistic than she felt, Goldie said, "Hi, Ollie. Have you got good news?" The slight smile broadened until she was grinning. "That's great, just great. Thank you so much. Of course I know you'll do everything you can." There was a long pause while Ollie kept talking. Then Goldie said, "Yes, of course, we'll leave everything up to the police. No, no, we won't put ourselves in danger. Promise. Bye."

She turned to Godiva. "Bingo! One of the people at the ferry terminal in Ketchikan recognized our goons. She even remembered the names on their passports. Get this—now they're now traveling as Vladimir Minsky and Uri Pinsky. She said she remembered because the names rhyme and she thought that was funny."

"There's only one way they could have gotten those passports."

Goldie's voice caught. A little sob escaped. "And that's if the Dumkovskys killed them and set fire to the warehouse. Poor Uri and Vladimir."

Godiva hesitated before saying in a cynical tone, "Your pals Uri and Vladimir could have been part of it. A smuggling ring, maybe. Did you ever consider that?"

Goldie pursed her lips and shook her head. "No way! They were very reputable. They would never team up with thugs like that."

"Well, maybe they did and that's why they were killed. By the way, did the lady at the ferry terminal say where were they headed?"

Goldie sniffled. "Umm—Bellingham. That's where the Alaska ferries dock. It's about ninety miles from Seattle. The agent said they just managed to get on today's three o'clock ferry. If they missed that one, they would have had to wait two days for the next one."

"How long does it take to get to Bellingham?"

"Ummm, it's about two-and-a-half days, so they should get into port on Friday morning."

"Okay, Sis. You know what that means. We've got to check the schedule and get there by the time the ferry docks to find out where they're headed. We certainly can't rely on your pal Ollie. He's probably happy to have them out of his hair. If we're right and they're after something in those samovars, your customer in Seattle will be next."

Goldie made a note to herself to look up the woman's number and call her to warn her. "Ollie mentioned something about leaving it to the cops in Washington State, but I can't remember exactly what he said."

"Look, I do need to get those columns done." Godiva looked at Goldie's pathetic old laptop and rolled her eyes. "Let's see if we can get out on a flight tonight. When we get to Seattle, I'll just buy a new laptop to work on while I'm there. When I'm done I'll give it to you to replace this old piece of garbage. That way, at least I can catch up on enough work to keep ahead of my commitments."

Goldie raised an eyebrow, feeling just a bit jealous that her sister could buy an expensive laptop with less thought than Goldie would give to buying a blouse on the bargain rack at Fred Meyer's. But then, Godiva wouldn't have all those millions if it weren't for her dear departed husband, Max DuBois, one of the most obnoxious men Goldie had ever encountered. Just the thought of being married to that uncouth loudmouth for so many years quashed the little flash of envy. "Leave tonight? You're kidding, aren't you?"

Godiva put her hands on her hips with mock indignation. "No, I'm serious. I'm partly packed and it shouldn't take you long to throw a few rags in your duffel bag. It's about five thirty now. We can be out of here in half-an-hour. Call Rudy and tell him to open the shop tomorrow. We were going to Seattle anyway, so we'll just check into the hotel a few days early."

Goldie warmed to the idea. "Well, I guess Mom and Uncle Sterling would really be surprised to see us waiting for them when they arrive tomorrow afternoon."

"There you go. I just know they'll be delighted to have some extra time with you while I'm sitting in my comfortable hotel room typing on *your* new laptop, instead of sleeping in a sardine can and trying to coax a few words out of this jerry-rigged contraption." She gestured toward the old computer. "Then on Friday morning you can drive us to Bellingham."

"Back up for a minute, why will I be the one to drive to

Bellingham?"

"Because I'll be sleeping in the reclining seat. You're an early riser, I'm not. You can't expect me to be all bright-eyed and bushy-tailed if we have to get up at four in the morning. So the way it works is, I pay for the car, you drive. Those Dumkovskys shouldn't be hard to spot. Let's get moving. Do you know when the next flight leaves?"

Goldie threw up her hands in frustration. "I can call and find out, but hold on a minute! This is the Alaska tourist season. Every flight is bound to be booked solid. Do you think you can just waltz up to the counter and buy two tickets?"

"Well, there can't be that many traveling first class."

Goldie felt like she was instructing a slow student. "Okay, here's the reality. First class seats are booked just as fast as the economy class by wealthy people like you, dear sister, who can't get a reservation for the regular seats. We have tickets on Friday's flight only because your precious Angel booked them a few weeks back. This may be one thing your money can't buy."

"Says you. Pack your bag and then get that old wreck of a car going and let's find out."

The terminal was swarming with summer travelers. Godiva elbowed through the VIP line, ignoring the protests and dirty looks from the people she pushed aside. Goldie leaned on one of her sister's Louis Vuitton traveling cases and worried that airport security would muscle her twin out of the airport. Godiva used every manipulative maneuver she knew but it was no use. The agent said they were booked solid with several standbys ahead of them. As Goldie predicted, even first class was full.

They decided to have a cup of tea in the coffee shop and brainstorm their next move. One thing was certain—if they took their scheduled flight it meant they would definitely miss the Dumkovskys' arrival in Bellingham.

As they waited for the tea, Godiva overheard the lady in the booth behind them say that she would give anything to stay even one more day before going back to Seattle. Godiva winked at her sister and slid out of the booth.

As she passed the table beside them, a woman pointed to Godiva and asked her companion in a stage whisper, "Is that someone I should recognize?"

Her companion turned in Godiva's direction and fixed her with a stare, then snapped her fingers and said with a heavy New York accent, "Hmmm. Well, it's not Mae West. She'd be much older. Yeah. I think it's what's-her-name? Wait, it's coming to me. Oh, yeah, she looks like that picture in the paper. You know, the advice column, *Ask G.O.D.*, or something." The other woman started to get up. "Maybe she'll give me an autograph." Godiva pretended not to hear them and kept walking. She had a mission.

She approached the folks in the adjoining booth and greeted them with her sweetest voice. "Hi. My sister and I are sitting behind you and I overheard you say how you wish you could stay a little longer. I have a good proposition for you."

The man, clad in a loud Hawaiian shirt with hula girls on it, stiffened his back and began to speak, "Look lady, if you..."

Godiva held up her hand. "Nothing fishy, sir. You see my sister and I have first class tickets for Seattle on the ten o'clock flight Friday morning, but we have an emergency and have to be there tonight. The problem is there are no seats available." She flashed a million dollar smile. "If you were willing to switch with us, I'd make it worth your while. Our first class tickets for your economy tickets and I'll even give you enough money for two nights in a hotel. What do you say?" She discretely made no mention of the fact that finding a hotel room would be like trying to find a diamond on the beach.

The woman gave her husband a pathetic puppy dog look, and he shrugged. "Uh, yeah, sure. The wife really wanted to stay a few more days, but it better be enough for a good room. No flea trap."

With victory at hand, Godiva reached into her purse and held up five one-hundred dollar bills. "Do I look like someone who would stay in a flea bag? Is it a deal?"

She strode back to the table triumphantly. "Okay, our plane

leaves in two hours. We'll have to sit in the cattle car, but at least we got on. Myra and Norton over there," she gestured toward the couple behind them, "will go over to the ticket counter with us and work it out when they finish their snack."

Goldie shook her head in disbelief. "You're amazing. I would have bet money you couldn't do it."

Her sister smirked. "Ah, money. That's the magic word."

Goldie pretended not to hear and reached for her cell phone to call the shop. Rudy picked it up on the first ring and chirped, "Silver Spoon Antiques, if it ain't old, we ain't got it."

"Hey Rudy, we're at the airport, getting ready to chase those Russians to Seattle. They boarded a ferry in Ketchikan and we're going to beat them to Bellingham. You're in charge of the shop until I get back."

Rudy didn't sound too surprised. "Yeah, I figgered you gals were up to somethin'. Belle came by a while ago and said she talked to Ollie. Then she commenced to tellin' me about you trackin' the Ruskies and visitin' Taku in jail."

"That's my mother-in-law. News travels faster than a speeding bullet when Belle gets hold of it."

Myra and Norton dabbed their chins with their napkins and stood up to pay the bill. Goldie jumped up. "I gotta go, Rudy. I'll call you from Seattle."

Before she could disconnect, Rudy shouted into the phone, "Almost forgot to tell 'ya boss. Ollie said they fished two more o' yer samovars outta the channel."

Chapter 15

The Alaska Airlines jet rolled into in Seattle at 10:37 pm. Godiva was starting to wind down and get grumpy as clumps of cases tumbled down the chute. Hopeful passengers elbowed their way past the twins and hugged the rim of the baggage carousel, probably praying their luggage actually made it. One particularly large man stomped on Goldie's foot. As she hopped up and down in pain she spotted her beat up duffle.

Goldie grabbed the handle, pulled it over the edge and thunked it down on the floor. "What luck. Mine came right away."

Godiva paced, clearly beginning to lose her cool as most of the other passengers rolled their suitcases away. "Great. Wouldn't you know it? Your crappy duffel bag comes down right away and I don't see my Louis Vuitton bags anywhere. With my luck, they're probably lost again."

"Calm down, Godiva. You're getting upset. Think positive," Goldie said in a soft, soothing tone. "Breathe from your diaphragm. Go like this." She demonstrated by closing her eyes, thumb and middle fingertips touching on each hand, and hummed a soft "Oommm."

Godiva wailed, "Eeeeyyaahhh!"

"No, no, Sis. Try saying ooommm."

"Oommm, my ass! Open your eyes, dammit! There are my bags. Look, that one has a big rip from one end to the other."

Godiva stormed over to the baggage claims desk where the clerk kept insisting they could fix the damage so it would hardly show. She demanded to speak to the supervisor and a few moments later issued veiled threats to convince him that "a repair that hardly showed" just wasn't acceptable for a suitcase of this quality. Beaten down, he finally approved a replacement and completed the claim form.

Luckily, the car rental presented no challenge. The Town Car Godiva requested was ready and waiting at Hertz, and by 11:30 that evening they arrived at the luxurious Hotel Monaco on 4th Street in downtown Seattle.

Goldie looked around the lobby in amazement. "Wow, Sis. I thought we'd be staying somewhere nice, like the Hilton, but this is fantastic. It must be costing you a mint."

Godiva sighed. "Goldie, it's my favorite place in Seattle. The Convention Center is pretty close so I figured why not stay here? We've got a car and I can afford the best. I discovered this place on my last trip here." After they got into the elevator, she kept chattering. "I booked the Mediterranean Suite for myself and deluxe adjoining rooms for you, Mom and Unk. Wait till you see them. Mine has a spa tub to die for and they give you these cute animal print robes to wear."

Goldie patted her sister on the arm. "Well, la-dee-dah. I've gotta say, you sure know how to spend your late husband's money."

"It may have been Max's money, but I earned every penny by putting up with him all those years!"

As they got off the elevator Godiva said, "By the way, would you like a goldfish companion?"

Goldie stopped dead in her tracks. "A what?"

"A goldfish companion. Their Guppy Love program will send one up to keep you company during the stay and the staff takes care of it. Watching fish is very relaxing, you know. I think I'll get one myself."

"Ummm, think I'll pass on the fish."

"Mom and Unk will be here tomorrow in time to take advantage of the hotel's *Hour of Indulgence,*" Godiva said as she opened the door to her suite. "They'll love it. So will you."

Goldie opened her own door and admired the room, then stepped back into the hall. "Hold on a second, *Hour of Indulgence.* What's that, a meet and greet wine tasting or something?"

Her sister shook her head. "No, my dear, it's way more. Not

only do they serve fine wines and boutique beers, but they have chair massages and fortune telling and Lord knows what else."

"Fortune telling? Wow. Mom will just love it. We left in such a rush, I didn't even have time to do our charts."

Godiva stepped into her suite. "Night. See you in the morning. We'll go shopping for that new laptop."

Minutes later they were both fast asleep in their respective beds under extra fluffy goose down comforters.

As soon as she awoke, Goldie tried to call Mrs. Wurlitzer, the Seattle customer, but all she got was the woman's voice mail. She made a mental note to try again a little later. During breakfast they planned out the rest of the day, as Goldie jotted notes on her yellow pad. The first order of business was to warn Caesar and Mrs. Wurlitzer that they were now the owners of some very dangerous merchandise.

Godiva reached for her cell phone and punched in Caesar's number. When she got the voice mail, she said, "Caesar, honey, call me when you get this. I've got to talk to you about that samovar you bought from Goldie." She shrugged her shoulders. "I sure hope he calls me as soon as he gets the message. Guess it's time for Plan B."

She opened the phone again and called her old boyfriend, Ricky Thompson, a former Special Forces operative who now owned a security/bodyguard company. Ricky and his hulky business partner Ivan guarded Caesar and Chili during a tense time the year before at the Gourmet Gladiator Tournament. Now it was time to call on him again. Caesar had the seventh samovar and that put a big X on his back.

When she hung up, Goldie said, "I'm glad you asked Ricky to guard Caesar and Chili. No telling what might be in those samovars, or who might be after them."

"Don't worry," Godiva said with a wink, "Ricky will keep an eye on them."

"Tell you what, Sis, if I wasn't married, I wouldn't mind

keeping my eye on Ricky. He sure turned out to be a hunk. Nothing like the psycho kid from high school who opened beer bottles with his teeth."

Godiva looked a bit dreamy. "Yeah, our senior year was really something, wasn't it? You going to love-ins with your hippie friends and me going to poker games with Tricky Ricky. Man, that guy could kiss!"

While her sister made some calls, Goldie tried Mrs. Wurlitzer again, with the same result. This time she left a voice message. "Mrs. Wurlitzer, this is Goldie Silver from Silver Spoon Antiques in Juneau. If you are back from your cruise, please call me, I must talk to you right away." She left her cell phone number.

Godiva gathered her things and clapped her hands, "Let's go. I simply must write my columns this afternoon, or I'll be in hot water." On their way out, Godiva put in her request for a goldfish, a fantail if possible.

Chapter 16

Godiva wasted no time at the huge computer warehouse. She headed right for the laptop with the most bells and whistles and tapped a few buttons just for show. "This one looks like it'll do. What do you think, Goldie?"

Goldie fingered the price tag. "Much too expensive. What about this one here? It's half the price and comes with a free case, too."

"Sorry, Sis, it's an off-brand, bound to cause trouble. Just look at that free case. I wouldn't be caught dead carrying that."

"But you won't be carrying it, I will."

"What if someone found out I gave you a cheesy computer in an ugly case? It would be so embarrassing." Godiva caught the clerk and told him to ring up the shiny silver laptop, but first she asked for the manager and convinced him to throw in a leather case as a bonus.

When they got in the car, Goldie tried Mrs. Wurlitzer one more time. Still no answer. "I don't get it. Mrs. Wurlitzer told me her cruise would be over by yesterday."

"Maybe she didn't go straight home. Might have stopped somewhere along the way to see a friend or something. Don't worry, Sis, if she's not home, the Dumkovskys can't find her either."

Goldie hugged herself tight. "I just hope nothing happened to her."

In the early afternoon, Godiva stayed at the hotel and worked on her column while Goldie took a walk down to the Pike Street Market. After watching a famous fish monger toss a few whole salmon across the counter to his helper, she poked around in the shops and stalls for an hour or two, then headed back to the hotel in time to meet her mother and uncle when they arrived.

At a few minutes past four, Flossie and Sterling Silver strolled through the lobby doors. A bellman followed rolling their large wardrobe case filled with costumes and props for the magic act they were scheduled to give at the Icons of Illusion banquet. Flossie, all dolled up for the trip, was wearing a pantsuit the color of pink cotton candy. Every blue-rinsed hair on her head was in place. She flashed her dentures at the young bellman. "You look like such a nice boy, but darling, you don't look like you're eating enough. You need a little meat on those bones." She pressed a ten dollar tip into his hand. "Here, honey, buy yourself a nice big pastrami sandwich and make sure they give you a good kosher pickle with it, too."

Sterling, dressed in a casual plaid shirt and chinos, took his sister-in-law by the elbow and nudged her along. "Come on Flossie, old girl. Don't harp on the poor kid like a Jewish mother. He looks healthy, and I'll bet he's got some biceps, hauling around those bags all day." The young man shot Sterling a grateful look.

Goldie and Godiva sat in chairs with their backs to the lobby doors. As soon as they heard Flossie trying to fatten up the bellman, they turned around and chorused, "Aren't you those famous magicians, Flossie and Sterling Silver?"

Flossie clasped her hands. "Oh, my beautiful girls." Then she hugged each of her daughters while fighting back tears. "You came, both of you. It's a sight for sore eyes to see you two together." She stepped back and admired her identical daughters. Then she surveyed the hotel lobby. "And such a fancy hotel, Godiva, I feel like the Queen of Sheba with her two princesses!"

Sterling folded his arms and grunted, "And what am I supposed to be? The Sheik of Araby?"

Flossie ignored him and went right on talking, "You know girls, your father—he should rest in peace—would be in heaven if he could receive that award himself tomorrow night."

Sterling grunted again. "He's already in heaven, Flossie, that's why we're here to accept it for him."

Goldie hugged her mother. "It's so exciting, Mom. Imagine our Daddy, Harry Silver, being honored as one of the greatest magicians of all time."

Sterling waved his hands in a theatrical flourish. "Now I ask you, how many guys can say their brother was one of the greatest names in magic? It sure gets me respect at the Magic Castle!" He turned to Godiva. "And I must thank you, Lady Godiva, for providing us with lodging fit for royalty. By the way, do we have time for a little nap before dinner?"

"Sure. Let's get you both checked in so you can rest up for the *Hour of Indulgence.*"

Sterling raised an eyebrow and fixed Godiva with a questioning look. "Hour of...."

"Indulgence, Unk. Don't even ask, but you'll enjoy the massage and I'm sure Mom will give the fortune teller a run for her money. I just hope you old ducks behave yourselves, don't get drunk on the wine, and please leave your tricks in the trunk until tomorrow night."

They completed the registration and Godiva said to the desk clerk, "Give them each a fish."

"A fish?" Flossie said, "Are we cooking in the room? If this is one of those rooms with a kitchen, I'd rather have chicken than fish, wouldn't you Sterling? You'd think in a fancy place like this everyone would eat in the restaurant."

Goldie couldn't hold in the laughter. "No, Mom. Godiva is ordering a pet goldfish in a bowl for each of you. She says it's relaxing. The staff takes care of them. You just watch them swim around."

Flossie shrugged her shoulders. "Hmmmph. Some classy joint! What will they think of next? I did our charts this morning and mine said I would be in for a big surprise, this must be it."

"Come on, old girl," Sterling said simply. "We need to get our beauty sleep." He turned to Godiva. "Do I really need to take the fish?"

She answered as sweetly as possible, "Trust me, Unk, you'll like it. Just don't make it disappear."

They piled the two oldsters into the elevator, and steered them to their rooms. The plan was to meet in the lobby at six.

An hour later, the sisters sat in Godiva's suite, sipping tea and nibbling on biscuits from a silver tray. Goldie pulled a yellow pad out of her huge carpetbag.

"Let's figure out where we stand." She started to make another list. "We don't have to worry about Caesar and Chili because Ricky will be keeping an eye on them. Before we left, Belle mentioned that one of the ladies she met at the National Mad Hatters' Convention last August is married to a captain on the LAPD. She gave me her number in case we need some help in L.A., but with Ricky on the job, maybe that won't be necessary. Belle seems to really like this woman. Said they were like the Bobbsey Twins at the convention."

"Just what I need—another Belle." Godiva groaned. "Well, put her number on the list. We'll have it handy if we need it in California. You never know. What's next?"

Goldie tapped the pad with her pencil. "I tried calling Mrs. Wurlitzer a few times with no luck. I guess she'll be back tomorrow, so I'll just put her on the list, too. And, of course, our trip to Bellingham tomorrow morning. I called to check, and the ferry comes in at about eight a.m. If we don't see the Dumkovskys get off the ferry, we need a fallback plan, don't you think?"

"Well, I hope we spot them, but even if we don't, we know where they're headed. Mrs. Wurlitzer's address was on the paperwork they swiped from your shop. The question is, even if we spot them, what can we do to stop them? Maybe we should ask Ollie to alert the police in Seattle."

"I'm way ahead of you, Sis. Ollie told me it probably wouldn't do any good. Since the crime wasn't committed in Seattle, they won't even pay any attention to us. Nope. If anything is going to get done, we'll have to do it. I promised Ollie again that we would stay out of trouble."

Godiva raised an eyebrow and her thought echoed in Goldie's head. *And will we?*

Chapter 17

"You know, that fortune teller wasn't half bad," Flossie said, smoothing the folds on her flowered jacket. "She said I was going to be the center of attention somewhere—maybe a theater. I'm telling you, Sterling, it's like she saw you and me on stage Saturday night."

"That's hogwash, Flossie," Sterling said. "You should have gotten a chair massage, instead of that half-baked fortune. My shoulders feel like a couple of limp noodles. All you got was the same line she probably tells everyone."

Godiva stepped between them. "Okay, children, let's not fight." She couldn't hold back her laughter. "Make nice and we'll all get something to eat."

They headed for the hotel's gourmet restaurant. During dinner, the twins filled Flossie and Sterling in on everything that had happened in Juneau. Sterling seemed more interested in Belle's salmon bake than the murder. Flossie wanted to know every detail of all of the crimes, and made her daughters repeat the description of the Russian villains.

"So you see," Goldie said, "that's why we're getting up early tomorrow morning and driving to Bellingham. We want to see if those Dumkovsky brothers get off the ferry. Don't worry, we'll be back in time for the Icons cocktail party."

Flossie beamed. "Oh boy. Some excitement. When do we leave?"

"Sorry, Mom, this doesn't include you. Goldie and I will leave at five in the morning. The drive takes about two hours. She'll drive and I'll sleep. And you two will be safely snuggled in your comfy hotel beds."

"Darn tootin' we will," said Sterling.

"But you girls might need a little help," Flossie protested.

"No way, Mom, we're just going to make sure they were on that ship. After that, we plan to follow them and get a license number or something, so we won't need any help. Besides, you two need to save all your energy for your performance and the banquet."

Flossie slumped in her chair, and fiddled with her dessert. "So I guess we're grounded. Just a couple of old shirts hung out to dry."

"It's okay with me," Sterling said, "I'll hang out around here anytime. Besides, I'm not getting up at five o'clock to go on some wild Russian goose chase."

As they rode the elevator up to their respective rooms, Goldie vowed to try Mrs. Wurlitzer one more time, Godiva groused about having to work on a column before bed, and Flossie said she was ready to "hit the hay." Sterling nodded off in the elevator and Flossie poked him in the ribs when they reached their floor.

Godiva opened the email from Angel and skimmed through several cries for help until one caught her eye.

Dear G.O.D.,

I've been dating Wally for about four months. People have said we look more like brother and sister than boyfriend and girlfriend, and now I know why. Last night we started talking about our youth and showed each other pictures of our parents. Omigod! Turns out we both have the same father. Mom always said Dad was a regular Romeo, but I guess he led a double life. What should I do?"
~In Love with My Brother

Godiva pushed back in her chair trying to come up with a solution. This one wasn't easy. Finally, she started to tap out an answer.

Dear In Love,

I'm sorry but this one doesn't have a fairytale ending. I think you and Wally have to face the music and be happy you've found each other as brother and sister. There are lots of other fish in the sea, but if you live in a small pond, you better move up-river to do your fishing. For all you know, your dad may have romanced every woman in town.

~G.O.D

She shut down the laptop, and climbed into bed feeling a bit sorry for poor *In Love with My Brother*. It seemed like only moments had passed when the jangling phone woke her up. A mechanical voice chirped, "Good morning. This is the wakeup call you requested."

She struggled into her clothes, first putting her Donna Karan tee-shirt on inside out and backwards. She was almost too tired to dab on a little makeup, but when she looked in the mirror she changed her mind and dragged out the cosmetic bag. Glancing out the window she saw there was a light drizzle, but grabbed a pair of sunglasses anyway to cover her half-open eyes.

The sisters both opened their doors the same time—Goldie as perky as a sunflower on a summer day and Godiva dragging her tail. They headed down the hall and stopped short. Flossie and Sterling stood in front of the elegant elevator doors.

"It's about time." Flossie stood there tapping her foot. "We've been here for ten minutes waiting for you, haven't we Sterling?"

Sterling threw his hands in the air. "Sorry, girls. It was all her idea. I wanted to sleep in, but she came banging on my door. You know your mother. Stubborn as a mule."

During the drive to Bellingham, while Godiva snored in the seat beside her, Goldie filled the oldsters in on more of their mission. They sat in the backseat studying the copies of Maurice Flambeau's drawings.

Flossie took off her glasses and looked closely at the

sketches. "So these are the guys we're looking for?"

"Yeah, Mom," Goldie answered. "The first sketch is the Dumkovsky brothers; the second one is what they look like wearing women's clothes."

Sterling pointed at the first drawing. "Geez, I'd hate to meet these ugly mugs in a dark alley." Then he looked at the other sketch. "But it'd be even worse to meet these women in the daylight."

"Yeah," Flossie squeaked, "they look pretty rough. Betcha I could spot them anywhere."

They got to the ferry terminal about ten minutes before the *Columbia* docked. The place was jam-packed, and it was hard to see much. They elbowed their way through the crowd for a better look at the disembarking passengers.

Flossie inched her way over to Goldie and held the drawing of the disguised Russians under her nose as if it were a secret CIA document. She said in a stage whisper, "There they are. Don't look right away, but it's those two big women schlepping those duffel bags. No one else could look that ugly."

"But, they don't have beards," said Goldie.

"*Oy vey*, have you never heard of razors? People would question beards, wouldn't they?

Clouds darkened the sky and the dock was really crowded, but in the end they all agreed it was definitely the Dumkovskys. Goldie ran to the parking lot to pull the car around while the others trailed behind the slow-walking pair. She pulled up just as the two big women got in line to hail a cab.

Godiva and the oldsters piled in. "Follow that cab!" said Sterling in a voice reminiscent of James Cagney in an old gangster movie.

Minutes later they were trailing the yellow taxi at a discreet distance. Everything seemed fine until just past Everett, when the cab turned east heading toward Snohomish. This was not the route to Seattle, so where were they going?

It didn't take long to learn the answer. The cab turned onto a side road and after a mile or so it stopped in front of a fancy gate. A tastefully lettered sign over the entry said: *Full Monty*

Mountain Resort—A Clothing Optional Retreat. Flossie squinted at the sign. "Clothing optional? What's that mean?"

Godiva let out a big sigh. "It's a nudist colony, Mom. I think we might have made a dreadful mistake."

"You mean those Russians are going to take off their clothes and romp around naked?" Flossie clucked her tongue.

"What the heck?" said Sterling.

The two ungainly women finally got out of the cab. Flossie took another look at the drawing of the Dumkovskys in women's clothes. *"Oy vey,"* she said and passed the drawing around. After closer observation, they all realized they had followed the wrong people.

"Well ladies," Sterling said, "it looks like we really barked up the wrong tree. Turn the car around, Goldie. Let's skedaddle fast before they get undressed."

Flossie moaned. "I'm sorry girls. It's my fault. They're just two ugly old ladies, not your Dumkovsky brothers after all. Guess I need new eyeglasses."

Even though this was a real setback, Goldie couldn't help laughing. "Yeah, right, Mom. They had us all fooled, so don't feel too bad."

"Well, at least we know those bums weren't headed for this nudist colony," said Sterling, "so what do you suppose happened to them?"

Goldie thought for a moment. "Well Unk. Could be one of two things. Either they got off at Prince Rupert instead of Bellingham, or we got so fixated on those women we missed the real thugs."

She pulled off on the shoulder and dragged out her cell phone, "Mrs. Wurlitzer still hasn't called back. Now it's becoming urgent." She tried the number again, but it didn't go through. "Guess I'll have to wait till we're back in range. I just hope we reach her before they do."

Godiva didn't reply. She was fast asleep.

Chapter 18

When Goldie's cell phone played *Chattanooga Choo-Choo* she reached into her carpetbag and took a quick peek at the screen. Mrs. Wurlitzer had finally called back. She flipped up the cover. "Goldie speaking. Is this Mrs. Wurlitzer?"

An aggravated voice replied, "Yes, this is Elvira Wurlitzer. Frankly, Ms. Silver, I can't imagine what could possibly be urgent enough for you to disturb me with so many messages. Surely there wasn't a problem with my credit card."

"No, there was no problem with the credit card, Mrs. Wurlitzer, it's about the samovar I sold you—"

Goldie was cut off before she could finish her sentence. "Well, about that samovar, I might as well tell you, after I unpacked it and put it in the drawing room, I decided I really didn't like it very much. A bit too gaudy on my Chesterfield sideboard. It is authentic, isn't it?"

"Of course it is."

Mrs. Wurlitzer prattled on, "I'm thinking I might ask the museum if they want it for their Russian exhibit and take a donation credit. At any rate, I really can't talk right now. I'm on my way home from the spa, and I don't like to talk on my cell phone while I'm driving, so please get to the point. Just what was so important?"

Goldie saw a chance to get her hands on one of the wayward teapots. "Ummm, look Mrs. Wurlitzer, if you don't like the samovar, why don't I just take it back and credit your card?"

There was a moment of silence. "Are you here in Seattle?"

"Yes, I'm in town for a few days. Would you like me to pick it up? I'd be happy to come and get it in the morning." She said a silent prayer.

Suspicion crept into Elvira Wurlitzer's voice. "Well, I don't know, Ms Silver." She hesitated, and then sounded cagey. "I'm having second thoughts about giving it away. I haven't really decided yet. I'd like some time to think it over. I'll call you back if I'm interested."

Goldie heard a click and the connection was broken. She rolled her eyes in a fit of frustration. She would wait a while for Mrs. Wurlitzer to return home and try again.

It was almost time to leave the hotel for the Icons of Illusion banquet, so Goldie went next door to Godiva's suite. When her sister answered the door, she pulled Goldie into the room and marched her to the computer. "I just finished reading this email from Angel. I love that girl. Every time I give her an assignment, she's like a bulldog with a bone. She's been checking the Vladivostok papers for clues on the warehouse fire, and I think she hit pay dirt." She pushed Goldie down in the desk chair. "Here, Sis, read this."

Goldie stared at the translated news article attached to Angel's email.

Minsky & Pinsky Warehouse Fire Covers Up Smuggling Ring

Fedor Zorankovitch, head of Russian Federal Sur-veillance Service for Compliance with the Law in Mass Communications and Cultural Heritage Protection, say recent Minsky & Pinsky Import/Export fire very sus-picious. Investigators suspect Vladmir Minsky and Uri Pinsky part of crime ring smuggling Russian treasures to buyers in United States by passing through Territory of Alaska.

Officers with the RFSSCLMCCHP have spent last fifteen months tracking long lost national treasures. Most valuable are Seven Stars of Siberia. Seven perfectly matched large Siberian alexandrites set in Tiffany tiara, missing since fall of the Romanovs. These priceless gems very rare. No other matched stones like them in whole world. Early last year agents traced stones to Minsky & Pinsky. Warehouse was under surveillance when fire occurred. Two persons seen escaping burning building, but not found for questioning. Government officers refused making further comments.

Goldie looked at Godiva in astonishment. "Vladmir and Uri smugglers? I can't believe it. They seemed so honest and likeable."

Godiva interrupted her and closed the lid on the computer. "I'll tell you the rest in the elevator. Mom and Unk will have cat fits if we're late." She picked up her little black leather bag and hustled Goldie out the door.

"I knew there was something inside those samovars! I'll bet it's those priceless gems. Seven of them, just like the samovars."

The elevator lurched to a stop and they spotted Flossie and Sterling pacing back and forth in the lobby.

Flossie started to scold her daughters for lollygagging, but Goldie took each of them under the arm and steered them outside. The valet opened the doors of the Town Car and hustled Flossie and Sterling into the backseat.

Even before Goldie settled herself in the front passenger seat, Flossie began to complain, "We have to schlep over to the Hilton for the banquet, and you girls are late. You know this is a big deal for us and such an honor for your father, he should rest in peace. How would it look if they say, 'and now an illusion from the famous Silvers,' and it turns out the illusion is that we're not there?" She waved her hand for emphasis.

Godiva turned around and patted her mother's arm. "Calm down, Mom. We're right on time. Your trunk with the props is already at the banquet and it's a short drive to the Hilton. You guys must have gotten down to the lobby way early."

"You know your mother," Sterling grunted. "If you're not there twenty minutes early, by her standards you're already late."

"Well, I got a very important email from Angel just as we were about to leave." She filled the old folks in on the story from the Russian newspaper.

Sterling scratched his head. "What did you call those gemstones? Alexandrite? Never heard of them."

"I hadn't either," said Godiva.

Goldie raised an eyebrow. "What? There's some kind of jewel my sister hasn't heard of? Say it isn't so."

Godiva ignored the dig and went on. "Angel sent me a description, too. I guess it's a pretty amazing stone. In daylight it's a beautiful green like an emerald, but as soon as it's under artificial light the color changes to a sort of ruby red or purple. The better the stone, the more intense the color, and anything over five carats is really rare."

"So where do these magical jewels come from?" Flossie asked.

"These came from Siberia. But, according to Angel, those mines closed years ago. That's one reason the missing stones are so rare. The gems on the market today come from places like Brazil."

Sterling perked up. "So how much would Siberian rocks like that be worth?"

"Well, Unk, a big one might be worth more than a fine diamond or emerald. But, a matched set of seven, well, I guess the sky is the limit."

"Woo hoo!" Flossie shouted. "We're not talking about spare change."

Goldie snapped her fingers. "By the way, in all the rush I forgot to tell you, Mrs. Wurlitzer finally contacted me. I might be able to get the samovar back from her. Seems it doesn't go with her décor. I told her I'd be happy to come and get it and refund her money. Then she started waffling and said she would think about it."

Her sister's voice was firm, "Goldie, you'll have to push her, even if you have to offer more than she paid. We have to get our hands on that samovar and see what's inside. It must be one of the gems."

"You bet, Kiddo! Sounds like that woman's life is in danger," Sterling said. "And you better call Caesar again, Godiva. Don't forget, he's got one of them, too. That makes him a sitting duck. And, as if that's not enough, our little Chili could be in danger when she's around him."

Goldie gasped as the reality hit her, but Godiva said, "Unk, don't worry. I've got Ricky Thompson and his friend Ivan guarding them, and besides, the Dumkovskys are still in Seattle. Those goons won't leave until they get Mrs. Wurlitzer's samovar, or at least what's in it. I'll call Caesar right after your act. In the meantime, I think we can trust Ricky and his crew."

"*Oy vey*, such intrigue," Flossie said. "Isn't Ricky's friend the one they call 'Ivan the Terrible'? If anyone can smack those Russian bozos around, he sure can."

They were almost to the Seattle Hilton, when Goldie's cell phone rang again. It was Mrs. Wurlitzer in a complete state of panic. She said when she got home, she found her maid bloody and unconscious on the living room floor. The ambulance came and rushed the poor woman to the hospital.

Mrs. Wurlitzer fussed and fretted. "I can't stay on the phone. Poor Emma. Promise you'll call me first thing in the morning. I'm on my way to see her now, and then I have to go to the police station and file a report."

Goldie had no doubt about what happened. Just before she hung up, Mrs. Wurlitzer said, "Ms. Silver, you better have a good explanation for this tomorrow. My beautiful home is a wreck, and it looks like the only thing missing is your blasted samovar!"

Chapter 19

Flash Fitzgerald, a 93 year old magician, was once known as the fastest hands in the magic world. As Flash shuffled onto the stage, leaning heavily on his walker, everyone in the audience rose to give him a round of applause that drowned out comments like, "My goodness, is that really Flash? I thought he died twenty years ago." Or, "Poor old Fitzgerald, the only thing movin' fast now are his knocking knees."

Two young magicians assisted him as he wobbled his way up the stairs to the stage. Basking in the glory of the old days, the great Fitzgerald was instantly transformed into a caricature of the wonderful entertainer he had been nearly sixty years before. Strobe lights flashed and magician's assistants in skimpy spangled outfits danced and pranced behind him on the stage. He was so excited, he almost spit out his dentures. With a flourish reminiscent of his days as the Flash, he gestured to the band to roll a fanfare, took a deep breath, then almost fell over, clearly exhausted from the effort.

He shuffled toward the mike and said in a quavery voice, "Welcome to the Icons of Illusion annual banquet." There was a burst of applause. "Tonight we are honoring the three great Harry's of Magic. Now, some of you may favor Houdini or Blackstone, but I say Harry Silver was the greatest of them all." The room rang with applause and shouts of praise for the twins' father. Goldie reached over and squeezed her sister's hand.

Flash started to tell a long story, but as it dragged on, the band drowned him out and he got the cue. Flash straightened up and squared his shoulders. "As a special treat, I am proud to present my dear friends Flossie and Sterling Silver, the remaining members of the Scintillating Silvers, who will now perform one of their famous illusions."

To the astonishment of everyone in the audience, including Goldie and Godiva, Flossie and Sterling bounced out on stage like two youngsters, wheeling a huge brilliantly decorated wooden box. Goldie nudged Godiva. "I can't believe it, Sis, look what Mom's wearing. I didn't know she still had that outfit. Look at her legs, she looks fabulous!"

Flossie, her tightly coiffed hair reflecting the stage lights, pranced to the middle of the stage in a gaudy blue and silver sequined outfit that barely cleared her slightly sagging bottom. She wore fishnet stockings and had covered her high heeled orthopedic shoes with silver sparkles. When she almost tripped, Godiva whispered to Goldie, "Let's hope she doesn't break a hip. I never would have thought she could squeeze into that outfit. It has to be more than fifty years old. But, I must say, she's still a babe."

"Yeah, well, an old babe."

Flossie tossed her silver blue curls and gestured to Sterling, resplendent in a deep blue tuxedo with silver spangled lapels. He opened the box and they went through the whole routine, with Flossie getting into the box, disappearing and then reappearing. Goldie said, "I am so proud of them. I only hope I'll be that sharp when I'm eighty."

Godiva raised an eyebrow. "When you're eighty? Mom runs circles around you now. Just kidding. Yeah, me too."

Magicians young and old honored the octogenarians as they completed the act. Then Flash Fitzgerald said, "Flossie, Sterling, it is my honor to bestow this year's Greatest Icon of Illusion award to our dear, departed Harry Silver, a legend in the world of magic."

The band played a rousing tune and Flash held out the trophy. A magnificent gold-plated rabbit emerging from a rhinestone studded top hat. The old magician almost fell over his walker as the spangled dancers gyrated behind him. Tears rolled down Flossie's cheeks.

In a brief, emotional acceptance speech, Sterling said, "On behalf of my dearly-departed brother, Flossie and I vow to carry on the Silver tradition in Harry's name, until we perform our final, permanent disappearing act." As they left the stage to change back into their normal clothes, there wasn't a dry eye in the house.

Later, Flossie plopped into the chair next to Goldie while Sterling chose the one next to Godiva. She patted her daughter's arm. "Whew, I'm glad that's over. Did you see? I almost tripped over my own feet? Some trick that would have been. *Oy vey*, girls, take it from me—it isn't easy being a sex symbol in your eighties. And I'll tell you another thing, that outfit was in the closet so long I think it shrunk a couple of sizes."

Sterling laughed. "If my boyfriend, Leonardo the Lion Tamer, wasn't so jealous, I might make a show of chasing after you."

Flossie patted him on the back. "Thanks for the compliment, Sterling, but stick with the boys."

"Anyway, old girl, you did great. I was just happy you were able to make it in and out of the box. If you had gotten stuck in there, we'd have been in a real pickle."

A very curvaceous young woman in a skin-tight evening gown extended her hand as she approached their table. "Ooh, I just had to come over to tell you how much I admire you two. Harry Silver was the best! An inspiration to all of us. When I was a little kid I saw your act in Las Vegas. I watched Harry turn a turquoise blue scarf into a peacock, and that's when I vowed I would do the same act one day. My mother finagled backstage passes, and he told me to follow my dream and signed an autograph. I still have it."

"So kid, do you have a gig now?" Sterling asked.

She inhaled and puffed out her ample chest. "Yeah, I work with four peacocks in my show and I owe it all to Harry Silver. Mara the Magnificent—you may have heard of me. I'm the headliner at the Glitz Palace on the Strip in Vegas. Of course, if I'd known those birds were so messy I might have chosen cockatoos. But, hey, everyone has cockatoos. I think I'm the only one in the business with peacocks."

She leaned over Sterling, her cleavage even with his nose, and tweaked his cheek. "If you get to Vegas, I'll get you some comp tickets to the show."

"You never know," Flossie joked. "My horoscope said I was going to take flights of fancy. By the way, these are my daughters, Goldie and Godiva. Gorgeous, aren't they? They're my best creation."

Mara looked from sister to sister. "Wait a minute, I know who you two are." She turned to Godiva. "Your daughter is Chili Pepper on the Flirting with Food Show. I love her. She's so quick with the comebacks, and I guess everyone tells you how pretty she is. I saw you in the audience once when I was watching the show."

Godiva gave her a polite smile and nodded.

Then the woman focused on Goldie. "And you. I'll bet you thought magicians didn't read advice columns. Well, I read your *Ask G.O.D* column all the time. I'd recognize you anywhere from your picture."

"Hmmmm...is that so?" Goldie said.

Mara beamed proudly. "I'm probably one of the only people you've met who can tell you two apart thanks to my keen powers of observation. After all, what's a magician without observation?"

Goldie held back her giggles and smiled as Mara's satin clad bottom wiggled away from their table. Godiva said with mock indignation, "Well, I hope her powers of observation are better when she does her bird act. Hmmmph. Thinking Goldie was me. I'll bet she can't tell a peacock from a pigeon."

Goldie snorted. "Are you calling me a pigeon?" They all had a good laugh. As the evening continued, other magicians came to their table singing Harry Silver's praises. On stage young illusionists tried, with varying degrees of success, to reproduce some of the best tricks attributed to the three great Harry's.

When the banquet came to an end, Godiva drove a very happy pair of elderly entertainers back to the Hotel Monaco. By the time they got there, Flossie was snoring in the key of C clutching the golden bunny to her bosom, and Sterling sounded more like an F-sharp.

Chapter 20

After the "headliners" were safely tucked into their beds, the twins went back to Godiva's suite and sat down at the table to brainstorm. Goldie dug around in her huge carpetbag purse and hauled out her yellow pad. While she scribbled on it, Godiva called Caesar.

"Darling, you won't believe what Angel found out about those samovars." She told him about the precious alexan-drites, and said, "Now that we've figured out the Dumkovskys are after something so valuable, I'm really getting worried about your safety. Even with Ricky and his men guarding you, I don't think you should keep the samovar there in the house. Thank goodness you have a good security system."

"That I do, love. You shouldn't worry so much, because you see—"

Goldie was gesturing to Godiva. "Tell him to keep an eye on Chili, too."

Godiva cut Caesar off in mid-sentence. "Um, Caesar darling, watch out for Chili till we get back. Your samovar is an open invitation. If those Russians manage to get past Ricky, they might try to break into the house or even the studio."

"There, there, Godiva dear. Aren't you being a bit melo-dramatic?" Caesar said.

"Not in the least, Caesar" Godiva shot back. "After all, one person is dead because of those damned teapots. And I'm beginning to think Father Augustine's murder might be related to the samovars, too. On top of that, three others have been attacked already and I don't want you or Chili to be next. We're pretty sure they're still in Seattle, but who knows. I'll be home tomorrow afternoon."

Caesar groaned on the other end. "I feel ridiculous having

bodyguards, *Cara Mia*. I can take care of myself. After all, I'm Romano. And besides—"

"Romano, schromano, I don't want my boyfriend to go from sitting duck to dead duck. Trust me. Goldie is coming back to Los Angeles with us, and we're going to get down to the bottom of this whole mess. Belle has a friend whose husband is an L.A. police captain, so maybe we can actually get some help from the cops this time."

There was a silence. Then Romano said, "Godiva, my dear, if you are done chattering, I've been trying to tell you that I don't have the samovar. Remember, I said I was buying it for my mother for her birthday? I've already had it packed up and sent to her in Palm Beach."

Godiva gasped. "Gone?"

"Yes, in fact she's already received it and she absolutely loves it. I can just imagine her serving tea from that beautiful samovar to all of her fancy bridge club friends. She even asked for Goldie's number to thank her, but my *mama mia* is a bit of a pest sometimes, so I told her I didn't have it."

Godiva hung up and turned to Goldie who was still scribbling on the yellow pad. "Caesar doesn't even have the blasted thing. He sent it to his mother in Palm Beach. What now?"

Goldie tapped her finger against her chin, lost in thought. Finally she said, "So, your Latin lover sent the samovar off to his *mama mia* in Florida? I suppose *la Baronessa Romano* will be serving tea to the grande dames of Palm Beach from a lovely Russian artifact with a smuggled gem inside by tomorrow. It sort of complicates everything, doesn't it?"

"Maybe it's a good thing that the Dumkovskys can't get their hands on it. On the other hand, they don't know that, so it doesn't get Caesar off the hot seat."

Goldie let out a big sigh. "How did we ever get mixed up in something like this? All I did was order a few samovars for the shop. The tourists love them—a real showy souvenir of Russian America. You know, some of them don't even realize that Alaska is a part of the United States!"

"Yeah, and you had to order those fancy teapots from a

couple of big time smugglers."

"Now wait a minute, Godiva. Minsky & Pinsky were legitimate antique dealers. I dealt with them for many years. I'll bet they were duped, or something."

"Right, or something." Godiva paced around the room, trying to sum up everything that happened. "Sis, have you ever noticed we seem to get into situations like this even when we're minding our own business?"

She ticked off the incidents on her fingers. "You order some samovars and the next thing you know bad things start to happen. Your friend Mimi is murdered, Rudy's friend Taku is in jail, poor old Father Innocent is beaten up..."

"Yeah," Goldie added. "Then Belle gets burglarized and takes a pot shot at the thieves who skip town dressed up like a couple of ugly women, and when they get to Seattle, they beat up another poor victim before we can stop them."

Godiva sighed again. "And it isn't over yet."

As Goldie scribbled a few more notes on her yellow pad, she glanced up and saw Godiva looking at her with a twinkle in her eye. "Well, there is one teensy little bright spot. Look how much we learned about alexandrite. I never heard of it before. Now that I know there's a rare gem worth more than diamonds or emeralds, I'll have to see if my jeweler at Bijoux de Beverly Hills can find one for me."

"Godiva, you are insufferable! This sucks, plain and simple. You're thinking about jewelry and there are human lives at stake."

"Speaking of humans, this human needs to turn in. It's after twelve and we have a busy day tomorrow." Goldie put the pad back in her purse, while Godiva went across the room to turn off the laptop. "You've Got a Message" was flashing, so she opened up her email and saw one from Ricky Thompson.

She read out loud, "Just wanted to let you know that your Romeo is safely tucked in bed—at least the lights are out in his house, and nothing strange has happened. Some guy was walking past on the other side of the street at about eleven and stopped to look at it for a while, but then he kept walking, so

I'm guessing it didn't mean anything. Nice looking place. That sculptured iron gate on Caesar's Palace is really a work of art. It's probably what the guy was looking at. Ivan is over at your house keeping an eye on Chili, so you can relax, at least for tonight. I've been—"

Godiva stopped reading abruptly, turned off the laptop and didn't say another word.

"Okay, out with it, Sis. What else did Tricky Ricky say? It's not like you to just stop flat like that. You know I'll pull it out of you, so you might as well read the rest of his message."

Godiva threw her arms around Goldie and then held her at arm's length. "You're always one step ahead of me, aren't you? Well, if you must know, Ricky said he's been thinking that he'd like to keep a lot closer eye on me. Somehow, it didn't seem like he meant security surveillance."

Goldie snickered. "Just what you need. A blast from your past."

Before she turned out the bed lamp, Goldie realized her cell phone was off. She had turned it off during the banquet and forgotten to turn it back on. Never one to miss a call, she hit the button and the little screen lit up. There were three voice messages.

First she played the one from Mrs. Wurlitzer. A still shaken voice said, "Ms. Silver, call me if you get this before midnight. Otherwise call me first thing in the morning. Emma is conscious, but in critical condition. She tried to tell the police what happened, and kept saying something about a foreign man with a funny accent. She's heavily sedated, so that's all she said. I thought you might want to know. The police will be talking to her again in the morning. I don't understand why someone would hurt poor Emma just to get a darn teapot."

The next one was from Belle. "Goldie, call me in the morning. There's some interesting news about Father Innocent and that fool Rimsky."

And the last one was from a number she didn't recognize. An unfamiliar woman's voice with a very thick Brooklyn accent said, "Hiya, Miss Silver, you don't know me. This is Rosario Burrito calling from Palm Beach. I'm Caesar Romano's mother. I wanted to talk to you about that lovely samovar my Benny...um sorry, Caesar, gave me for my birthday." She left a call back number.

Goldie played it again to be sure she'd heard correctly, then wondered why Caesar's mother had an accent that sounded more like a Puerto Rican from New York than Italian from Naples. Goldie looked at the clock on the nightstand flashing 1:30. The return calls would have to wait until morning. She'd call Mrs. Wurlitzer first and then call Belle and Caesar's mother. She made a mental note to tell Godiva about Mrs. Burrito's New York accent and that she'd called him Benny before correcting herself and saying Caesar.

Chapter 21

Goldie's brightly colored skirt, made from old quilt tops, fluttered in the breeze as she danced a lively two-step with Taku Ted. The bluegrass music playing in the background got louder and louder. A split second after she grabbed the pillow and put it over her head, Goldie realized the music came from her cell phone on the nightstand. She opened one droopy eye and looked at the clock. Five-thirty in the morning?

She flipped the lid and managed to croak, "Goldie speaking."

"I'm glad I caught you before you started your day." It was the woman with the heavy Brooklyn accent. Before she was able to say something sarcastic to her early caller, like *"Yeah, I'd better get up and milk the cows,"* the cheerful voice chirped on, "This is Rosario Burrito, but you can just call me Rosie. I'm sorry, did I wake you? You sound half asleep."

Goldie remembered that this woman purported to be Caesar's mother, so she resisted the urge to blurt out something nasty. "That's all right Mrs. Bur— um—Rosie. I guess you forgot about the time difference. It's only five-thirty here."

After a profuse apology, Mrs. Burrito said, "Ya know, my Benito—whoops—it's crazy, but no matter how many times he corrects me, I still have a hard time calling him Caesar. Ya know, like the Roman emperor." She gave a hearty laugh. "Anyway, he wouldn't give me your number so I could call you to tell you how much I love that gorgeous old teapot. Oh, wait a minute—he called it a samovar. Russian, isn't it? Said he'd thank you for me. But I just had to tell you myself."

Goldie, the sleuth, was now wide-awake. *Hmm. Seems like there's more mystery to Caesar than Godiva imagined.*

This woman hardly sounded like a wealthy Italian dowager who spent her youth in a lavish villa in Naples. She questioned Mrs. Burrito in a very friendly way. "If Caesar didn't give you my cell phone number, Rosie, how did get it?"

"Hey, Goldie, I'm a New Yorker. When you grow up in a place like Brooklyn, you learn your way around the block. So what if my snooty son didn't give me your number? It's not like it's a government secret."

No, but it looks like there are some other secrets around here.

"I called Juneau information like any person with half a brain would do. The name of your shop was on the gift box, ya know. By the way, Silver Spoon is cute. I like it."

Goldie sat up in the luxurious hotel bed and rubbed her eyes. "Oh, I see."

"Yeah, took no time. So much for Benny, er—Caesar and his airs. The guy who answered the phone at your shop surprised me with his Texas accent. Kinda strange for Alaska, I thought. So I told him I'm Caesar's mother and he says his name is Rudy Valentino, you're off traveling and he's watching the store. I just joked around and pretty soon we were yakking away. Nice guy, that Rudy. I asked him if he was named after the old silent movie star, Rudolph Valentino. Such a sexy guy. He died the year I was born, ya know."

There was a titter on the other end and Goldie pictured her Rudy with plaid pants and hot pink suspenders.

"Well, Rudy said he didn't look like a movie star, and he was never silent. Anyway he gave me your cell phone number. Hope you don't mind."

Goldie was picturing a very different Caesar Romano than the one she and Godiva knew. Now she was determined to ferret out the story. "So, Rosie, you said you grew up in Brooklyn. Did Caesar grow up there, too? For some reason, with that lovely accent, I thought he grew up in Naples."

Rosario let out a huge belly laugh. "That's my boy, Benny. Guess he had you fooled. Yep, he was raised right on Coney Island Avenue. That boy always loved to act. He played an Italian in the high school play, ya know, it was *Roman Holiday*."

"Well," Goldie ventured, "he does have a good stage presence."

"So you thought he was Italian? Well, I guess Puerto Rican isn't that far from Italian—sort of."

Goldie pressed on like a bloodhound. "Rosie, I never would have guessed. Imagine. Raised right on Coney Island Avenue? So where did he learn to cook like he does? And where did he get that wonderful accent?"

Rosario hesitated. "Uh, gee, Goldie, I'm not sure he would like me telling you all of this."

Time to nail it. "Look Rosie. With the romance he and my sister have going, we could be family some day. It will come out sometime anyway."

That's all it took to open the floodgates. "Well, we lived in this little apartment above a restaurant. His father, the creep, took off when Benny was only five. My Benny was always saying, 'Mom, it's gotta be better than this. Someday we'll have lots of money and I'll buy you a big house.' He made wild promises, like young kids do. But my Benny, bless his heart, he delivered."

"Wow, Rosie. I never suspected."

Rosario snorted. "Anyway, when your great Chef Caesar was fourteen, he goes downstairs and asks Luigi, the Lasagna King, to take him on as a kitchen helper after school. You shoulda heard Luigi spin the tales about Italy. So romantic. Benny would repeat every one like he was Luigi himself. He even mimicked the accent, said it was elegant."

Goldie was amazed. "So Caesar worked for Luigi and learned the business—"

"And the language, and the airs. You know what Luigi's last name is? Romano. And my boy has become just as pompous as old Romano himself. But I'm not complaining. You should see my place here in Palm Beach. It's like a palace."

After they hung up, Goldie reran the entire conversation in her head. The story would knock Godiva on her behind. Her elegant Italian stud was from Brooklyn, not Naples, and his real name was Benito Burrito. She almost told Rosario Burrito about how deadly the seven samovars turned out to be, but then thought better of it. No point in distressing the old woman.

Goldie was certain that Mrs. Burrito had a precious alexandrite in her possession, but she wasn't sure what they should do. The samovar would be safe with Rosario for the time being.

Unless they beat it out of Caesar, she felt confident there was no way the Dumkovskys could know their quarry rested on a shelf in a cantaloupe-colored condo in Palm Beach. Thank heavens it would be next to impossible for them to get past Ricky.

Goldie jumped into the shower and cleared her head as the warm water washed over her. The sisters had a lot to do before leaving Seattle in the afternoon, not the least of which was herding Flossie and Sterling to the airport.

She sat down on the edge of the bed in her hotel-issue fluffy terry cloth robe decorated with an exotic animal print, and pulled out her yellow pad. First on the list would be finding out what Emma had to say, if the poor woman was alert. Goldie reached for the phone to call Godiva in the next room. *She'll love this. A six thirty wakeup call followed by an eye-opener about her Latin lover. Hope she doesn't shoot the messenger.*

Chapter 22

Goldie decided to wait a few more minutes before dropping the bomb on her sister. She put the receiver back in the cradle and pulled out her cell phone. A moment later Rudy's phone rang nine hundred miles away. An old ranch boy, Rudy was usually up with the chickens, and surely would be awake and dressed. She pictured him puttering on some project before heading over to the City Café for the breakfast special.

His sleepy voice sounded like tires crunching on gravel as he growled, "Who are ya and whadda ya want?"

"Rudy," Goldie said sweetly, "why so grumpy? I didn't wake you, did I?"

"Goldarn it, Goldilocks, it ain't time to open the store yet, izzit?" She heard him fumbling for the bedside clock. "Hey! It's flippin' quarter-to-six in the mornin'. Did you forget the time difference?"

There was a quick intake of breath as Goldie realized she did the same thing to Rudy that Rosie had done to her. "I'm so sorry, Rudy, it's six forty-five here, I figured you'd be up."

"Well, I ain't."

"I have some hot news to share with you."

"Did ya catch them Ruskies?"

Goldie sighed. "No, not that kind of news. I thought we could have a good laugh about Caesar's mother. She just called me, and I haven't broken the news to Godiva yet."

"If you're gonna tell Miss Hoity-Toity that her Romano is really a Burrito, then you'd better duck when ya say it."

"Who would have dreamed my sister's classy Italian chef actually comes from Brooklyn, not Naples? I'm gonna love seeing her reaction."

With that Rudy let loose a big hee-haw. "Yeah, she'll love it like a bear loves a bee sting. It's a humdinger, ain't it Goldie? Fancy Eye-talian, my ass! I'd love to see Godiva's face when she hears the news. Might bring her down a peg or two. But, y'know, that Rosie sounded like a pretty nice ol' gal. Straight shooter, if ya ask me. A lot straighter than Godiva's lover boy."

"I agree. I liked her, too. So how're things in Juneau?"

Rudy snorted. "I'll tell you what, Goldilocks, I'm plumb worried. Went to see Taku at the jail yesterday, and I think he's goin' downhill. Like he gave up. Ollie doesn't seem to be doin' much. All he keeps talkin' 'bout is how they found him with that derned bloody halibut bat. Last time I talked to him it didn't sound too good for Taku. You've gotta prove it was them goons, and not Taku that kilt poor Mimi. He couldn't have done it. I was up all night worryin' 'bout what could happen to him. Me and Jack Daniels finally came to an agreement, and I got a little sleep—till you called."

"Look Rudy, if it makes you feel any better, all of us, even Mom and Sterling, are chasing after those Dumkovskys. And Belle's got a Mad Hatter friend in L.A. whose husband's a police captain. I'm going to call and see if we can get some help from him."

"I gotta tell ya, the prospect of Flossie and Sterling and Belle helpin' out doesn't make me feel a whole lot better."

Goldie changed the subject. "How's everything at the shop?"

"Fair to middlin.' Lotsa tourists. There was somethin' weird, though. Went to look up one o' them Russian icons in the ledger book and the whole dern sheet with the samovars sales on it was missing. Did you take it?"

She gulped. "I most certainly didn't. It was there when I left Juneau. Do you think someone might have taken it while you were waiting on a customer?"

"Don't know. I was pretty busy. How was the banquet?"

They talked for a few minutes about the award and Flossie and Sterling's performance. Then he asked, "So, how's the chase going?"

"It isn't good. Yesterday they beat another poor woman

senseless, and then grabbed the samovar our cruise ship customer bought. We're going to the hospital to talk to her before we fly down to L.A. Maybe she'll be able to tell us something."

Rudy harrumphed. "So they beat up that snooty Mrs. Wurlitzer, did they? I remember that old snob with her nose in the air. Maybe she got what she deserved. There just ain't no justice. Got poor Taku locked up, and them Dumkovskys runnin' all over tarnation, beatin' people up and stealin' them cursed teapots."

"It wasn't Mrs. Wurlitzer, Rudy, it was her maid."

"There you go, another breech of justice. She let her maid take the punches for her, eh?"

"The lady wasn't home. Anyway, we figure they're on their way to California next. Godiva has her old high school boyfriend Ricky Thompson and his crew guarding Caesar and Chili. And since Rosie's got the samovar, at least for the time being the Dumkovsky brothers won't get their bloody hands on that one."

"The way I look at it, Caesar might need that Ricky Thompson to protect him from your evil twin when she finds out he's not an Eye-talian stallion."

Goldie rolled her eyes skyward, knowing that Rudy was right. Her sister had one heck of a temper. "Well Rudy, my first challenge is to figure out how to get the hot potato out of Rosie's hands."

"I don't know what's so special about them teapots, but if anyone can get it back from Rosita without rufflin' her feathers, it'd be you. Don't let your sister near that poor woman, or fur will fly."

Goldie left Rudy in the dark about the contents of the samovars. The sisters hadn't discussed the theory about the hidden alexandrite gems with anyone but Flossie and Sterling. The less people who knew, the better.

She thanked Rudy for his help with the store, and made him promise to call if there were any problems. He gave her a few choice tidbits about Belle and then he said, "Ya know,

them church ladies was in again the day after you left, wantin'
to know didn't we have another samovar. I told 'em no, we
didn't, and they'd have to wait till you got back. But you know
how pushy that Nora can be. She stomped right to the back of
the shop and started pawin' through everything. Like I was
hidin' one back there."

"Oh well," Goldie said, "that's Nora."

Rudy continued. "I figured I'd let that old busybody see for
herself. No samovars. Anyway, while she was in the back, I had
a good talk with Dora and she said the old priest jest ain't been
the same at all since he was banged up."

"Isn't Rimsky looking after him?"

"Nah. Dora said they couldn't find him anywhere. He
prob'ly up and quit. It's a lot of work takin' care of a sick old
guy."

By the time Goldie called Godiva, it was 6:55. Getting past
Rudy's grunting was nothing compared to breaking through
Godiva's stupor. After a few attempts to engage her sister in co-
herent conversation, she finally decided Godiva needed a java
jolt.

"Listen, get your pampered posterior out of bed. Now! We
have a lot to do today before we head to L.A. I'll call room
service and have them deliver some breakfast and a pot of
strong coffee to your room. Then I'll call Mom and tell her we'll
be leaving for the airport about one. We can slip out and talk to
Emma at the hospital before Mom and Unk even know we're
gone."

Godiva answered with a mumble that sounded like, "Good
luck slipping past Mom."

"Cut that out, Sis. Listen, room service should take about
half an hour, so get up and get ready. I'll be knocking on your
door at 7:15. If breakfast comes sooner, let me know. I'm
starving."

"Yeah, coffee. That should wake me up."

A little smile played around the edge of Goldie's lips. You're going to need some strong coffee when you hear what I have to tell you.

Chapter 23

Goldie came down the hall just as a young woman in a crisp hotel uniform pushed the room service cart into Godiva's suite. She slipped past the server and crossed the sitting room. A weak morning light filtered through the dainty sheers.

The woman laid out the food on the dining table while Goldie sat on the edge of a blue satin chair, half anticipating but half dreading what would happen when she told Godiva about her conversation with Caesar's mother.

Godiva tipped the server and called out, "Well, if it isn't Little Miss Sunshine. Have you finished feeding the chickens?" She poured herself a cup of coffee, and motioned Goldie over to the table, now laden with eggs, fruit, toasted bagels and small pots of jelly, orange juice, coffee and tea.

"I'm glad you ordered the Lumberjack Breakfast, Sis. For some reason I'm really hungry this morning." She sipped her coffee. "And do I ever need this caffeine! Give me a few minutes, and then you can lay out your plan."

Goldie took her time spreading butter and strawberry jam on a bagel. She said between bites, "The hospital. That's the main thing. We need to talk to Emma. Find out what really happened."

Godiva forked in some eggs, then took a few sips of coffee. "Goldie, I think that's a waste of time. We know who broke in and took it. The Dumkovskys, of course. It's a sure bet they'll be going after Caesar next, because they have no way of knowing he doesn't have what they're after. It's all such a no-brainer. What could we find out from Emma that would be of any importance?" She rubbed at a little spot in the center of her forehead, and Goldie hoped her sister wasn't getting a headache.

"You know what Mom always says, you never know until you ask."

"Well, I say we have better things to do, like, maybe, going back to sleep."

"And, I say we need to talk to Emma. She might be able to tell us some little details we *don't* already know. When I think of poor Mimi..."

Goldie wiped her eyes with the edge of the tablecloth. "If she had only survived."

"All right, Goldie, let's talk about our next moves on the way to the hospital. I guess we do owe it to Mimi, and Taku, to track down every lead."

As Godiva went into the bedroom and pulled out her teal and taupe raw silk pantsuit, Goldie leaned against the doorway, her arms folded across a vest that was made of 1950's upholstery fabric. She cleared her throat. "Um, I have something else to tell you and—well, it's about Caesar. I'm afraid you won't like it."

Godiva buttoned her blouse. "Goldie, don't be silly. What could I possibly not like about my sexy Italian stallion?"

Goldie took a deep breath and prepared for the worst. "Well, for one thing, your stallion isn't Italian!"

"What are you talking about?" Godiva slipped her feet into a pair of Prada pumps. "Of course Caesar's Italian! Where do you think he got that magnificent accent?"

The words just tumbled out of Goldie's mouth. "He's Puerto Rican and he got that accent from Luigi, the Lasagna King on Coney Island Avenue in Brooklyn."

Godiva balled up her fists and took a step toward her twin sister. Goldie held out her two palms and stepped back. "Wait a minute, I'm not making this up. If you want to go after someone, try Caesar's mother, Rosita Burrito. She called me at 5:30 this morning to thank me for selling him such a wonderful samovar."

Godiva sat on the edge of the bed. "Tell me I'm having a nightmare."

"Would I lie to you? Your Latin lover's real name is Benito

Burrito. He grew up in Brooklyn and loved acting. He and his single mom lived above a restaurant and when he was a teenager he worked for the guy who owned it, Luigi Romano. Caesar learned how to cook, mimicked his accent, and even took his last name."

Shock and anger spread across Godiva's face like puddle of spilled red ink. "She told you all this?"

"I admit, when I found out who she was, and heard that Brooklyn accent, I pumped her for information."

Godiva's voice grew very cold and flat. "From Brooklyn. I can't believe it. My dashing *Romantic Chef* is from Brooklyn. He isn't even Italian. Now that's a laugh." But she wasn't laughing. Her eyes flashed, and Goldie could only imagine what her sister was thinking. Or plotting. This was one time the twin ESP hit a short circuit.

Goldie almost got frostbite from Godiva's icy voice. "Looks like it's time to have a little talk with that imposter!" She snatched her exquisite raw silk jacket from the bed, slammed the bedroom door with a thunk and said through clenched teeth, "Let's go. We have work to do. I'll deal with Caesar later."

The morning went from bad to worse. As elevator doors opened on the Lobby level, they couldn't miss the figures of Flossie and Sterling sitting patiently in the two wing-backed chairs that faced the elevator.

Sterling held his hands up. "Not my fault." He sheepishly pointed to Flossie. "The she-devil here called and said that when Goldie called, she said you girls were taking the morning easy and to be ready at one. But, you know your mother. She called back, but Goldie wasn't in her room." He snuck a look at Flossie who was grinning like a Cheshire cat. "So she woke me up."

Flossie squirmed a little. "Well, yes, I called and told him to get his *tuchas* out of bed. I figured you girls were up to something, and I didn't want to miss out on the action." She got up from the comfortable lobby chair and pulled Sterling to his feet. "I don't know what you girls are doing this morning, but count us in." She put her handbag over her shoulder and marched to the lobby door.

Sterling tried to protest but, as usual, Flossie overruled him.

Godiva sighed in resignation, mumbling, "I should have known better than to think we could sneak out. Okay, you old geezers can come along. We're off to visit Mrs. Wurlitzer's maid, Emma. If she's conscious, maybe she can tell us what happened."

They drove to Humana Hospital at the end of John Street and found Emma Poletzski's room. Emma, her head swathed in bandages, appeared to be sleeping and there wasn't a nurse in sight. Flossie approached the maid's bed and touched her arm, then recoiled as though she felt an electric shock. Flossie turned around to her daughters and said, her voice quavering, "This woman is cold as a carp."

They all drew closer and it was quite obvious that Emma wasn't sleeping. She was dead. Just at that moment, Mrs. Wurlitzer flew through the door with a nurse in tow. Tears were streaking down her carefully made up face. "You see?" she said to the nurse as she pointed to poor, cold Emma. "Don't you people ever check on your patients?" The nurse approached the bed and confirmed that her patient was indeed beyond help.

Mrs. Wurlitzer suddenly became aware that there were four others in the room. "What are you people doing here?" She spat out each word.

Flossie put her arm out and said in her best Jewish mother way, "My girls just came to check on your poor maid, Mrs. Wurlitzer. I'm their mother, and this is their uncle." She motioned toward Sterling who was trying to melt into the wall.

"We're all so sorry."

Mrs. Wurlitzer turned on her with fury blazing through the tears. "Your daughter and that awful samovar! If it wasn't for her, my poor Emma would be dusting and vacuuming right now. Instead, well, look at her." She extended her finger toward the still figure in the hospital bed.

Goldie tried to say something, but she was cut off by another angry outburst.

"Ms. Silver, do you have any idea how hard it is to find a good maid in this town?"

When Mrs. Wurlitzer finally calmed down enough to talk, it was apparent she cared more about her personal comfort than the fact that her maid had been beaten to death. She showed no interest in locating the dead woman's family in Poland and grudgingly agreed that she would call Emma's friend who worked for her neighbor, Mrs. Bettington.

While the hospital staff bustled about the room, preparing Emma for transfer to the morgue, the sisters dragged Mrs. Wurlitzer to a quiet corner of the visitor's lounge. Goldie got her attention long enough to ask if Emma said anything before she died. The woman hesitated for a moment and said, "She was talking a bit last night. I really thought she was going to be okay. Emma said she came in with the groceries and found the front door ajar. She apologized for not being more careful."

She looked over at Flossie and said, "Hmmph. Emma really was a careless girl. Help is all the same, don't you think? I tried to impress upon her how important it was to lock up every time she went out, but did she listen?"

Godiva headed off her mother's inevitable lecture about treating others with kindness by saying, "So last night she was awake and talking about what happened, and this morning the poor dear was gone. How sad! Did she say anything else?"

Wrinkling her brow, Mrs. Wurlitzer tugged at an emerald earring. "After she mumbled something about bringing the bags in, she said she finished putting the groceries away, and then I think she said there was a knock on the door."

All of the Silvers perked up. "Are you sure? The burglars actually knocked?"

Mrs. Wurlitzer's anger flared up.

"Well! I'm not sure. After all, the woman was babbling and mumbling. Hard to tell if any of it made any sense. It seems she remembered someone pushing his way in, and demanding the samovar from Alaska. When she couldn't find it, he hit her."

Mrs. Wurlitzer bit her lip. "Emma lapsed into Polish, said something I didn't understand, and then drifted off to sleep. I guess that was the last thing she ever said." A crocodile tear slid down her cheek.

Goldie offered support. "Is there anything I can do for you?"

Mrs. Wurlitzer looked up and snapped, "Yes. You can give me a refund for that stupid samovar. And while you're at it, find me a new maid!" She turned on her heel and headed for the elevator.

Chapter 24

They went back to the hotel and did a last minute check of all of the rooms; then called the bellman.

Flossie settled into one of the plush chairs in the lobby to wait for the Town Car. "*Oy, Totelahs,* I hate to leave. A woman could get used to this luxury. People doing all the tidying up and fussing over you."

Sterling glared at her. "What are you talking about, Flossie? Martina and Lupe do all the housework and cooking. The only time you have to lift a finger is when you treat us to some of your home cooking. And now that you've taught Martina to make chicken soup better than any Jewish mother, you don't even have to do that. Thanks to your daughter and all that money Max left her, you get fussed over by everyone." Sterling poked his finger toward her, "Listen, Sister, you've got it good, and don't you forget it."

"Gee, Unk," Godiva said, "thanks for the vote of appreciation. But it looks like Mom really doesn't want to leave. What's eating you, Mom?"

Flossie bit her lip and said nothing.

Goldie walked over to her mother and gave her a hug. "Come on. What is it?"

Flossie's eyes watered. "I'm gonna miss Harry once we leave, that's what."

They all looked at each other, afraid Flossie had gone around the bend.

Sterling said gently, "Flossie, my brother died years ago, you must be seeing things again. I'll bet the banquet knocked you for a loop." He patted her shoulder. "Come on, old girl. Buck up."

Flossie became indignant. "No, I am not seeing things,

you bozo. Of course my Harry's been gone for years. I know that." She pointed at the reception desk. "I'm talking about the goldfish they put in my room. I named him Harry. I'm gonna miss the little guy. That's all. He kinda looked like your brother, you know."

Sterling rolled his eyes and let out a guffaw. "Now that I think about it, I did call my brother 'old fisheye'. Don't worry, when we get home I'll drive you over to the Fish-o-Rama on Fairfax and you can pick out a dandy goldfish."

When they got to SeaTac and checked their flight on the board, they discovered it was delayed for two hours. "Well, since we have time to kill," Goldie said, "we might as well go to the snack bar and knock a few ideas around."

They bought some cold drinks and snacks and found a table for four by the huge windows where they could watch the planes take off. "First thing I need to do is check in with Ricky. I'm guessing the Dumkovskys are in L.A. already, so something bad could happen any time." Godiva pulled out her cell phone and looked around for a quiet corner where she could talk without being overheard.

"While you have him on the phone," Goldie called out, "find out if he knows Captain McNab over at the Westside LAPD. He's the husband of Belle's friend. If Ricky knows him, maybe he can tell us if McNab's the type of guy who will help us."

Godiva nodded and gave her a thumbs up as she slipped off to make her call. When he answered the phone, she said, "Listen, Ricky, we're at SeaTac and our flight is going to be late. I just wanted to check in with you to see if anything has happened. I'm pretty worried. The maid—" Her voice cracked and she took a deep breath. "—well, she died, and all she was able to say was something about a big foreign man. Those guys are really dangerous."

She hesitated, then said, "Ricky, we think we know what

they're after, and it's really huge." She lowered her voice and for the next few minutes she filled him in on their theory about the Seven Stars of Siberia.

Ricky whistled. "Man, this is way bigger than I thought it was. How many stones do you think they have already?"

"We don't know if they found the gems hidden in Mimi's samovars, but if they did, then the only one they're missing is Caesar's, and that one is in Florida. I'm convinced they'll do anything to get what they're after."

Ricky tried to reassure her. "Like I told you, I've got men covering everything. So far we haven't seen anybody in the vicinity fitting their description."

They discussed it a bit more and then Godiva said, "Hey Ricky, do you know an L.A. police captain named Harley McNab?"

Ricky chuckled. "Ole' Harley? That guy's a legend! Why did you ask?"

"Actually I don't know him. His wife Nellie is one of Belle Pepper's Mad Hatter friends. Belle thought Nellie might be able to convince her husband to help us even though the Dumkovskys haven't committed a crime in L.A. yet. What do you think?"

After a short silence, Ricky said, "Yeah, Harley and me go way back. Remember when I rode with the Ghost Riders?"

"Isn't that where you learned to open beer bottles with your teeth?"

"You still remember that? Didn't know it made such an impression. Anyway, he never really joined the Riders, but he had the biggest, meanest Harley you ever saw and an attitude to match. His real name is Thurston, but I don't think anyone dared call him that. He really cleaned up his act after he married Nellie and joined the force. He's a good cop. It wouldn't hurt for you guys to call his wife. If we can get Harley's help, it would be a plus."

"Ricky, do you think there is any way the Russians could know that Caesar sent the samovar to his mother? Maybe that's why they haven't showed up?"

Ricky said, "I don't think there's any way they could know that, Godiva. They probably were delayed. We have no idea how they're traveling. Maybe they're avoiding airports and driving or taking the train. We'll keep our surveillance going. If they make a move, we're on it."

Godiva closed her cell phone and returned to her family. Flossie leaned across the table. "Godiva, I've been wondering, is that the same Ricky you dated in high school? That wild boy with the noisy motorcycle?"

"Yes, Mom," she said with a little wink, "I think he still has the hots for me."

Flossie knitted her brow. "*Oy vey!*"

Chapter 25

Godiva tucked the cell phone back into the small pocket on the side of her Italian leather shoulder bag and addressed the little group. "Ricky raised a good question. How are they traveling? Maybe they aren't in L.A. yet because they're driving or taking a train."

"Well, if they're hitchhiking in those women's clothes," Sterling said, "they're probably still standing on the highway in Seattle."

Godiva laughed at the thought. "Anyway, Ricky knows Harley McNab. He says it would be a good idea to contact him. Lord knows, we need all the help we can get."

Flossie started to say something but Goldie interrupted her. "Hold on a minute, Mom, this is important. I guess I'm the logical one to call Nellie, since I'm Belle's daughter-in-law."

"Heaven help us," Sterling groaned. "My nieces are at it again. Listen you two, these guys are bad news. I'll feel a lot better if you can get the police involved. I don't want you jumping into something you can't wiggle out of. Instead of chasing criminals, Godiva, you should be churning out snappy answers for your column. And Goldie, why don't you look for some more old crap for your shop? Take my advice. Leave capturing killers to the professionals."

Flossie kept clearing her throat. Finally Goldie said, "Mom, is there something wrong?"

"You bet there is. Listen up, Sterling, you are such a wimp. Always running away from a little excitement. Having this McNab guy help us would be great, but shouldn't we stay in the game, too? After all, we're magicians and they're nothing but *dummkopfs*, just like their name. With four minds like ours, and some muscle from Ricky, we can help the police get these guys." The light of adventure was back in her eyes.

Sterling mumbled, "Stuff it, Flossie."

Before the conversation went any further, the boarding announcement for their flight blared over the loudspeakers. Sterling took a last sip of his diet soda, Flossie wrapped the rest of her chocolate chip muffin in a napkin, shoved it in her tote, and they headed for the gate.

Two and a half hours later they joined the jostling crowd around the baggage carousel at LAX. While the ladies waited for the bags, Sterling headed for the outsize baggage area, saying a silent prayer that their disappearing box and other paraphernalia made it. By the time the normal luggage was collected, Sterling hadn't returned. The women found him engaged in verbal combat with a disinterested baggage agent.

The crate with all the props and costumes was on the floor beside him, but the trunk containing the disappearing box was missing. They entered the office in time to hear him say, "Look here, Missy, I know the regulations. Los Angeles isn't the final stop for this flight. It's headed down to San Diego, isn't it? Now, there's half an hour left before that plane takes off again. You know what that means?"

She snapped back, "Maybe you can quote the rules to me. Sounds like this 'disappearing box' of yours has done what it was designed to do, so why are you makin' such a fuss?"

That was the final straw. In a very measured tone Sterling said, "Young lady, I've been through this before. If baggage is missing and the city where it is missing is not the final destination and there is time left before takeoff, I can request a search of the cargo area to see if the missing piece is still on board. That's the rule, line and verse. I hereby request a search!"

At that moment, two fellows who had been waiting in line behind Sterling loomed up on either side of him and glared at the agent. They looked like poster boys for the Sumo Wrestling Federation. One put his arm around Sterling's shoulder and growled, "Lady, our bags are missing, too. If Pops here is right about searching the plane, you better pick up that phone and make the call, or you'll be sorry." The bigger of the two slammed their baggage checks on the counter and the agent started to tremble.

Flossie shook her fist and flashed her dentures at them. "You tell her, boys."

Fifteen minutes later all of the missing cases magically appeared, including those of the two hulks. One of them slapped Sterling on the back with a "Thanks, Pop" that almost knocked him off his feet. Then they turned around and rolled their cases out.

Through all of this, the driver of the limo Godiva had hired waited patiently outside the baggage claim office. Now he and an airport Redcap pushed the trolleys laden with baggage and crates to the stretch Lincoln while the Silver family trailed behind. When Sterling looked back at the baggage clerk, she was scowling at another unhappy traveler. Parked at the curb behind the limo was a rental van with a uniformed driver. The chauffeur settled his passengers in the limo, and then helped the van driver load the crate and disappearing box.

Goldie said, "Sis, you've really got it made. If I was traveling by myself, I'd be schlepping all of this stuff and then standing in line for a cab." She gave a wicked smile. "Makes me think maybe I should have married someone like Max, too."

Godiva laughed. "Don't kid yourself. You haven't got it in you. Besides, gold digging isn't as easy as it sounds; living with Max was damned hard work! In a way it was a blessing he had a bad heart. I wouldn't have gotten as much out of a divorce settlement, if it ever came to that. And besides, having Uncle Sterling as Torch's role model was so much better than Max's influence would have been. Instead of becoming a cold-hearted wheeler-dealer like his father, my son followed Unk's path, went into showbiz and became an award winning FX man with a heart of gold."

Sterling smiled at Godiva. "Thanks for the pat on the back, honey." Then he turned to Goldie, "Sweetheart, you know you would never trade marrying Red for hooking a filthy-rich jerk like your sister did. Your Captain Pepper is a real *mensch*. And that's priceless."

Goldie smiled. "And don't I know it?"

They pulled through the gates of Godiva's Beverly Hills estate, and the driver's first stop was at the cozy gardener's cottage Sterling now called home. Gardening was Sterling's passion, and he loved taking care of the grounds for Godiva with the help of three Mexican gardeners. The rose garden was his personal domain and no one touched the roses but Sterling.

Flossie got out of the car at the former guest cottage. Several years ago during a séance, Flossie swore she heard her dear Harry telling her to take a chance and change her life. So the twins' mother sold the kitschy house that she and Harry bought for $10,000 in the late 40s to a porn movie producer for more than $500,000. Since the neighborhood, now called "The Grove District," was becoming gentrified, the producer thought he got a bargain and Flossie figured she made a killing.

After Flossie took Godiva up on her offer to live in the guest cottage, Godiva hired a decorator who artfully arranged a collection of *tsochkes* and chintz to reflect the comfort of Flossie's old house. It was a good move. Flossie loved being near her daughter, grandson and brother-in-law while still maintaining her independence.

At the end of the driveway, Goldie and Godiva got out and trudged up the marble stairs toward the massive front door. As Godiva reached for her key, the door swung open and Chili flew out with her cousin Torch right on her heels. They stopped short at the top of the stairs, each looking at a different twin, and shouted, "Mom!"

After a couple of brief hugs, Torch said, "Hey, it's great to see you Aunt Goldie, I was sure sorry to hear about your friend's murder. Guess you two are playing Nancy Drew again, huh?"

Godiva frowned at her son. "You make it sound so trivial, Torch. I'll have you know this is serious business. Where are you two going?"

Chili was already halfway down the stairs. "Torch got tickets to a concert. Hope you don't mind if we take off."

Before the twins could answer, the cousins were gone.

The twins crossed the grand foyer, making their way to the cozy family room. Goldie preferred the warmth of this charming room with its English country décor. She was uncomfortable in Godiva's formal living room—a room so big that the whole first floor of her house in Juneau could fit into it with space left over.

As they passed the former library, now the command center of *Ask G.O.D.*, Godiva didn't even glance in that direction because she wasn't up to looking at the mountain of mail yet. Angel could be counted on to have all the letters worthy of publication neatly sorted and stacked in the middle of her boss's desk.

Godiva's maid, Guadalupe, took Goldie's shabby duffel bag upstairs. Passing the blue guest room, the pink guest room and the purple guest room, she deposited the lone bag in the room she knew Goldie loved because of the antique furniture and beautiful view of the rose garden. It was done in soft yellow and was across the hall from the room Chili now called home.

The cook, glided into the family room carrying a tray of coffee and tea and a dish of small snacks. Goldie snuggled into the oversized flowered sofa, kicked off her shoes, and reached into her carpetbag purse for the ever-present yellow pad to take notes. She was beginning to write, when she felt a moist nose nudge her hand. The nose was attached to a very large dog of questionable parentage, who wiggled like a kid on Christmas. He whined something that sounded like, *"Wheeeere weeerre youuu?"*

"Why, Waldo old guy, I missed you, too." She stopped writing long enough to pat his fuzzy head. From the time he was a gangly puppy, Waldo the Wonder Dog helped Flossie and Sterling with the act they performed every Thursday at the Home for Hollywood Has-Beens. Most of the family members agreed that Waldo could talk, but were careful not to share that fact with skeptics.

"Daaaanccccce?" The dog's tail wagged wildly.

"Sorry, fella, our waltz will have to wait. We have a real problem on our hands." The dog hung his head and padded away.

"Waldo sure loves it when you pay attention to him," Godiva said.

Her sister nodded. "Yeah, I love him too."

"Guess we should call Belle and ask for tips on talking to Nellie McNab." She picked up the phone and handed it to her sister.

"And I suppose 'we' means 'me', huh Sis?" Goldie glanced at her watch. "Well I guess this is as good a time as any." She took a deep breath and dialed.

Godiva went upstairs to her sitting room to call Caesar. She was still miffed at discovering Caesar's secret identity, and looked as if she might do battle with him as soon as he answered the phone. There would be plenty of time to chew out Caesar and check in with Ricky Thompson before Belle was done bending Goldie's ear. She marveled at the amount of small town news Belle could find to gossip about.

Chapter 26

Belle answered after three rings, sounding a bit breathless.

With the greetings out of the way, Goldie said, "Did I take you away from something? You sound like you're out of breath."

A husky voice boomed in her ear. "Nah, nothing much. I just got home. I met those pests Nora and Dora on the street by the Russian church and they jumped on me again. Those women are driving me nuts!"

"I know what you mean. Those two can really be a handful. How is the old priest? Is someone taking care of him? Last time I talked to Rudy, he said Rimsky took off. Did he finally show up?"

Belle snorted into the phone. "Rimsky, that worthless guy? I haven't seen hide nor hair of him. Dora said she was glad he was gone—that he wasn't much help anyway."

"Maybe that's true, but they must be a little concerned."

"If you want my two cents, I think those ladies are more interested in your whereabouts than Rimsky's. Nora keeps asking if I've spoken to you and if you've found out anything more about Mimi's murder." She sighed. "They're always trying to steal my gossip and spread it around before I get a chance. Trying to upstage me! Steal my thunder! But this time my lips are sealed."

"Don't worry Mama Belle, no one can beat you at the gossip game. They probably keep bugging you to find out when I get back so they can pounce on me. I'm sure they're just anxious about the crime wave. By the way, have you heard anything more about Father Augustine's murder? Do the church ladies know when a new priest will arrive?"

Belle snickered. "No, on both counts. As for the murder,

well, you know Ollie is not the sharpest knife in the drawer."

Goldie steered the conversation to the real reason she called. "Speaking of cops, remember you told me about your friend Nellie McNab, and how you thought she might be able to get her husband to help us?"

There was a smile in Belle's voice. "Of course I do. I love that woman. She's my soul sister."

Goldie figured if she only asked Belle a few more questions she would learn the best way to approach her mother-in-law's "soul sister." But Belle took off down memory lane, explaining how it was fate that she and Nellie hooked up at the Hatter's conference. Every time Goldie tried to short circuit the seemingly endless story, Belle just talked over her.

In frustration, she finally blurted out, "Listen, Mama Belle, I'll be sure to tell Nellie what a good conversation we had about the conference. What I really need to know is the best way to get her husband's help. It turns out that Godiva's friend Ricky Thompson also knows Nellie's husband. But, it's still a little touchy considering the Dumkovskys haven't committed a crime in L.A. yet."

"Did Ricky tell Godiva that Harley almost became one of the Ghost Riders instead of a cop? You know, if it wasn't for Nellie, he would probably still be riding with that motorcycle gang. She said it comes in handy in his work sometimes."

"You're right. That's what Ricky said. Anyway, what do you suggest?"

There was a short silence, and then Belle said, "I gave you her phone number, didn't I?"

Goldie said that she did, and urged her mother-in-law to continue, hoping to divert her from launching into another story.

"Well, give her a call and tell her you're my daughter-in-law, and being as you're so devoted to me, you and your sister would like to take her out for lunch."

"That seems pretty easy. What else?" Goldie asked.

"Don't mention your motive, save that for later. She loves to eat out, and she loves to have a little glass of wine before the meal. Harley won't let her keep wine in the house. If I remember correctly, he's a recovering alcoholic, so I think a nice glass of Merlot will really soften her up."

"Okay, so when do we pop the question about getting her husband's help?"

Belle laughed. "Just about the time there's nothing left in the bottle. Truth is she loves to be involved in things just as much as I do. But she doesn't like to feel she's being used. By the time she finishes the wine, you'll all be great friends. She's like that."

Goldie heard Belle snap her fingers on the other end. Then Belle said, "I just remembered another plus. I think she's a fan of your sister's column."

Belle kept Goldie on the line another ten minutes bringing her up to date on the buzz around town about Taku, some mundane local news, and the fact that she had just donated ten thousand dollars to the Glory Hole so they could renovate their soup kitchen. As they were saying their goodbyes, Godiva charged into the room. As soon as the receiver hit the cradle, her sister said, "Are you ready for a new wrinkle?"

Chapter 27

The imaginary storm clouds above Godiva's head were about to burst as she plopped down on the sofa across from Goldie. "This is so damned confusing, Sis. I'm ticked off at Caesar for pretending to be something he's not, but on the other hand, I'm really worried about him."

Goldie got up and sat next to her normally tough-as-nails sister, who, at the moment, looked like she was ready to cry. She put her arm around Godiva's shoulder. "Okay, Sis, why don't you fill me in?"

"Actually, I think I want a cup of coffee first. I'm really beat." She rang for Martina. "Do you want some tea? I'll ask Martina to fix it."

"Thanks, Sis. Some Yerba Maté, if you have any."

"Hey, there are some brownies in the kitchen. To hell with the calories, let's eat them all. Are you game?"

A smile spread across Goldie's face. "Are you kidding? I could eat the whole batch myself!" She patted her ample hip. "That's where they'll go."

While Martina was fixing the snacks, Godiva filled Goldie in on her conversation with Caesar, saving what Ricky said for later. "They're here in L.A.," she blurted out, "Caesar's office at Food Broadcasting was ransacked last night."

"It had to be the Dumkovskys. I'll bet they're right here under our noses."

"Yeah, Caesar was pretty shaken up when he found the mess this morning. The studio called the cops, so now there is a crime on the books in L.A., or Hollywood if you want to be exact."

Goldie perked up. "Well, that means the police will get involved—that's a good thing."

139

Her sister didn't look quite so perky. "But that really doesn't help us much. The Hollywood cops will never believe that a simple break and enter at a studio is tied to a murder in Juneau and one in Seattle."

"Yeah, our track record with the Hollywood police isn't so good." Goldie rolled her eyes. "We had a heck of a time convincing them that Caesar wasn't a murderer when they thought they had an open-and-shut case." She shuddered. "If it was up to them, a nutcase would have gotten away with murder and the cops would have fried your boyfriend."

"Good thing they let him go. Now I get to wring his neck myself." Godiva muttered.

Goldie got back on track. "Okay, so we can assume that the Hollywood station won't be much help. The robbery and homicide divisions probably don't even talk to each other. What did they steal at Caesar's office?"

"Well, that's it, Sis. Caesar said the place was a total mess but nothing was missing. They ransacked his desk, but only took a few papers."

Goldie started to ask, "What papers—"

But Godiva talked over her. "I know what you're thinking, but the FedEx receipt for shipping the samovar to his mother was in his coat pocket, so they didn't get that. Of course, once his mother was mentioned, that led into a confrontation about who he really is, but let's save that for later."

Goldie let out an involuntary sigh. "I guess they went to Food Broadcasting because they figured since he's a chef, he would have the samovar where he works. I'm stumped. What should we do next?"

"Ricky and his boys are on the job. They're posted at Caesar's house and at the studio. Some police participation sure would help. The Dumkovskys can't possibly know that Caesar doesn't have the samovar, so their next move has to be breaking into his house."

With a shake of her silver mane, Goldie answered, "I don't know. I guess that's the logical move, but I think they'll probably be sneakier about getting into Caesar's place—that is if they're capable of being sneaky."

Godiva's shoulders sagged like a rag doll. "What did Belle say?"

"I'll tell you after you tell me about your talk with Caesar. Did he explode when you told him you knew his real name was Benny Burrito? Was he furious with his mother?"

"Let's just say his temper is even worse in Puerto Rican than it was in Italian. Elegant, sophisticated Caesar became Benito the street fighter in a matter of minutes. From the little Spanish I understand, I think he was cursing his mother's big mouth. I even heard a Brooklyn accent mixed in with the Spanish. I gather he told her time and again how important his image was. He was absolutely furious that she spilled the beans to you and spoiled his ruse with me."

"What did you say?"

"What could I say? When he finally calmed down, I told him I felt betrayed. I said I thought we were close enough by now to drop our guards. After all, I admitted to him that I only married Max for his money. He could have at least shared a few of his secrets with me."

Goldie shrugged. "I don't know. Godiva, I guess I can see his side, too. It could be risky. After all, you are in the newspaper business."

"I—I'm not sure I want to stay in a relationship with an imposter, although he does have his redeeming qualities, if you know what I mean." At this point she struck a pouty Mae West pose. "But I'll worry about that later." She shrugged. "A broken heart isn't as serious as a murdered boyfriend."

Goldie gave her sister a hug. It was unusual for a chink to show in Godiva's armor. She never betrayed her emotions, and this time she really did look like her heart was aching. When Godiva's hand snaked out, grabbed one of the brownies on the silver tray, and shoved it all into her mouth at once, Goldie knew her sister's pain was serious. But when Godiva started on her second brownie, Goldie knew she was on the road to recovery. After all, chocolate is the great cure-all.

"Um, Sis, we have to make a lunch date with Nellie McNab.

I had a good conversation with Belle and she coached me on how to approach it. I think we'll be able to get her involved. Of course, she regaled me with local gossip and I almost got sucked into one of her long stories. Fortunately, I cut her short. But, you know, as annoying as she is, she's still a great old gal in my book. Know what she told me she did?"

"Now, how could I possibly know what your goofy mother-in-law did? Oh well, I suppose you'll tell me."

"Yes, I'm so proud of her. She donated ten thousand dollars to the Glory Hole so they can update their soup kitchen. I've gotta say, she's anything but selfish—"

Godiva screeched, "*Like me*? She isn't selfish *like me*. Is that what you meant to say? I'll have you know I'm going to make a nice big donation to a women's shelter."

"Since when?"

"Um, since now. You just shamed me into it."

Chapter 28

The sisters were on their way out the door to meet Nellie McNab when Flossie shuffled up the walk waving her hankie. "Yoo-hoo, Darlings, where are you going?" Goldie and Godiva exchanged glances. *Oh boy, don't tell her anything.*

"Hi Mom," Goldie said. "We're just going to do a little antiquing. I need a few more things for my shop and I know how you hate picking through all that old stuff, so we didn't think you would want to come along."

"Darn right," Flossie grumbled, "most of the things you buy aren't even antiques—they're things that were new when I was a girl. My mother threw out old garbage like that." She raised one eyebrow, planted her hands on her hips and tapped her orthopedic shoe on the landing. "Wait just a minute! You're going antiquing? This is no time to go traipsing off to have fun. We've got work to do! We've got to figure out how to set a trap for those Russians."

"But this is business, Mom. We won't be gone long. I can't bring everything to a screeching halt while Rudy minds the shop. I have responsibilities, you know."

"Well, how about your responsibility to that poor Taku fellow? Sitting there in jail while you tend to business, humph! Monkey business is what it is. Priceless gems floating around, Russian thugs ready to pounce on Godiva's boyfriend. And you girls are going shopping! What's this generation coming to?"

The twins finally talked Flossie down, and she stomped off saying that she was going to confer with Sterling.

Godiva's Town Car crawled through Los Angeles traffic on its way to Westwood, the college town that houses UCLA. They arrived about ten minutes late at The Gardens on Glendon and scanned the people waiting to be seated. The sisters assumed

Belle's "soul sister," Nellie McNab, would be cut from the same cloth, and tried to spot anyone who looked something like Belle.

Godiva shook her head and motioned Goldie to an empty seat near the hostess station. "Maybe Nellie is late, too." She started to sit down when a slim, athletic looking woman who appeared to be in her late fifties, came rushing up to them. Her long blonde hair rested in soft waves on her shoulders and she wore a chic red leather blazer, designer jeans and ankle boots. She held her arms out to the startled twins. "I'm so sorry to be late. I don't think it's possible to be on time anymore in this town. Even when you allow an extra half hour, something happens."

Goldie found her voice first. "Nell—Nellie? Is that you?"

A smile crossed the woman's lovely face and her green eyes twinkled. "Yup, I'm the one you're looking for. I probably should have described myself to you, but from Belle's description of the 'Dynamic Duo,' I knew you twins would be easy to spot. So tell me, which one of you is lucky enough to have Belle as your mother-in-law? I just love that woman."

Goldie extended her hand for a little shake. "That would be me, Nellie. Goldie Silver. Thanks for agreeing to meet us. Belle has spoken so highly of you that I just had to meet you."

As if on cue, the hostess called "Silver, party of three. I can seat you now."

They requested a table in the Courtyard. Goldie admired the way the soft light filtered in from the glass-domed ceiling and cast a special glow on everything. She spotted a few celebrities discretely eating lunch, and noticed her sister looking here and there to see if anyone recognized her. Godiva was in her element.

As Belle suggested, the sisters plied Nellie with an excellent California wine, and by the second glass she had gotten quite chummy. "Godiva, I must tell you, I love your column. I've read it in the *Beverly Hills Blabbermouth* every week since it started, and just look at you now. A national celebrity."

"Thank you so much, Nellie. I was just in the right place at the right time. Maybe someday I'll be thought of in the same class as Ann Landers and Dear Abby, but for now, I'm just learning the ropes." Goldie was astounded by her sister's uncharacteristic modesty. Surely it was Godiva's way of getting Nellie on board.

The police captain's wife laughed and the ice was broken. "Godiva, you're in a class all by yourself. Forget about those old stick-in-the-muds Ann and Abby. Your answers are way better. By the way, weren't they twins too?" She turned to Goldie. "How about you Goldie? Gonna write anything for the *Juneau Fishwrapper*? I'll bet Belle could help you out."

Goldie shook her head vehemently. "Oh no, Nellie! Dishing out advice is not my thing. One of us is quite enough. Now, Belle, that's another story."

The server scooted between them and delicately placed the food on the table. Goldie admired the spread. "Look at this meat loaf platter. My mouth is watering." Godiva picked at Stevie T's Sliced Chicken, while Nellie attacked her Chinese Chicken Salad.

"Nellie, Belle said your husband is a police captain in West L.A. That's so exciting! Do you ever help him solve cases?" Goldie said.

"Well, sometimes the cases my Harley works on are pretty interesting, he likes to bounce ideas off of me." Nellie sipped at the wine glass that Godiva had refilled.

Goldie's eyes lit up as she snapped her fingers and faked a sudden brainstorm. "Hey, we're working on a case right now that's a real doozy. Want to hear about it? Maybe your husband would have some advice for us."

Nellie put down her fork and leaned forward, "Well, I—"

Without hesitation, Goldie jumped in and gave her the basics, beginning with the lost shipment of samovars. They had a bit of a chuckle describing how overbearing Dora and Nora had become.

"I never thought those church ladies would get so pushy," Goldie said. "They just about drove me crazy."

"If that happened in Los Angeles," Nellie said, "they could

have gone to a few dozen other stores until they found a substitute. But I suppose it's more difficult in an isolated little town like Juneau."

Goldie nodded and continued the story. By the time they described Caesar's office being broken into, Nellie was sitting on the edge of her chair.

The twins swore Nellie to secrecy before sharing some of the information Angel researched, leading them to the theory that each of the samovars concealed one of the Seven Stars of Siberia. Godiva finished by saying that if they couldn't stop the Dumkovskys, Taku would go on trial for a murder he didn't commit and the two louts would get away with a set of priceless gems.

"So let me get this straight. You think these Russian killers are here in L.A., and you guess they'll be going after Caesar Romano, the famous TV chef, to get the samovar that he doesn't have because he sent it to his mother?"

"That's about the size of it, Nellie, and we're afraid they'll hurt Caesar and maybe even Goldie's daughter, Chili, since she works for him."

Goldie twisted her napkin nervously at the mere mention of her daughter's name. "We've seen the two bodies they left in their wake. Two innocent people. When they go after Caesar, my Chili could be caught in the crossfire."

Nellie thought for a moment, tapping a French manicured fingernail against her chin. "Hmmm, I'd like to get Harley involved. Of course, he can't do anything officially because at this point it's all speculation." She cleared her throat. "I do know a little about these things. You see I studied criminal law and took the bar before I married Harley. I passed, but I've never practiced." She winked at Godiva. "Frankly, keeping up with my husband is a full time job."

Goldie felt a giggle escaping even though she tried to stifle it. "I've got to confess, Nellie, we know a little bit about your Harley. You see, we went to school with Ricky Thompson and—"

Nellie broke in. "Oh my God! You know crazy Ricky?"

Godiva smiled innocently. "Can you believe it? He was my boyfriend in high school. He told me how Harley got his nickname, and how you saved him from a wild life. Actually, I've hired Ricky and his team to guard Caesar and Chili."

Nellie nodded. "Well ladies, he's the best—except for my Harley, of course. Tell you what; I really want to help with this. I'll mull it over and maybe we can meet at your place tonight, Godiva. Where do you live?"

Godiva gave her the address. They ordered some mocha cappuccinos, discussed the situation a little more, and then agreed to meet at seven o'clock.

Chapter 29

While the twins were having lunch with Nellie, Flossie went into action. After she wished them good luck "antiquing," she stomped up the path to Sterling's cottage where she found him taking a snooze in one of the Adirondack chairs next to his beloved rose garden. She shook him gently and sat down in the other chair, waiting for him to wake up.

Sterling blinked at her in the dazzling sunlight, a puzzled look on his face, while she prattled on about her plan. "Hold your horses, Flossie. What in tarnation are you babbling about?"

"Catching those murderous thieves, that's what I'm babbling about. I've been plotting while you've been sleeping on the job."

Fully awake now, Sterling bristled defensively. "Now, hold on a minute, old girl. I most certainly am not asleep at the wheel. You know I do some of my best thinking in a semi-conscious state."

Flossie waggled an accusatory finger. "Hogwash, Sterling, you're semi-conscious half the time. Listen, the girls aren't taking this seriously enough." She leaned closer to him. "Know what they're doing right now? They're off antiquing, while those bozos are plotting God-knows-what. It's up to us to save Caesar."

"So, Mrs. Sherlock, just how do you propose to do that? And what makes you think Caesar will go along with it?"

Flossie threw her hands up in the air, exasperation coloring her wrinkled face. "Why must you always be so skeptical? Maybe that's why Harry was the star of the show. He was a man of action, and you always get mired in doubt. You need every single thing guaranteed before you jump in. Sometimes I wish you were more like your brother."

Sterling's mouth was set in a firm line. Finally he said, "Well, I got news for you, Flossie. Your Harry has transmogrified to the great beyond and left me holding the bag. So you'll just have to take me as I am. Think of me as your voice of reason."

"Voice of reason, my foot. Just keep that voice quiet and listen to what I came up with while you were off in dreamland." After Flossie laid out what she had in mind, Sterling had to agree that Caesar would definitely go along with it. He would probably love the theatrical flair. It never occurred to them that Flossie's scheme could place all three of them in real danger.

They huddled together amid the fragrant roses, plotting and planning how they could turn Flossie's inspiration into reality. Sterling said, "Good thing Goldie solved the problem of the samovar Caesar sent to his mother. One less thing to worry about. Maybe we'll actually get to see what all the hoopla is about."

Flossie stretched to ease an arthritic crick in her back. She smiled. "She's one smart cookie, my Goldie. Leave it to her to convince that Burrito woman to send the darned thing back to her at Godiva's house. All she had to do was suggest the samovar had historic significance and she needed it back to get her a proper Certificate of Authenticity."

Sterling nodded. "Yeah, she said Caesar's mama got it to the FedEx office in record time. Should be here this afternoon."

"You bet, Sterling. Goldie said Rosario asked why she should send it to Godiva's house instead of Caesar's, so my clever daughter told her that way she could work with it as soon as the samovar arrived."

"Okay," said the Voice of Reason, "let's keep on track, Flossie. You do tend to go off on side roads, you know. So, we're pretty sure the Dumkovskys will go to Caesar's house looking for the samovar—"

"Of course, they got his address from the break-in at Goldie's shop."

"We just don't know when they'll make their move, but it's

safe to bet they'll wait until dark. They may not even try tonight. Maybe they'll wait till tomorrow."

"See, there you go, waffling again!"

"I was pretty surprised that they went to Food Broadcasting, but maybe they're not as dumb as we think."

Flossie agreed. "Elementary, Dear Watson. Caesar is on TV every day. How hard is it to figure out he has an office at Food Broadcasting? Even they could figure that out. Those *gonifs* probably thought that since he's a chef, he would take the *farstunkener* teapot to work. Who knows, maybe they thought he bought it to serve some fancy tea on his show."

"Could be," Sterling shot back. "But how did they know? I find it hard to believe that a couple of thugs from Russia even watch TV cooking shows. Anyway, from what Godiva said, they didn't get anything there, so they'll show up at Caesar's house soon. Better for us if it's not too soon. Ricky and his men will be there waiting. But so will we."

Flossie sighed. "I wish Goldie had never ordered those blasted things. Stick to American junk, I say! Look how it's complicated our lives, not to mention leaving a trail of bodies along the way." But there was a twinkle in her eye.

Sterling smiled at her, knowing what the old sparkle meant. "True, but I've gotta say, old girl, you outdid yourself. Your plan is brilliant and we can pull it off with our eyes closed. Wait till Caesar hears what you've cooked up. He'll love it. Still, I'm a little worried about how the girls will react."

She shook her head back and forth like a wind-up toy. "Are you kidding? Do you have chicken *schmaltz* for brains? We can't tell them—not if we want to bust the bad guys. If we tell them, we'll get our wings clipped. Pulling off the illusion will be easy. The trick will be sneaking away from our jailers tonight and making it over to Caesar's."

Sterling rolled his eyes, feigning confusion while Flossie snorted. Then a smile broke across his face and he said, "Okay, but stop calling your daughters 'the jailers'. You know they're just looking out for us."

"Oh, Sterling, it'll be so exciting to pull a caper."

"Yeah, when we save the day we'll be back in the limelight again. Real heroes with interviews on TV. That is, if Caesar doesn't spill the beans to those overprotective nieces of mine."

"I think he'll play along. Caesar loves drama and this'll be like a movie of the week." Flossie held her finger up to her lips. "Quiet, I think I hear the girls coming. Think of an excuse for us to be out tonight while I keep them busy." As Goldie and Godiva came up the path, she called out, "Find anything you two?"

Seeing the gleam in Flossie's eyes, Goldie shot Godiva a look. *Better keep an eye on them. I think they're up to something.*

"Good thing you didn't come, Mom," Godiva said. "Watching Goldie paw through all that old junk is almost pitiful. Thank goodness we finally took a break and had a nice lunch. How was your afternoon?"

The oldsters locked eyes. Sterling said, "Oh, you know. Nothing much going on. I took a little nap in the sun."

"Well," Goldie said, "we just wanted to check in with you and let you know we're back. I'm going to see if FedEx came yet." She started back toward the main house.

Godiva started after her and said over her shoulder, "By the way, let's have dinner early. About five-thirty. A friend of ours is stopping by at seven, and we have lots to talk about, so it's better if we get dinner out of the way early."

Sterling called after his nieces, "Don't worry about us girls. We'll eat dinner at the Daily Grill. Your mother wants to see that new movie that's playing at the Beverly Center. Good thing I can still drive at night." He turned and whispered to Flossie, "See, sometimes things just work themselves out."

As the twins disappeared behind the rose bushes, Flossie said, "Now, let's go call Caesar and tell him we'd like to come over tonight."

Chapter 30

Goldie hustled up the path to the main house. Godiva, always competing for first place, put on an extra burst of energy. With her Prada pumps pounding the pavers, she passed her sister. As soon as they set foot in the marble entry hall, they saw the large FedEx package strategically placed on the French ormolu table.

"Well, Sis, I guess this is your cursed samovar," said Godiva. "Let's take it into the study and open it."

Guadalupe stood at the doorway between the entry hall and the living room. "Ah, *Senora*, I see you find the package. I tell the man to put it on the table, so you see it when you come in."

Godiva nodded. "I appreciate that, Lupe. I was hoping it would arrive today. Could you please tell Martina that we would like dinner ready by five-thirty? I have a friend coming over afterward."

"And, for *Senora* Flossie and *Tio* Sterling, *tambien?*"

"No, the old folks won't be joining us. They are going to eat out and see a movie tonight."

The maid smiled. "Oh, they so full of pep for two *viejos*. I hope I be like that some day. What about your kids?"

"Torch has a date, and Chili said she was eating out with some friends from the studio, so it will just be the two of us." The maid trotted off toward the kitchen to talk to Martina.

Goldie picked up the bulky Fed Ex box and they went into Godiva's study. Waldo padded after them, nudging Goldie while whining, *"Daaance nooowwww?"* She smiled and patted him on the head. "Later, Waldo. I promise." The big dog trailed behind wagging his tail.

Angel Batista was tidying up her desk in the large

mahogany-paneled room, preparing to leave "mission central" for the day. She called out, "Hey Boss, I put a couple of great letters on your desk. Will you have time to go through them?" She turned around and added, "Oh I see you found your package, Goldie. What's inside?"

"If you stick around, you'll see." Godiva closed the study door and turned the lock. "Don't want anyone walking in on us." She fished around in her handbag and came up with a little gold penknife.

Goldie and Angel watched Godiva carefully slit the packaging. Styrofoam peanuts spilled all over the floor when she lifted up the exquisite samovar and let out a low whistle. Waldo chased the fluffy little squiggles all around the room, unaware of the treasure they had surrounded.

"Ohhhh, is that one of the samovars? When Lupe said a special package came for Goldie, I didn't realize that's what it was. Can I touch it?" Angel's eyes widened behind her huge glasses.

"Sure, Angel," Goldie said.

She crossed the room, looking like she was almost afraid to get too close. "So, this is one of the deadly teapots, eh? Wow. It really is beautiful though, isn't it?" She walked around the desk and examined it from all angles, admiring the ivory handles, lion's paw feet and delicate grape vines entwining the polished bronze urn. "Where do you think the gems are hidden? After reading about it, I'd love to see what a real-life alexandrite looks like."

Godiva turned to her sister. "Goldie, you're familiar with things like this. Where do you think it's hidden?"

"I don't know. Let's start at the top, and work our way down." She removed the tape that secured the little teapot to a pedestal on top of the urn and peeked inside, even though she knew that was too obvious a hiding place.

She took off the samovar's lid, held it under the desk lamp, then looked into the large conical body. There was nothing unusual inside. She turned it over to study the underside.-She visualized Belle's dented samovar sitting on a table at the Glory Hole after Jack fished it out of the dumpster. Goldie remembered it looked like something had been torn off the bottom. Exerting just a little pressure, she ran her finger around the lower edge.

A tarnished plate attached to the fancy legs suddenly sprang open. Inside the hidden round cavity rested an old tobacco tin with Cyrillic lettering on it. Godiva and Angel stood by wide-eyed as Goldie removed the tin carefully and twisted the lid. Crumbs of stale tobacco spilled on the desk. For a moment, none of the three women moved. Nestled in the mound of remaining tobacco was a large, brilliant, blood red gemstone that looked a lot like a fine ruby.

"Now, Angel, you're sworn to secrecy. No one else can know we have the samovar and this stone."

Angel looked her squarely in the eye. "Hey Boss, you're talking to me. I'm the one who helped you figure it out. Remember? I haven't said anything yet, and now that I've seen it, not a word will pass my lips." She made a hand gesture across her mouth as though she was closing a zipper.

"Okay, I'm satisfied."

A tear slid down Goldie's cheek. "I forgot how nice this one was." Then with a little break in her voice, she said, "Sorry, but just looking at this samovar makes me realize how much I'll miss Mimi." Waldo nuzzled her hand as she blinked away tears.

Godiva jumped in and changed the subject. "Angel, tell us about alexandrite again."

"Well, when I was doing my research, one of the articles said a small vein was found in an emerald mine in the Urals back in the early 1830s and it was named after Alexander II. Anything over a one carat Siberian alexandrite is rare, and one over five carats has almost never been seen. This big rock must be over five carats. I can't even imagine how much seven stones like this would be worth. Probably priceless."

Godiva flashed her showy canary yellow diamond ring. "This one is five carats and, see," she held the deep red gem beside it, "this alexandrite is much bigger. What else did you find out about these stones, Angel?"

"Well, when they're seen in different lights, the most expensive ones do a complete color change from brilliant emerald green to a blood red color—just like this one. Some only change partially. It said the best way to see the color change is to darken the room and put it under a fluorescent light, because that's like looking at it in daylight. Then, if you switch to incandescent light, you can see the color change. Let's try it."

The twins nodded in unison. Angel pulled the draperies and Goldie turned off the wall switch for the overhead fixture. The room was cloaked in darkness. Godiva clicked the switch on the large fluorescent desk lamp and the stone slowly changed to a brilliant emerald green. She turned it off again and Goldie flipped the wall switch to turn on the overhead light. All three gasped as they watched it change back to a sparkling deep ruby color.

Angel made the sign of the cross. "You know, I'm actually getting kinda creeped out. One of the things I read said the royal family was executed in 1918. Tzar Nicholas II died first, his daughters were shot too, but they were still alive. One man tried to finish them off with a bayonet, but that didn't work. Finally, they were all shot in the head."

Goldie let a little gasp escape as she plunked the gem back in the tobacco tin. "So, what has that got to do with this stone?"

"Well, when the men came to undress the bodies, they found that all of the women were wearing gold bodices covered almost entirely with diamonds, emeralds, and other precious stones."

"Nothing like insurance for a rainy day," Godiva said.

"Yeah, Sis, a lot of good it did them."

"Anyway, besides the bodices," Angel continued, "the Tzarina's tiara with the Seven Stars of Siberia disappeared, too. Most people thought it was stolen by one of those guards."

"Wow, that is creepy," Godiva said. "And, you think this stone came out of that tiara?"

"Yep, that's what I think. According to one of the articles, they found the remains of a platinum tiara in the rubble at

Minsky & Pinsky, and if alexandrites this large and pure in color are so rare, what are the odds of there being two sets of seven?"

Goldie nodded sadly. She hated admitting to herself that her kindly Russian friends were really criminals. "Well, it looks like the investigators who were watching Vladimir and Uri really were on the right track."

A silence fell over the study as they thought about the slaughter of the royal family of Russia, and the looting of the precious gems.

Waldo had gone to sleep on a pile of plastic bubbles and was snoring gently.

Godiva finally said, "Do you suppose we'll ever find out how the Seven Stars got from that 1918 massacre to your crooked importers' warehouse?"

"I'll keep digging," Angel said. "If there's anything's out there, I'll find it, but some secrets never come to light."

Angel looked at her watch. "Man-oh-man, I've gotta run, Boss. I'm supposed to meet Nathan for dinner in—oh no, fifteen minutes ago. Thanks for letting me see the stone. You guys better put it someplace safe."

Godiva ushered Angel out of the study and locked the door. She walked over to the mahogany bookshelves lining the side wall, reached for a large bible on one of the upper shelves and the bookshelf swung open revealing a hidden room.

"This is the only thing Max ever used the bible for."

Goldie's eyes widened as she peeked into the little room, filled with valuable paintings, jewel boxes and a fireproof file cabinet. Before she could say anything, Godiva said, "This is my insurance for a rainy day. It will be a good hiding place."

Chapter 31

They had just finished dinner when the intercom buzzed. The security camera showed Nellie McNab at the gate. Godiva pressed the remote button and both twins jumped up to greet her in the foyer.

Nellie breezed through the massive front door dressed in a very stylish purple pantsuit with a matching cashmere turtleneck. Perched on her head was a lavender cowboy hat with a rhinestone-studded hatband adorned with so many feathers it looked like she was ready to take flight. She pointed to the hat and chuckled. "I was just a few blocks away from you at a Mad Hatters' dinner meeting. Do you like my outfit?"

Goldie laughed. "Well, your hat's not as flashy as most of Belle's, but you look great. Would you like some coffee or tea?"

"You know, I'd love a cup of coffee if it isn't too much trouble."

Nellie followed them into the comfortable family room. "I've been going all day without stopping, and I didn't stay for dessert and coffee because I was anxious to get over here. How often do I get the chance to be part of something like this?" An engaging smile broke across her handsome face.

Godiva rang for Guadalupe and asked her to bring their guest some coffee and a slice of peach pie.

Before either sister could say another word, Nellie jumped in. "I was pretty worried about this whole situation. After all, Caesar Romano is one of my favorite TV chefs, so I talked to Harley about it. I hope you don't mind, but I've asked my husband for a favor."

Goldie raised a suspicious eyebrow. "Do I want to hear this, Nellie?"

Her chuckle sounded like a tinkling bell. "After getting to

know you at lunch today, I think you girls will love it. It's your kind of thing."

They huddled in a bit closer and Nellie continued, "You know Harley can't do anything in an official capacity at this point. But that doesn't mean he can't ask some of his friends in the Ghost Riders to give Ricky Thompson a helping hand."

"What exactly do you mean by 'helping hand,' Nellie?" Goldie asked.

"A bunch of the guys are going over to Caesar's house to team up with Ricky and his men. They'll keep out of sight, but his place will be surrounded in a tight circle. They'll walk the bikes in so the engines don't give them away. If your Russians show up and try to get into the house, they're going to get a real surprise. Let's just say, I think your Italian Stallion will be very safe tonight."

"That sounds like a good precaution," Goldie said. "Those Dumkovskys are ruthless. What do you think, Sis?"

Godiva nodded. "Yeah, I agree. We have to make sure those bad boys are stopped, because if they do get into Caesar's house and discover there's no samovar, well, no telling what a couple of mad Russians are likely to do. I may be upset with Caesar, but I don't want him to get hurt."

They both smiled at Nellie. Goldie shook her hand. "Welcome to the team."

Chapter 32

Sterling steered the mammoth '59 Cadillac toward Caesar's house while Flossie sat beside him and offered unwanted advice.

"*Oy*! Sterling, step on your brakes!" she shouted, clutching the dashboard. Since Flossie never actually learned to drive, Sterling figured out long ago how to tune her out. But he tapped the brake a little, just to shut her up.

In between her commands, he managed to say, "Listen, old girl, we have to get to the point with Caesar right away. No going off on stories about the old days, you understand?"

"So what do you suggest, Mr. Toastmaster? We should just barge in and tell him a couple of *alter kockers* are ready to save his life because the police aren't going to do a thing?"

"Well, not in so many words, but we do need to stay on track." He drew a sharp breath and slammed on his brakes as a young guy in a silver Lamborghini cut in front of him. "It's a mystery to me where those damn kids get the money for a machine like that. I was happy to have a used Model T when I was his age."

Flossie tittered. "And you were saying about staying on track..."

"Okay, you got me there, I did get distracted. Anyway, the idea is to wait until those big bozos break in."

"Who knows, maybe they'll just waltz up to the front door in their cute little dresses and say they're selling Girl Scout cookies." She snickered at her own joke.

"Pay attention! As soon as we see the whites of their eyes, we set off the first illusion and 'boom' we trap them in the steel net from our Neptune and Nemo act just as they're about to grab the fake samovar."

"You got the net in the trunk? Did you get Godiva's big coffee urn to use as a foil?"

"Well not exactly," said Sterling a little sheepishly, "Martina loaned the damn thing to her church for a party, so I found a fertilizer can in the shed that's about the right shape."

"I don't know, sounds a little shaky to me. What do we do with these guys once we get them in the net? Who gets to call the cops, me or you?"

"I dunno, Flossie, maybe Caesar should do that."

"You mean let him get all the credit?" She folded her arms across her chest and pouted until they arrived.

They waited impatiently in front of the security camera until Caesar buzzed them in. They were unaware that Ricky and his guys, backed up by a contingent of the Ghost Riders, were watching from their hiding places around the perimeter of the property.

When the private line rang, the twins were deep in conspiratorial conversation with Nellie.

"I'll bet that's Ricky." Godiva zoomed across the room and grabbed the receiver. She listened while her eyes got wider and wider. She kept saying, "I don't believe it." Finally she hung up and said, "Saddle up, ladies. Mom and Unk are at it again."

"I thought they were having dinner at the Daily Grill and going to a movie," said Goldie.

"They skunked us, Sis. Those old goats are over at Caesar's. Ricky spotted them as they drove up. Of course Uncle Sterling's big old Cadillac isn't exactly a stealth missile." She balled up her fists as she tried to calm her temper. "Darn them. They could ruin everything."

Caesar welcomed Flossie and Sterling, then led them into the luxurious living room. Deep burgundy leather sofas and club chairs flanked a huge walnut coffee table arranged in front of an Italian tile fireplace. A signed Picasso print graced the opposite wall. The air was scented with a delicious aroma drifting in from the kitchen.

"Sit down, you two. I was just experimenting with a new creation. Would you like a taste? I know you have something important to talk about, but first you must sample my recipe."

Flossie answered for both of them. "Of course we want a taste. My mouth is watering already just from one whiff. We can talk afterwards."

Sterling gave her a warning look. "No, this can't wait. This is very important Caesar. It's about that samovar you sent your mother. Did Godiva tell you people who have them are dying?"

Caesar nodded. "Well, she said there was some danger, but the blasted teapot isn't even here. Besides, Ricky Thompson's out there." He pointed toward the window. "So there's nothing to fear."

Flossie waved her arms to get his attention. "Yes, there is Caesar. Yours is the last one. The Russian killers don't know you sent yours to Florida."

Sterling broke in. "Listen old man, you're a target whether you like it or not. But we have a plan. Very dramatic. And I guarantee, we'll catch those guys."

"It'll be fun for you, too," Flossie said.

"The girls don't know we're here," Sterling resumed in a businesslike way. "I suppose they told you the cops won't help until a crime's committed. But we've seen what those guys will do. It's not pretty, Caesar. You don't want to wait until your house is a crime scene."

Caesar considered that. Then he said in his flawlessly accented stage voice, "If it's really that dangerous, why haven't Ricky and his boys been more visible? I've barely seen them."

Flossie chuckled. "Of course you haven't. That's the way he works. Under the radar. We didn't see anyone when we drove up, but if they're here I'm sure Ricky saw us come in. Since we're obviously not the enemy, he let us pass. After all, you're my daughter's paramour, so I'm practically your own Jewish mother!"

Caesar sighed. "I'm not so sure about paramour anymore, Flossie. But why don't we move into the dining room and I'll get a plate for each of you. Jewish mothers aren't the only ones who feed you when you visit."

Once they were seated Flossie took one bite and raised her eyebrows. "Caesar, what is this? It's *soooo* good."

A charming smile broke across his face. The heavenly scent of tomato, oregano and anise filled the room. He placed a heaped silver platter on the table in case his guests wanted a second helping.

"I don't have a name for it yet. I was just playing around with some veal and vegetables and spices. Perhaps I'll name it for Godiva. She has such an elegant sounding name."

Sterling smacked his lips. "I tell ya what, anyone who cooks this good ought to be somebody's wife. What do ya say we get married?"

Caesar bellowed with laughter. "I'm afraid you're too old for me, Sterling."

"In that case, let's get down to brass tacks. Here's our plan, we've got the stuff in the car..."

The sound of the security buzzer interrupted Sterling. Caesar excused himself. He peered at the camera monitor and pressed the voice button. Then he said in a booming voice, "What is it?" He followed that with, "Isn't it a little late for Food Broadcasting to send a messenger?"

Caesar was wasting valuable time by yakking away with someone from the TV network. Flossie and Sterling were ready to unveil their brilliant plan, and got more and more impatient.

Sterling said in a stage whisper, "Keep calm, Flossie. It sounds like Caesar is getting a delivery from the studio. A few more minutes won't make a difference; it gives me enough time to have a second helping. Please pass that platter."

Caesar's voice sounded disturbed. "Just leave it by the gate. I'll get it later."

After a short silence, he said, "Since when do they require a signature? That Manny Manicotti is a real pain. Hummph. Dinner hour." Another pause while the messenger spoke. Then,

"Okay, I'll open the gate, but no chit chat, got it? I'll let you in, you give me the package, I'll sign and you leave. Manicotti's got some nerve."

Caesar popped his head into the dining room. "Sorry. There's a messenger from my studio out there. I've got to let this guy in so I can sign for something. Shouldn't take a minute. Help yourself to some more food."

The heavy door groaned a bit as he swung it open. The next thing they saw as they craned their necks to peek around the corner, was a stocky man who looked like Edward G. Robinson wearing a Food Broadcasting cap and jacket. But something was very wrong. He had a gun shoved in Caesar's back.

Chapter 33

Caesar avoided looking in the direction of the dining room as the man pushed him forward.

Meanwhile, Flossie and Sterling worked their way back to a far corner of the room, out of the intruder's range of vision. They might have been able to hide, if Sterling hadn't stepped on Flossie's toe, causing her to screech "*Oy vey!*" The intruder whipped around, searching for the source of the high-pitched cry of pain.

Unfortunately, Flossie followed up her initial outcry by shouting, "You *klutz,* watch where you're going."

The man pushed Caesar into the dining room and said sarcastically, "Hmmm, what do we have here, Mr. Fancy Pants Chef? Your mother and father, maybe?" He waved the gun in their direction, keeping one big paw clamped securely on Caesar's shoulder. Then he shoved the bewildered chef forward while Flossie and Sterling tried to inch back, which was impossible. They were already plastered against the wall.

The man poked Caesar with the gun and the color drained out of his handsome face, turning it a ghostly shade of pale olive. The stranger shouted, "Okay, where is the samovar?"

Flossie rolled her eyes skyward and said, "Not those *farstunkener* teapots again! Is that all anyone thinks about anymore?"

"Button yer lip, Grandma," the stocky man growled. "No stalling. I want that samovar, now!"

Caesar couldn't seem to make his mouth work. The lips flapped up and down, but no sound escaped. He raised an eyebrow at the oldsters, as if to ask, "Where's your clever plan now?"

Sterling cleared his throat, stalling for a bit more time.

Then, he took a deep breath and in as soothing a tone as he could manage, said, "I guess you really don't work for Food Broadcasting, do you?" He didn't wait for an answer. "Well, never mind. The samovar isn't here, is it Caesar?" The chef's head bobbed from side to side like a robot with a short circuit.

A brilliant shade of scarlet crept from the stranger's neck up to his forehead. In a quick motion, he drew back a fist as big as a wrecking ball.

"Shame on you, you big bully," Flossie scolded. "You don't need to get so rough." She reached over to the silver platter on the table, nudged it toward him. "Here Mr. Burglar. Why not try some of this delicious food? Maybe it will calm you down."

Caesar found his voice. "It's quite good. One of my new creations." He tried to ooze a little charm, but it was a miserable failure. His chattering teeth distorted the words.

The phony messenger raised his voice, clearly furious. "Cut the crap, Chef. I don't want food. I don't intend to be nice. I want that damned samovar!"

With that, he flung the platter to the floor spraying the off-white carpet with veal, vegetables and red sauce.

"Don't play games! I know it was sold to you, and it wasn't at your studio, so it has to be here somewhere. I'll get it if I have to tear the whole place apart. If you don't cooperate, I'll pulverize you and these two old farts." He waved the gun in the air. "Trust me, this isn't an idle threat."

He pointed the gun at Flossie. "You, Grandma—take those ropes holding back the drapes."

She moved as though in a trance, carefully removing four tiebacks. "Now, take two of 'em and tie up this old coot. One for his hands and one for his feet. You better make it tight—or else."

Flossie did as she was told, but she tied the ropes with a special trick knot they used in one of their escape illusions. To the average observer, it looked like a normal knot, but Sterling would easily be able to slip out of it.

The tough guy smiled with satisfaction, showing tobacco-stained teeth with a chip on one of the front ones. "That's good, you old bag. Okay, now come over here—very slowly."

Without thinking, Flossie snapped, "Watch who you're calling an old bag. You're no pretty boy yourself, you know." Then her eyes sparked with fear. A smart remark could cost her dearly. In a meek voice she said, "Sorry," and moved toward the other side of the room.

Caesar sat in a chair, eyes glazed over with pain and frustration, while the stranger stood behind him and once again clamped down on his shoulder with that meat hook of a hand. His mouth moved, but no sound came out. Perspiration dotted his forehead. The man said to Flossie, "Give those other two ropes to Chef Romeo here."

Caesar finally found a shaky little voice. "That's Romano, not Romeo. Who the hell are you, anyway?"

"Never mind who I am, Fancy Pants. Take those and tie up the old lady." He yanked Caesar from the chair and shoved him toward Flossie. "Okay, Grandma, don't get no funny ideas. Just behave, and let the good chef here tie you up."

She started to protest and he whacked her across the face, knocking her glasses off her nose. A slight trickle of blood worked its way down her wrinkled cheek.

"Don't mess with me you old bat, or I'll forget myself and really let you have it." For once in her life, Flossie shut her mouth.

Sterling mumbled something under his breath but no one could understand what he was saying.

Caesar tried to control his shaking hands and he finally tied Flossie up. She attempted to signal him not to worry by winking. However, instead of winking, her flurry of continuous blinking looked more like she had something in her eye.

The man moved over to Sterling, got right in his face and said through clenched teeth, "Be good Pops, or you'll wind up dead." He whacked Sterling on the side of the head with the gun and laughed when pain flashed across the old man's face. Satisfied that the seniors were out of commission, he left Flossie and Sterling tied to the dining room chairs, grabbed Caesar again, and yanked him to his feet. He jammed the gun into the stunned chef's back, then commanded, "March!"

Outside Ricky and the bikers still watched for some sign of the Dumkovskys. The plan was to let them get inside and then Ricky, Ivan and half of the bikers would storm the house and the others would standby to wait for the signal. In the end, the criminals would be handed over to the LAPD. At that point the various police jurisdictions involved could quibble over who got them.

Ricky tapped Ivan on the shoulder. "If that Food Broadcasting guy doesn't come out pretty soon, we may have to go in and get him. Can't have him getting in the way."

One of the Ghost Riders said, "He was carrying a pretty big package. Maybe he had lots of papers or something for the chef to go over."

"I don't know," grumbled Ivan. "It sounded like Caesar just had to sign something and send him on his way."

A beat up turquoise Chevy with "Rent-a-Wreck" stickers on the rear bumper cruised past them and parked halfway down the street. Two big hulks got out and started toward Caesar's house. The messenger was quickly forgotten, as Ivan signaled everyone to keep quiet.

Both of the men were dressed in black from head to toe. One threw a grappling hook with a rope over the wall surrounding the property and literally walked up the wall, then swung over. The bigger of the two struggled after him. Ivan whispered to Ricky, "So much for security walls!"

Ricky, Ivan and the twelve Ghost Rider volunteers drew into a tighter circle.

The Dumkovskys smashed the leaded glass in the front door, reached in and turned the handle to open it. When the first intruder heard the noise, he stopped walking toward the living room and spun Caesar around, just as the two big guys lumbered into the elegant hall. Now they were all face-to-face. Igor grunted in amazement and stopped short. Boris rammed into him. They both stared at the man terrorizing Caesar and chorused in unison, "Rimsky?"

Rimsky sneered at them. He spat out in a mocking tone,

"Yes, you stupid oafs. It is me, Rimsky." He pointed the gun at them while keeping a firm grip on Caesar. "How convenient for you to show up right now. That makes it a lot easier to hang a few more murders on you. Move it." Turning the gun in a circular motion, he indicated the direction of the living room.

Sterling whispered to Flossie. "Okay old girl. I don't know what the hell is going on out there, but they're far enough away now for me to get untied. Good job with the knots." He loosened the ropes with a few quick movements and threw them aside. He rubbed his numb hands and feet and then untied Flossie.

The octogenarians crept toward the doorway, careful not to make any noise. There was a loud scuffle going on in the living room, with three gruff voices shouting in Russian. Somewhere in the house, a phone was ringing. Flossie grabbed a big brass candlestick off the sideboard and followed Sterling into the hall. When one of the thugs spotted her and bellowed, Flossie swung the candlestick with such force that she knocked the man to his knees. She wound up halfway across the room, upside down on the sofa.

At that moment, a mighty roar arose outside, rattling the windows and shaking the house. "Just what we need right now, a damned earthquake!" muttered Sterling as he braced himself in the doorway.

Ricky had given the Dumkovskys a few minutes to enter the house before he carefully opened the gates just enough so that Ivan and the motorcycle gang could walk their bikes forward, taking care to be as quiet as possible. According to plan, once through the gates, they regrouped in the gigantic courtyard and arranged the bikes in a semicircle pointed toward the house.

Blinding light streamed in through the leaded glass side windows and the broken glass in the entry door. Everyone froze in their tracks. The phone rang again.

Ivan and Ricky crashed into the hall. Half a dozen giants in black leathers followed close on their heels, while another half dozen revved the engines of the bikes in the courtyard until the roar became earsplitting. Confused by the lights and roar of the Harleys, Rimsky started shooting blindly into the hall from his position in the living room.

Neighbors streamed out of their houses and shouted to each other. Some called the police on their cell phones to complain of bikers disturbing the peace. The scene in the street escalated into something that resembled a sleazy movie.

A sleek blond in a designer dress screamed, "Murder, murder..." and her husband tried to calm her down. An aged former movie star clasped his heart and pleaded, "Get me an ambulance," and parents pushed their kids back toward the imposing homes lining the street. Several of the enormous Ghost Riders stood beside their bikes and very courteously cautioned the local gentry to return to their homes so they wouldn't get hurt.

Chapter 34

What should have been a fifteen minute ride to Caesar's house seemed to take forever. While Godiva battled L.A. traffic, Goldie kept dialing Caesar's number, but each time his voice mail answered.

"Goldie," Godiva said, "are you sure you're calling the right number? Ricky said Caesar was in the house."

A slight trace of annoyance crept into Goldie's voice. "Of course it's the right number, unless you have the wrong one programmed into your phone. I'm pressing five for speed dial, just like you told me to."

"Okay, why don't you try calling Sterling on his cell? Maybe the old dear actually remembered to turn it on. I think he worries about alien sound waves, or something."

Nellie interrupted from the backseat. "Look you two, while you're trying to get them, why don't I call Ricky? You have his number, don't you?"

Nellie dialed, as Godiva dictated the number.

Impatiently stomping on the gas pedal, Godiva thought if she speeded up she could make it into the next lane where the cars were zipping along. Unfortunately, just at that moment, a big blue truck filled with tools pulled alongside her and she clipped its bumper with a resounding *whack!* The three women watched in awe as the front bumper of their Town Car flew over the truck, and landed on the parkway with a loud clatter. Traffic came to a halt all around them.

"What the..."

Goldie's voice sounded a little shaky. "Umm, Sis, you hit the truck next to us. Guess we better get out and see how bad it is." They stood in the middle of the road and stared at the bumper still teetering back and forth on the grass.

The other driver got out of his truck, looking a bit dazed. Aside from a little dent where their bumpers kissed, he and his truck didn't seem to be any worse for wear. He looked concerned. "Are you ladies okay?"

Before anyone could answer, he squinted at Goldie and said, "Hey, wait a minute, I saw your picture on the back of a bus. Don't you write some kind of newspaper column?"

Goldie shook her head and pointed to Godiva who was now walking around the car. "Column? Oh, that's my sister. She's the writer."

Nellie stepped between them. "Look, we have an emergency here. The twins' mother is in great danger, and Godiva is really upset. That's probably why she wasn't paying full attention. Can you guys just exchange information so we can get going? Every minute counts."

He smoothed his thinning brown hair over an obvious bald spot and gave them a sympathetic look. "Well, I'm not hurt, and there actually isn't much damage to my truck, although..."

Godiva came up beside him. "Although my bumper is over there on the grass, and it looks like that's our biggest problem at the moment."

The driver scratched the stubble on his chin and said, "Look, lady, some people would really give you a hard time and lawyer up. You weren't looking, you know. On the other hand, I think my wife reads your column." He slowly walked around the Town Car.

Godiva turned on every ounce of her charm. "Thanks so much for your understanding, Mr.—"

"Banger. Chet Banger. No comments please. This time you're the one who's the banger." He slapped his knee and let out a big guffaw.

While giving him her best smile, she said, "That's a good one, Chet. Look, maybe I'll write a special column about the kindness of strangers. I'll put your name in if you want me to."

"Nah. Don't use my name. I'll tell you what. I'll give you my card. It's got my address. Why not just send me an autographed picture for my wife. Her name is Hannah." He ran his hand along the small dent in his bumper. "Ya know, if you don't want a black mark on your insurance, I have a buddy who can probably fix this for a pretty reasonable price."

"That would be great, I'll pay whatever it costs. I'm really worried about my mother. Look, I'll include a little extra for you if you can help us get going. I'll write all of the information on the back of my card."

Chet fiddled in his pocket and brought out a slightly crumpled card of his own. He took her pen, scribbled some information on the back, and handed it to her. She read the front out loud. "Beat it to Fit—Paint it to Match—call Chet Banger, Handyman Extraordinaire. So you're a fix-it man, huh?"

"Yep, and now I'm gonna fix you ladies up and get you back on the road." He walked over to the grassy parkway, and picked up the bumper as though it weighed nothing. He pointed to Goldie and Nellie. "If you two will open the back doors, we'll just maneuver it into the back seat somehow, and you can drive off." He looked it over and said, "My friend might even be able to bang out the dents and fix it." Then he looked Godiva up and down and added, "But I'm guessing you'll want a new one."

They jockeyed the cumbersome bumper back and forth until it was finally secure in the back seat, with one end of it extending out of the rear side window. Because Nellie was the slimmest and most agile, she volunteered to wiggle in and share the space with the bumper.

He called after them, "I'll send ya the bill. Don't forget the picture, and I hope your mother's okay."

Goldie said, "You lucked out, Godiva. Let's get out of here."

A few heads turned, watching the Town Car continue along Sunset Boulevard with its bumper sticking out of the side window. By the time they came to Carolwood Drive and approached Caesar's house, the street was filled with flashing red lights, large men in motorcycle gear, distraught neighbors and detectives from the LAPD.

At first, two of the officers eyeballed them suspiciously and wouldn't let them turn onto the street, saying it was a crime scene and only residents were allowed to pass.

"Omigod," gasped Godiva. "Did anyone get hurt—"

Goldie chimed in, "Or killed? My mother and uncle are in there, you know."

"And my boyfriend, too," said Godiva.

At that point, Nellie poked her head around the bumper and called out to one of them, "Officer McPherson, is that you?"

He whipped around, apparently surprised to see Captain McNab's wife.

She said, "Listen, McPherson, you've got to tell me. What happened in there?"

"Well, ma'am, I'm not supposed to say anything, but seeing it's you, Miz McNab, I guess it's okay to assure you that no one's been killed. Outside of a couple bumps and bruises, everyone's fine."

They got out of the car just in time to see the two Russian goons and a smaller stocky man being led out of the house in handcuffs.

Goldie tugged at Godiva's sleeve. "Omigod, Sis, I can't believe it. Do you know who that shorter one is? That's Rimsky, Father Innocent's helper. What's he doing here?"

Chapter 35

The twins and Nellie hustled toward the front door, where two uniformed officers approached them. The heftier of the pair held up his hand. "I'm sorry, ladies, you can't go in." His arm swept the courtyard, which was still filled with assorted bikers and cops. The police cruiser, with Rimsky inside, started to pull out of the circular driveway. "As you can see, this is a crime scene. How did you get past my officers, anyway?"

He was interrupted by his partner, a young man with a shock of sun-bleached hair who didn't look old enough to be a cadet, let alone a uniformed cop. "I think it's okay, Mike," the baby-faced cop said in a surprisingly authoritative tone. He gestured at Nellie and said a little louder than necessary, "I guess you didn't recognize Captain McNab's wife."

Goldie put her arm around Godiva and addressed the younger cop. "You know those two old folks inside? They're our mother and uncle. And my sister's boyfriend is Chef Romano. Please, you have to let us go in—we're so worried about all of them."

Just then, Flossie wobbled to the partially open front door with Sterling right behind her. She clutched the doorframe and poked her head out. Godiva noticed she wasn't wearing her glasses. Steadying herself against the door, Flossie called out, "Oh, it's my dear girls! I'm so happy to see you." She put her hand to her face and felt around where her glasses should have been. "Well, actually, I can't see you very well at all, but I sure can hear you."

Goldie sprinted up the stairs and gave her mother a bear hug. "Oh, Mom, we were so worried about you." Then she noticed Flossie sported a real shiner. She touched her mother's cheek gently. "What have those ruffians done to you? You've got a black eye and a cut on the side of your face."

Flossie fingered her brow and winced. She balled her hands into fists and threw a mock one-two punch. "If you think this is bad, you should see the other guy!" She looped her arms through those of her daughters and tut-tutted, "Black eye, schmack eye. It'll heal up. Just wait'll we tell you what happened."

Sterling shook his head as if to say, *Your mother and her crazy ideas.*

The twins' mother waggled her finger at the fuzzy image of her brother-in-law, and chattered away. "Your uncle and I were just like a pair of comic book heroes, weren't we Sterling? You see girls, I got this idea for a real doozy of a trick to—"

Sterling harrumphed. "You and your ideas will get us killed some day, Flossie. I don't know how you manage to talk me into these things."

Godiva shook her head, looking at the broken glass in the front door. In spite of the ordeal, Flossie was radiating excitement and seemed much younger than her eighty-one years. Even though Sterling leaned heavily on his cane, there was also a spring in his step.

"What am I going to do with you two? You're worse than a pair of wayward teenagers."

Nellie patted Godiva on the arm. "I know what you mean. Harley's folks are a handful too. They're in their mid-eighties and, of all things, they've taken up skydiving. I worry about them every day. But my mother-in-law just says, 'I used to be afraid that skydiving might kill me, but now that I'm so close, I figure, what a way to go!'"

The group made their way to the living room, carefully stepping around the mess in the long entry hall. Caesar settled Sterling into an easy chair, brought an ice bag for the bump on his head, and a cool damp cloth for Flossie's wounds. Then he sat on the sofa next to Flossie and dropped his head into his hands. Two LAPD officers, still in the house, continued to wrap things up.

In a voice filled with fury, Godiva shouted, "Caesar, how

could you do this? You knew the house was under surveillance. You knew those thugs were going to come after the samovar, and still you allowed my mother and uncle to be in this dangerous situation." She raised a balled fist in his direction. "No one but you was supposed to be in the house. You all could have gotten killed."

He raised his head and flashed an apologetic half-smile, holding his hands up in protest. "*Cara mia*, I know you're mad at me, but that isn't quite how it happened. Just let me tell you—"

Sterling broke in. "Listen girls, your mother and I take full responsibility. First we lied to you about going to dinner and a movie. Heck, I have no idea what movies are playing at the Beverly Center tonight, but it sounded good. Then we bullied Caesar into letting us come over, because Flossie hatched a clever plot to catch the villains."

"Yeah, and it would have worked, too," said Flossie, "if it wasn't for that other guy. I thought there were only two."

"And what about the motorcycle gang! Where did they come from, anyway?" croaked Sterling. "I almost peed my pants when they revved things up."

"Well Mom," Goldie said, "you won't believe it, but I know who the third guy is. He's Rimsky, the fellow who took care of Father Innocent back in Juneau. Belle said he disappeared a few days ago. When she told me the church ladies couldn't find him, I didn't think anything of it. After all, I hardly know him, and he struck me as a kind of stupid guy. I have no idea how he's involved in all of this or if he even knows the Dumkovskys."

"Don't let him fool you," Sterling snorted. "That guy is one smart cookie, and he's after those cursed samovars, too. He arrived here first, disguised as a Food Broadcasting messenger. When those two other goons broke in, they all seemed to know each other. If I remember right, they called him by name and he called them Igor and Boris." He readjusted the icepack, positioning it around the spot where Rimsky hit him with the gun. Although he made a point of appearing to tough it out, a small groan escaped.

After that, everyone started to talk at the same time. Finally Caesar put two fingers to his lips and let out a shrill whistle. "Stop, stop. This isn't getting us anywhere. Settle down and let me tell all of you what happened."

The twins sank down into the lounge chairs on either side of the fireplace and stared at him stony-faced. Nellie pulled up a side chair. Both officers stopped what they were doing and stood a little closer, arms akimbo, waiting for Caesar to begin.

He cleared his throat, and then cleared it again, stalling for time. When he cast a hopeful glance at Godiva, she did not smile back at him. "Well, like your uncle said, the shorter guy got here first. He's a mean one, that—what was his name? Ritzsky?"

Goldie's voice dripped icicles. "Rimsky."

"Anyway, Sterling told him I didn't have the samovar, but he was still demanding that I give it to him when your Dumkovskys came along and smashed the window. As soon as they came face-to-face, like Sterling said, they recognized each other. Then it got pretty rowdy with all of them shouting at each other in Russian."

"Cursin' each other, if you ask me," Sterling said under his breath.

Flossie reached over and patted Caesar's knee. "You're not telling the whole story. You left out the part where the first guy pretended he had papers from your studio."

"We said he got here first, dressed like a messenger," he answered through clenched teeth.

"Yes, but you didn't say how he got into the house." She smiled triumphantly at her daughters. "Pretty clever saying he needed a signature. While Caesar went to the door, your uncle and I waited in the dining room."

Sterling perked up, "At least we got to sample that wonderful dish you made. You should take a taste, girls."

"It was good wasn't it? I used some vegetables, veal—even told your mother I was thinking of naming it after you, *Cara Mia*. Now it's all over my nice white carpeting."

"Enough, Caesar! Sure it was good," Flossie said, "but we were about to tell you our scheme to catch the crooks when that *schlemiel* barged in. Instead of dazzling you with our clever plot, we see this guy with a gun shoved in your back pushing you down the hall."

"Anyway," Sterling added, "we were doing a pretty good job of hiding in the dining room until I stepped on your mother's toe, and she shouted that I'm a klutz. Of course, the minute he heard her shrieking, he knew Caesar wasn't alone."

The old woman hung her head and mouthed, "Sorry."

"But she made up for it when he told her to tie me up. That old girl used the Knot of Deception, you know, the one your Dad invented. Anyway, he didn't suspect a thing and as soon as he left the room, I was able to wiggle out of the rope and untie Flossie. Then we—"

"Sterling. Flossie. There is time for that later." Caesar appeared to be miffed that the oldsters were stealing his thunder. "Here's the important part. After the Dumkovskys broke in and saw the other guy here, one of them began to strangle him. That was some fight! Two against one, but that Rimsky was not one to tangle with. I tell you, what he lacks in size, he makes up for in nastiness."

Everyone in the room waited for the chef to continue his story. Caesar walked over to the window and started pacing, clearly struggling to remember the events of the evening. Finally he tapped his finger against his chin. "All of a sudden, one of the Dumkovskys spots a leather bag hanging around that other guy's neck." Caesar grabbed at the air. "He lets out a roar and yanks it off."

"A leather bag?"

"Yeah, it was a sort of like one of those Indian medicine bags or something like that. He spits in Rimsky's face, and shouts in English, 'Traitor!' Then he tosses the bag to his brother who yells something back in Russian. The second guy takes a little tin out of his pocket, opens it up, then looks inside the bag and nods. After that, he stuffs the bag into the tin."

Flossie wiggled around like a kid who needed a bathroom

break. Without her glasses, she was squinting so much that her eyes were nearly closed. "Don't forget my part." She turned in the direction of the twins. "I tell you girls, I was just like Wonder Woman, wasn't I, Caesar?"

"I'm getting to that, Flossie. Calm down." He stopped pacing and sat down on the sofa again. "The second Dumkovsky is standing there looking at the box in his hand, when your mother comes out of the dining room swinging a big brass candlestick and whacks him right in the face."

Flossie clapped her hands and chuckled with delight. "Yep, I ended up ass over teakettle there on the couch. Good thing I had my new Lollypops underwear on!"

"You should have seen your mother. She really gave him a good one. Blood's dripping everywhere; he's holding his nose and cursing in Russian. That's when those motorcycle maniacs busted in whooping and hollering, while more of them were out in the courtyard making a god-awful racket with their engines."

"We thought it was a damned earthquake!" Sterling squeaked.

"It was like a crazy movie. The cops came blasting in right behind the bikers." Caesar took a deep breath, then sighed. "You know the rest of the story."

Nellie spoke up from her chair by the fireplace. "I'm just glad everyone is okay. Sounds like the Riders had fun, too. They love a good fight. I'm glad my husband called them."

"Yeah. So am I." Goldie looked lovingly at her mother and shook her head. "Mom, I can't believe you did that. You really whacked that big Russian?"

She nodded, holding up her right fist like a champ. "To tell you the truth, it's a wonder I hit anything. I lost my glasses when that creep hit me, so I just came out swinging. I figured I'd hit someone. I was praying it wouldn't be you, Caesar."

Everyone sank back into their seats looking exhausted, while the policemen took reports to wrap things up. Nellie said, "Well, Flossie and Sterling, you've had quite a night. We should be getting you home, don't you think?"

"What should I do about the broken window in my front door?" Caesar threw his hands in the air, looking helpless. "I'll never get anyone out to fix it this late."

"Calm down. Surely you have a hammer and a few nails around here somewhere," Goldie said. "Maybe there's a piece of wood in your garage we can nail over the opening."

He shrugged. "I guess I can find something. But who can we get to put it up?"

She patted him on the arm. "No big deal. I can do it for you." One of the cops stifled a chuckle and Godiva received the message from her sister loud and clear: *He's useless.*

Caesar stalked off to the garage and came back with a hammer and nails and a piece of wood from an old packing crate. He insisted he could do it himself, but after hitting his thumb twice and bellowing in pain, he surrendered the hammer to Goldie. She finished the job in less than five minutes and put the hammer on the hall table. "Okay, let's get going."

"Oh, by the way, my front bumper is in the backseat of my car," Godiva said, "so I think I'll leave it here and ask the dealership to pick the car up tomorrow."

Caesar's eyes opened wide and he looked at Godiva with alarm. "What happened to your car, my love? Did you have an accident?"

"Just a little fender bender on the way here, nothing to worry about. I suppose Sterling's old Caddy can hold all of us."

Sterling's shoulders sagged. He looked down at his feet and sighed, "I'm sorry girls. I'm just too tired to drive it home."

Goldie got up and put her arm around her uncle's shoulder. "No problem, Unk. I drive Red's truck all the time. Your Caddy should be a piece of cake. We'll put two of us in the front, and three in the back. What do you say?"

He put down the ice pack and nodded.

Godiva turned to Caesar and said in a flat tone, "I'll call the dealership tomorrow morning to pick up my car. We'll come back in the roadster to meet them and sign whatever paperwork they need to haul it away."

Caesar reminded Godiva that he had to be at the studio

early in the morning to make preparations for his show. He tried to put his arm around her waist, but she threw it off, still angry.

"Godiva, I'm sorry. Flossie and Sterling said they had such a good idea, and I never even got to hear it."

She snapped, "And you won't!"

He reached in his pocket and then pressed a house key in her hand. "Here, *Cara Mia*, just use this tomorrow. That way you can wait inside for the driver."

Chapter 36

On the way home Flossie tried to convince Godiva not to be too hard on Caesar. Sitting beside her in the backseat of the behemoth Caddy, Sterling rested his wounded head on Nellie's shoulder, snoring in alternating tones of C-sharp and F-flat.

Flossie leaned forward and tapped her daughter on the shoulder to get her attention. "Godiva, darling, pay attention. This is your mother speaking. After all, it was my idea that got your uncle and me into such hot water. Think about what a fantastic chef your Caesar is. And such a handsome, cultured gentleman to boot. With the way he cooks, and the way you love food, it's a match made in heaven."

Godiva shook her head as though her mind was made up. "Yeah, Mom, I could look the other way if tonight's episode was the only thing, but there's more to it. I don't want to go into details right now. It might be a long time before I forgive him—if I ever do."

Driving at exactly the speed limit, Goldie chimed in. "It looks like Godiva's love life will have to take a backseat, Mom. We have so many other things to do. I have to call Perry Pinkwater tonight and tell him the L.A. cops have the bad guys. He'll get hold of Ollie first thing in the morning and do whatever's necessary to get Taku out of jail. Godiva needs to take care of the Town Car in the morning, and there are a million other things—"

Nellie broke in. "Plus, the big question is, where *are* the rest of those gems? Not that it's really my business, but you know what they say about curiosity."

"And *my* big question is, where are my glasses?" Flossie squinted, trying to clear up the fuzzy images that surrounded her. "When you go back to Caesar's place to meet that car guy tomorrow, be sure to scout around for them because I can't see a darn thing. They have to be somewhere in his dining room." She made a big show of crossing her fingers and saying a little prayer. "With any luck, they won't be broken."

Goldie steered though the imposing gates and dropped Flossie and Sterling at their cottages. Back at the main house, Nellie gave each sister a hug and bid them good night. "This is more excitement than I've had in a long time. I have to remember to thank Belle for giving you my number. Let me know what happens."

The twins each returned the hugs. "We have you to thank for the Ghost Riders," Goldie said. "Bet Ricky didn't expect that kind of backup. I'd love to tell Red about them, but that's probably not a good idea. My husband always worries when I'm in L.A. In fact, it would be a big favor to me if you tone down what happened when you talk to Belle. I know she'll get Red all riled up."

Early the next morning, Godiva gave Angel her marching orders for the day, and scribbled answers to a few of the letters. Then she pulled the silver Mercedes roadster into the driveway, and waited while Goldie went back to the family room to retrieve her yellow notepad.

As she slid into the passenger seat, Goldie said, "I don't know, Sis. There are still too many loose ends here. Like Nellie said last night, where are those gems? Maybe when Mom conked that big Russian on the noggin he dropped the sack or tin that Caesar mentioned. I'll betcha anything when we locate that little tin, all the beautiful alexandrites will be in it."

"Or maybe they're hidden somewhere else. The police might even have found them in one of those thugs' pockets."

They pulled into Caesar's driveway a little after ten. When Godiva called the dealership on her cell, she was told it would take between forty-five minutes and an hour for their man to get there. She winked at her sister as she placed Caesar's spare key in the lock. When the door swung open, she extended her arm. "Shall we?"

The minute they were in the house, Godiva made a beeline for Caesar's office and started riffling through the papers on his desk, while mumbling to herself.

"How dare you, Godiva? Those are his personal things. You have no right to spy on him." Goldie grabbed her sister's arm and tried to pull her out of the room.

"Him, who? Caesar Romano or Benito Burrito?" She dug in her heels. "Come on, after the way he lied to me, I have the right. Well, maybe not the right to dig through his papers, but I should have the right to find out what else he's hiding."

Goldie grabbed a sheaf of papers out of her hand and plunked them back on the desk. "Sorry, but this is where I draw the line. You'll have to find out his secrets in some other way. Come on, we have to look for Mom's glasses and that little leather sack."

They found Flossie's missing glasses among the fronds of a potted palm in the corner of the dining room. Godiva said, "This is the last place I would have looked. Bless your attention to small details." Close inspection showed no damage, so Goldie wrapped the glasses in a green linen napkin from the sideboard and placed them in her tote bag. Then they both made their way to the living room.

Their ample derrieres bobbed up and down as the twins crawled around on their hands and knees at opposite sides of the room. They felt around under every piece of furniture in hopes of finding the bag or the tin. It was beginning to seem like a lost cause, when Godiva felt something under one of the skirted sofas. She fished it out and held it close to get a better look.

Goldie called across the room, "What did you find?"

"Yahoo! It's a Russian tobacco tin, like the one we found in Rosita's samovar." Godvia twisted the lid and let out another whoop when she saw a small brown leather pouch on a thong nestled inside. She set the tin on the seat of the sofa and struggled to her feet. "I think we hit the jackpot."

She was about to take the little leather bag out and open it, when two things happened simultaneously. The man from the dealership buzzed at the front gate, and Godiva's cell phone belted out a jazzy tune. A glance at the display showed that Angel was calling. She reeled off instructions to Goldie about what to do to let the man in, and flipped open the phone. Angel wasted no time on a greeting. She spoke so fast everything ran together. "Slow down, Angel, I can't understand a word you're saying."

There was a deep inhale on the other end. Then, "Well, Boss, we got a very interesting call after you left. You're gonna love this. Your Russian caper made the *LA Times* this morning, but that's not all. Apparently the story was also spread across the whole front page of the *Juneau Fishwrapper*. With all the tie-ins to local folks like Goldie, the Rimsky guy, and that poor sucker, Taku. By the way, it says they're letting him out of jail today."

She took a breath. "The story plays up the fact that the Dumkovskys and Rimsky are the real crooks. Anyway, it went on and on. You won't believe what Police Chief Oliver said. He made it sound like he was the one who cracked the case. Here's his quote."

Angel cleared her throat and adopted a deep-throated voice. "Oh, I suspected all along that the Mendoza murder had something to do with the Russian samovars." She paused before saying, "But the reporter wasn't fooled, because the story said it was Goldie who helped catch the criminals."

Godiva said, "Good, so Goldie got the ink. Did it say anything about me, by chance?"

"Yeah. It did mention you and the name of your column at the end. Said you helped your sister." She waited for the predictable explosion on the other end.

"Hmmmph. Helped? I should have gotten equal billing. Anyway, what were you going to tell me about the interesting call we got?"

Angel began to answer when Godiva heard her sister calling to her. "Wait a minute, Angel. I have to help Goldie. They're here to pick up the car and need me to sign the release. Tell you what. I'll call back in a minute." She snatched the tin from the sofa, replaced the lid and put it in her pocket.

After the man drove off with her bumperless Town Car, she said, "I'd better call Angel back. She said the story about Rimsky and the Dumkovskys is all over your little rinky-dink paper in Juneau, and she's all wound up about some kind of phone call that came in after we left."

Angel answered immediately, and continued where she left off. "Here's what I was trying to say—"

"Just a minute," Godiva broke in. "I'm putting this on speaker." She pushed the button, and held the cell phone between them. "Tell her what you told me."

"Hi, Angel," Goldie said. "Go ahead, I can't wait to hear this."

Angel chattered about the newspaper articles for a couple of minutes and then she said, "Apparently as a result of the investigation of Minsky and Pinsky, a couple of Russian antiquity officials had tracked the Seven Stars to Juneau, and for the last few days they have been questioning everyone they could find who came in contact with the samovars."

"I'll bet Belle gave them an earful about her encounter," Goldie said. "I saw a message from her, but with everything going on, I figured I'd call her back later today."

"Yep. When you talk to her, she'll probably give you an Academy Award version starring Belle Pepper. From what I could gather, after the *Fishwrapper* splashed the story all over the front page this morning, these investigators saw it and one of them called here asking for Goldie. Frankly, the fellow had a very heavy accent, but I think I got that part right."

"Well, that is an interesting call. So the bloodhounds are on the trail."

Goldie added, "With priceless national treasures at stake, it makes sense. Did he say anything else?"

"He said when they contacted the LAPD they were told that no gems were found at the crime scene. He described the seven alexandrites to them, and demanded they return to Caesar's house and do a more thorough search. Then he says, and I quote, 'We go to *Cal-ee-forn-i-a* now. When we talk to old heroes and chef, we get real story.'" Angel giggled at her own Russian imitation.

"Anyway, Rudy gave them this number to contact you and to reach Flossie and Sterling. They're flying out tomorrow afternoon or the next day, whenever they can get tickets, and want to talk to all of you. I guess even Russian officials have to wait for a seat on Alaska Airlines."

"So Angel, did it sound like maybe those investigators think we have something to do with the missing gems?" Goldie laughed nervously as she eyeballed the little bulge in her sister's pocket.

"No, nothing like that. They probably think Caesar and your mom and uncle might know more than the police do. Here's the kicker: the Russian government is offering a reward for the return of the Seven Stars—if all seven are recovered, it's five million rubles."

Both sisters let out a low whistle at the same time. Godiva reached into her pocket and held up the tin. "Five million rubles, huh? Well, Angel, you never know, maybe we will be able to help them after all." Then she said, "Wait a minute, Angel. How much is that in U.S. dollars?"

There was a silence. "Don't know, but I'll find out."

Chapter 37

"Wow, Sis. Who would have ever thought a simple order of Russian antiques would wind up like this?" Goldie shook her head in amazement. "I wonder if they'll pay our reward in U.S. dollars."

Godiva opened the tin and removed the leather pouch. It dangled from her hand, swinging back and forth on the thong like a pendulum. She reached into the little bag and one by one removed four alexandrites, just as big and sparkly as the one they fished out of Rosita's samovar. The gems were a beautiful deep ruby red under the glow of Caesar's fancy chandelier.

"I've got to admit, Sis, those are really impressive." Goldie leaned over the stones and took a closer look. "Are the other two still in the bag? With the one at your house we'll have all seven."

"Sorry, that's it. There aren't any more. Which means?"

"Mimi's aren't here." A tear welled in her eye and skittered down her cheek. She gulped. "I guess poor Mimi died without giving up her secret. They must still be hidden somewhere in her shop, but where?" Goldie sighed and rubbed her temples. "I thought we did a pretty thorough search, but I guess we just didn't dig deep enough. I haven't got a clue where she could have put them."

Godiva placed the pouch with the alexandrites in the zippered pocket inside her purse. "You know what? We better get out of here before the police come back to search for these little troublemakers."

She gathered up her paperwork and headed for the front door.

The sisters decided to stop at The Cheesecake Factory on Beverly Drive for a bite of lunch before returning home. Godiva clutched her designer handbag close to her side.

With her mouth watering for a slice of their famous cheesecake, Goldie teased her sister by saying, "I guess you chose this restaurant because of their great salads. Are they still as good as they used to be?"

"Yep. They're the best. I figured if we each have a salad, we won't feel so guilty when we order the cheesecake."

"That's you, always looking for the angles."

After finishing her salad, Goldie tapped a spot on the menu. "We should order two kinds and split them. Craig's Crazy Carrot Cheesecake sounds interesting to me. What sounds good to you?"

Godiva fluffed her silver mane. "You mean you had to ask? The Godiva Chocolate Cheesecake, of course."

While they savored the rich desserts, Godiva's cell phone vibrated. When she answered, Angel said, "I found out what five million rubles is worth. It's only two hundred and fifty thousand U.S. dollars. A few less zeros, but still not too shabby."

"No, I guess not, but I do prefer those seven digit numbers." She told Angel she would be home shortly, and closed the phone.

"Well, it turns out the five million ruble reward is only worth about two hundred and fifty thousand dollars."

Goldie's eyes sparkled. "*Only* two hundred and fifty thousand? Well, that might not seem like much to you, Mrs. Rockefeller, but it does to me. We could do something really nice in Mimi's memory and still have a little left over. Of course, that's if we manage to find the two stones Mimi hid. Angel did say the reward was for the return of all seven."

Always interested in making a deal, Godiva raised an eyebrow. "Wonder if they'll give us three and a half million for five of them?" She patted her purse.

When they returned to Godiva's estate, Angel practically flew through the front door, her huge glasses bouncing up and down on her tiny nose. She was usually very much in charge of herself, so the twins knew something must have happened.

She dragged them back into the study, where she plunked down on a wing-backed chair. The sisters sat across from her on a leather sofa, eager to hear the news.

"New developments," she sighed, "I don't know where to start."

Goldie reached over and patted her hand. "How about the beginning?"

The frazzled Angel took a deep breath. "Okay. I guess I'll start with the news about Flossie and Sterling. A reporter called right after I rang you at the restaurant. She wants to interview them live on the evening news."

Godiva put her arm around her sister. "And do they want to interview us, too? I really could have used more notice. My hair—my makeup..."

"Uh, no, Boss. They just want Flossie and Sterling." She tapped her finger to her forehead. "The reporter, what's her name, again? Oh yeah, Margery McGonicle. She said she's doing a senior spotlight or something like that. You know, 'don't underestimate the elderly' kind of thing. In fact, the crew is due here in—" she checked her Mickey Mouse watch, "—two and a half hours."

"So where are the superheroes?"

"Chili tried to talk them into going to the doctor to have their bumps and bruises checked out, but they flatly refused."

"Sounds typical," said Godiva, "I'll have that nice Dr. Finkel come over tonight and check them out. He won't mind making a house call for me. He's always trying to get me to contribute to his pet projects."

Goldie got back to the question at hand. "So, where did they go?"

"Flossie talked Chili into driving her over to Mr. Beau on Fairfax for a rinse and set so she can look glamorous. You know your Mom, she always wants to look her best in public. And your Uncle Sterling took Waldo to the groomers for a bath and a red bow. They'll be back way before the reporter comes."

Godiva glared. "Waldo gets into the act, and we get treated like nobodies? My sister and I had a big hand in solving this, you know."

"Oh, lighten up," Goldie chuckled. "You get plenty of publicity, let them enjoy the limelight. Between this and the award banquet, they must be walking on cloud nine. Imagine that, the evening news!"

"So, Angel, what else? A little thing like a spur-of-the-minute TV interview wouldn't have you in such a tizzy."

"You're right about that!" Pushing her glasses up on her nose, Angel said to Goldie, "Your mother-in-law called and, boy-oh-boy, she really lives up to her title as the best gossip in town."

"Leave it to Belle. What is she up to?"

"Well, it's not what she's up to. It's what's going on in Juneau. As they say, 'now the plot thickens'."

"Get to the point, Angel." Godiva was growing impatient.

"Okay, she said she forgot to tell you that Father Innocent's replacement came the day after you left. Apparently this new priest, Father Inquisitive—very mousy looking according to Belle—is a studious young man. Dora told her he's very detail-oriented and determined to clean up the church's bookkeeping."

Goldie got up and started to pace the room. "So, with the new priest already there, I suppose that means I'm going to be on the hook for a replacement samovar for Father Innocent." She looked distressed. "Maybe I can find something and ship it home by Fed Ex."

Angel waved her hand. "Oh, that's not it. Nobody said anything about the gift. Let me get to the big news. While he was checking the accounts, Father Inquisitive found some cryptic notations written by Father Augustine before he was killed. That's when the new guy started digging."

"Did he find anything?"

"Bingo! Belle said he discovered that Rimsky has been running a smuggling operation out of the Russian Orthodox Church for quite some time. It's the hot topic around Juneau today."

Godiva broke in. "Wow! A real smuggling operation? You

mean it wasn't just this one shipment?"

"Not by a long shot! On top of being a thief and a smuggler, looks like Rimsky's probably the man who killed Father Augustine."

"Did Father Innocent know about any of this?"

"Belle didn't think so, but according to what they found out so far, it's big. There has to be at least one more person in Juneau involved, but they don't know who that is yet. Belle said she'd keep the Church women at bay until you get back, Goldie."

"And pump them for as much gossip as she can get out of them, no doubt."

Angel smiled. "Yep, Belle said someone had to carry on your snooping while you're out of town. She said to call her tonight and she'll fill you in on everything she's found out."

"Well, Angel, I guess sometimes it pays to have a mother-in-law who sticks her nose into everyone's business. One thing is for sure. She and Nellie will have plenty to talk about at the next Mad Hatter's Convention."

Godiva started to get up from the couch. "So, is that all of it?"

Angel sighed. "I wish. The phone has been ringing off the hook all day. The Russian officials will be here day after tomorrow in the late morning. I told them they could come right from the airport. I hope that's okay."

Godiva hesitated. "Sure. No problem."

Except that we only have five stones. Goldie winked, having read her sister's thoughts loud and clear.

"After that Rudy called. He said to tell you he's picking Taku up at the jail this afternoon, and wants to put him up in his apartment over the shop for a few days. Said he didn't think you would mind. From what I could gather, Taku is pretty shaky and Rudy was worried about him."

"No wonder he's shaky. Look what he's been through."

"Anyway, he said to tell you they're going to stop by Mimi's shop first. It's been locked up tight, but the police tape is finally down. Taku says he knows where the key is hidden and wants to pick up his backpack and a few things." Angel looked at her Mickey Mouse watch again. "Listen, I've gotta go meet Nathan. I was really late yesterday. I hate to do that again."

Godiva folded her arms across her chest. "Now what am I going to do about my columns? The next three have to be sent out before tomorrow afternoon, you know. I shouldn't have gone to Belle's party." She waggled her finger at Goldie. "Look what you got me into. You're supposed to live in a quiet, backwater town, Sis, not crime central. I hate to work at night, but I have to get this done." She looked at her assistant expectantly.

"Gee, Boss, I'm sorry I didn't get a chance to do all work you left for me, but don't worry, I managed to get enough done for the next three columns. It's on your desk. The pile in the middle has six letters that are sure things. Your readers are gonna love them. I put the maybes in the yellow basket and the definitely-nots in the green one. Honestly Godiva, you're so slick you'll probably have it all knocked out in an hour." Angel grabbed her purse and headed for the door. "Oh yeah, and Caesar called three times, says you didn't answer your cell phone. Bye!"

Before Godiva sat down at her desk to check the piles of hot, lukewarm and cold letters, Angel was gone.

Chapter 38

Godiva finished reading the six letters while Goldie made more notes on her yellow pad. Who could possibly be involved with Rimsky? Who was actually in Mimi's shop the day they encountered the intruder? How did the Dumkovskys know Rimsky, and where did Minsky and Pinsky fit in? She scratched her head—it was like a giant jigsaw puzzle.

Her concentration was interrupted by Godiva's laughter. "Take a break from your pondering, Goldie. I've got to read you this last letter."

"Okay, I'll never get to the bottom of this anyway. I could use a good laugh."

Godiva cleared her throat and held the letter at arm's length so she didn't have to put on her reading glasses.

Dear G. O. D.,

My brother and I are in love with the same bi-guy. Recently we went to the movies with this friend and he sat between us. We both flirted with him and held his hand. I think he liked all the attention, but he said he couldn't eat his popcorn. My brother thinks I scared him off and wants to try again with him. He asked me to cool it. We've always been so competitive, fighting over the same dolls, dresses, etc. that I hate to give an inch. Should I let my bro win this one or hold my ground?

~Straight Sis

"Wow. Some triangle! Guess I've heard everything now."

"Not by a long shot. You'd be surprised at what some people write. At least there's no dog involved. I thought I'd answer like this, what do you think?

Dear Straight Sis,

I think both of you should give your friend a break and stop using him like a ping pong ball. This is clearly about your brother stealing your dolls when you were six years old. Get over it. No matter who wins this tug of war, no meaningful relation-ship can come of it."

~G.O.D.

"Right on, Sis. Makes me glad that you and I never fought over lovers."

By the time Godiva finished her work, Goldie had jotted a whole list on the pad. She glanced at her watch. "I guess the TV crew will be here soon for the interview. Should we just stay out of their way?"

Godiva put on a sexy pout. "They might want to ask us a few questions, so let's hang out in the kitchen in case they need us. Besides, you never know what we'll find in there to munch on."

A few minutes later Flossie, Sterling and Waldo waltzed into the living room, ready to meet the press. Waldo was growling something that sounded like *teeeveee* as he pranced around showing off his new red bow. He smelled like lavender. Flossie's rinsed and styled hair glistened with a tinge of light blue, which contrasted with her black eye and bruised cheek. Sterling carried a large bouquet of his roses in a plastic vase. His head looked a little lopsided with the reddish goose egg showing through his thinning hair.

Goldie was glad she suggested that they bow out and let the oldsters enjoy the notoriety. Sterling puffed out his chest and struck a Rambo-like pose. "Do I look tough enough, girls? Guess they're going to call us the senior swat team or something like that for this interview."

Waldo licked Sterling's hand and snuffled *heeerrrrooos* as his tail wagged furiously.

Sterling held out the bouquet. "These roses are for Margery McGonicle. I figure if I give the woman flowers, it'll soften her up. My boyfriend Leonardo does lots of TV interviews—says it works every time."

"I'm sure she'll love them Unk." Goldie cupped a particularly beautiful bright red one and inhaled its perfume. "We'll be in the kitchen if you need us."

Fifteen minutes later, the elegant living room was flooded with the news crew, acting like they owned the place. While the perfectly coiffed and powdered Margery interviewed Flossie and Sterling, and even Waldo when it sounded like he was trying to say something, the twins nibbled on the delicious cinnamon apple coffeecake that Martina whipped up that afternoon. They definitely didn't count the calories. Godiva had freshened her makeup, just in case, but the reporter's story was strictly about Flossie and Sterling. Not once were they asked to join the group.

After the short interview, Flossie and Sterling poked their heads into the kitchen. They were still on a high, but it was obvious their energy was ebbing.

"Well, that's over," Sterling said. "It took them longer to set up all their junk than it did for Margery to interview us. We talked a few minutes at most. You girls can watch it on the news. I'm beat. I've gotta hit the hay." He started toward the door. "By the way, Leonardo was right. Margery loved the roses."

Flossie nodded. "Yeah, she said some very nice things about us, and the camera guy got a real good shot of my black eye." She glanced at the kitchen clock. "*Oy*, it feels like midnight, but it's still so early. I think I'll go lie down, too."

The two celebrities toddled off to their cottages leaving an exhausted Waldo spread out on the kitchen floor like a Greek Flokati rug.

About nine o'clock Godiva answered the phone and heard Rudy's voice on the other end. "Well, howdy-do, yer Highness. Better rustle up Goldilocks and put yer phone on speaker. Have I got a tale to tell ya. You ain't gonna believe it." She could hear another voice in the background and figured it was Taku. Just what she needed. Two drunks wanting to tell them a story. She motioned Goldie over to her desk, and punched the speaker button.

"Are ya both listening now?"

Together they said, "Yes."

"Well hold on to yer hats ladies, here goes. I tol' yer little Angel I was pickin' up Taku at the jail, an' that's what I did. Then Taku and me stopped by poor Mimi's shop. Oh Lord, it didn't seem right without her there. Pore ol' Taku just broke down an' bawled."

"I felt the same way when I went there to look around," said Goldie, "It's so sad."

"Anyway, ladies, Taku didn't want to stay there very long. Never saw the ol' boy look so miserable. He grabbed his backpack from the storeroom—it was still right where he left it— gathered up a few other things and we skedaddled. Are ya with me so far?"

"Of course we are, Rudy. Go on."

"Well, we got us a bottle of scotch and figgered we'd celebrate Taku's freedom and have our own little wake for Mimi at the same time. We set down on the sofa and turned on the TV. They was talkin' about catching those Ruskie killers and sure enough they showed the same guys what came into our shop, and Rimsky, too. Who woulda thought it? Rimsky? A smuggler and a murderer! Didn't seem smart enough to me."

"I agree, I always thought he was a little dimwitted, kind of crazy, really."

"You know what Mom would say," said Godiva, "crazy like a fox."

"You got that right, Lady Godiva. Anyway, back to the big news, listen up now. They was tellin' how these guys were part of a smuggling ring who were chasin' after some kinda fancy jewels—treasures from the Russian Tzar, they said. Anyway, the police ain't found them baubles yet, so they showed pictures of what they look like. It's the darndest thing the way they change color in different light, ya know. 'Course, I figger that's what them two Ruskie officials were trackin' down the last few days. Them bulldogs gave me a pretty good grillin', but they didn't seem too satisfied with the results."

"To tell you the truth, Rudy," Goldie said, "we kind of figured out a while back that those stones were in the samovars. Angel found some articles online that seemed to point to it, but we didn't want to mention anything until we knew for sure."

"Well, here's the thing, Goldilocks, I think Taku and me got two 'o them fancy gems. We was just settlin' back when Taku says why don't we have a chaw. He reaches into his backpack and when he thinks he's pullin' out his Old Copenhagen tobacco, he's got some beat up old tin with Russian writin' all over it, instead."

The twins gave each other knowing glances and let Rudy continue with his story. "Go on."

"Taku takes one look at this strange tin, and he starts a-weepin' again. 'My poor sweet Mimi,' he says. 'Looks like Russian tobacco. She musta put this in here thinkin' I would enjoy it.' He opens up the tin, and there is one 'o them big, sparkly, color-changin' jewels. Jest a sittin' there in that ol' dry tobacco like a diamond in a dung heap, they was."

"Wow!" the sisters said in unison.

"Yeah, that's what we said. So, Taku still wants a chaw and he reaches into the pack again and what does he git? Another one 'o them old Russian tins with another stone in it. Well now he dumps out the whole backpack to see if there's any more, but that's it. Just his own junk, so he grabs the real can of Copenhagen and we had us a good chaw."

Goldie could hardly contain herself. "Are you sure those are the missing alexandrites?"

"Well, Taku asks me, didn't they just say on the TV that the missing stones change color under fluorescent light? Ya know, a different color than what it looks like with regular light bulbs lit. So we did jest what any fool would do, Goldie. We took 'em down to the shop and turned on the fluorescent light by my work bench."

Both sisters held their breath.

"Danged if them rubies didn't turn into emeralds right before our eyes! Not a trace of red left. The way I figger it, one of the last things Mimi did was to hide them jewels in Taku's backpack. So, what do we do now?"

Goldie tapped her index finger against her front tooth for a few seconds, then her face lit up, "Listen carefully, Rudy. Neither of you can tell a soul about this, absolutely no one, you understand?"

"Yes'm."

"All right, now go into the shop and take a few pieces of that gaudy costume jewelry out of the front case, and wrap them up along with the alexandrites in that tacky French jewel box on the back shelf. Package it up and take it to Alaska Airlines Cargo first thing in the morning. Send the package by Goldstreak Same Day Express. Be sure to arrange for the DHL Courier to pick up the package as soon as it arrives at LAX and hand-carry it to Godiva's address. That way it will be here before the Russian antiquity officials show up. If anybody gets curious, it will just look like junk jewelry."

"I got ya, Goldilocks. I'll have it there when they open at seven am. What are you gals gonna do with 'em? Give 'em to the police? The FBI?"

"Nope, we have the other five here in L.A., so with those two we can give the whole set back to the Russian government and collect the five million ruble reward. It comes to about two hundred fifty thousand dollars. And, since Taku found two of them, he's entitled to get almost thirty percent of that."

There was a whoop on the other end after Rudy shouted to Taku, "You're gonna be rich."

"Taku may get a big surprise when they read Mimi's will," Goldie said. "She told me she was going to leave her little building to the Fishermen's Benevolent Society when her time came. You know she always worried about Taku, and part of her bequest was going to be that the Society allows him to live in the apartment upstairs. I kidded her about making plans for the hereafter too soon. But she said she had a premonition that she would die young, and didn't want to leave any loose ends." Goldie began to sob. "Oh, Rudy, that was just a few months ago. Who knew?"

Chapter 39

Goldie tapped her pencil on the yellow notepad, which was now filled with pages of notes. "I don't know. There's still something missing, and I can't quite put my finger on it. I've gone over this list again and again."

"I know what you mean. It's like there's still another actor hiding behind the curtain. So even though they're turning off the footlights, this play isn't over yet. Do you suppose your illustrious Chief of Police has any leads on an accomplice?"

"Not Ollie. If I know him, he's probably just sitting back in his chair drinking cold stale coffee, and hoping he doesn't have to chase down any more suspects in this case. If the Dumkovskys killed Mimi and if Rimsky bumped off Father Augustine, that's two murders solved and everyone's satisfied. If he's really lucky, Seattle will want the Dumkovsky brothers for murdering Emma."

"Or, Russia will want to extradite them for murder and arson in Vladivostok."

"And Ollie will be able to relax and go back to the really important stuff like who stole Cassie Custard's underwear."

A determined look crossed Godiva's face, "Well, there's no way *this* crime-busting team will be satisfied until we have the final piece of the puzzle. Agreed?"

Goldie nodded and high-fived her sister. "Agreed."

Godiva sat at the kitchen island and finished off the last of the cinnamon apple coffee cake. "I've been thinking, Goldie, when those antiquity officials get here, how do we know they're for real? Maybe they're actually from some Russian crime ring, and this is a cheap way to get their hands on the crown jewels. Maybe there is no reward at all. And even if they do give us two hundred and fifty thousand, it'd still be a steal for them."

"You know, that never occurred to me, but now that you mention it, I guess we do have to ask them for credentials or something."

Godiva's answer surprised Goldie. "Credentials won't do it."

"Why? That should prove who they are."

"Poor little country mouse, big city folks know that counterfeit credentials are a dime a dozen. Why, for a few bucks, I could be a Russian antiquities official myself, or anything else I want to be. Besides, the credentials would probably be in Russian, so for all we know, they could be official dogcatchers. No, we need something better."

They were both silent while they thought about how to qualify the Russian visitors before handing over the stones. Then Godiva snapped her fingers. "Okay, here's what we do. I'll have Angel call the National Antiquities Agency in Moscow and verify their identities."

"Really? You think she can do something like that?"

"Sure. She'll find the complicated name of the department on the Internet and if anyone can find a way to reach them, Angel can. They must have someone who speaks English. If not, she can probably find a translator. I have complete faith in that girl—she can do almost anything."

"Well, it's a good idea. It must be nice to have an assistant like Angel. I can't picture Rudy carrying off anything like that."

Godiva chuckled. "No, I can't either, but then again, I doubt that Angel could fix an antique clock. Back to the subject, though, I think we have to insist they wire the money to my bank from an official Russian government account. Then I can have my banker verify the source. That should only take a day or two. Once the money is in my account, I'll ask Oscar Goldensheim to be a witness when we turn over the stones. That should do it. Bottom line, they don't get the stones until we have the money signed, sealed, delivered and verified.

They've waited all these years. A little while longer shouldn't make much difference."

Goldie was polishing off the last of a particularly delicious slice of fresh peach pie. "I guess you're right, Sis. I don't always think like you do when it comes to high finance and con artists. I just want these national treasures to return to their proper place. They should be on display in a Russian museum. But if these guys balk, we should threaten to call the FBI and hand the Seven Stars of Siberia over to them."

"Goldie, I swear you're getting craftier in your old age."

"Wait a minute, Godiva, I just had a terrible thought. If they are crooks, what's to prevent them from killing us and grabbing the gems? After all, three people are dead already because of that treasure. You better call Ricky and Ivan to stand by with the big guns."

Godiva winked at her sister. "Already did."

She put her plate in the sink, returned to the richly upholstered barstool and put her hands on the counter, palms down in a businesslike manner. "Okay, so now for the next bit. Assuming everything goes as planned, and we get the reward, we need to agree on who gets what."

Goldie considered the question quietly for a moment. "Well, Taku definitely gets his fair share for the two stones he found. Let's see, that's two-sevenths. Ummm..." She scribbled a few numbers on the yellow pad. "Twenty eight and a half percent—"

Cutting her off in mid-sentence, Godiva snapped, "But if Mimi actually made sure Taku has a place to live, how much could a guy like him really need? You and your big mouth, you shouldn't have told Rudy how much the reward is. Maybe we can get away with just giving him a few thousand. After all, I've already spent quite a bit on his lawyer."

"No way! Maybe you would treat someone like that, but not me!"

Godiva threw her hands in the air and mumbled, "Okay, Miss Goody-Two-Shoes, you win." She did some quick math in her head. "So that comes to a little over seventy grand, which leaves nearly ninety for each of us."

Goldie shot her sister a look of astonishment. "The heck it does! What about Mrs. Wurlitzer's poor maid Emma? She lost her life over those stones; we need to do something in her memory. I'll bet that mean old bat probably put her in a pauper's grave. We have to make sure she gets a nice headstone. Maybe her friend who works next door can tell us if Emma had a relative back in Romania to send a little something to. I know we don't have to, but you can't be that cold-hearted. You know it's the right thing to do."

After a bit of grumbling, Godiva had to admit her sister was right. She consented to put ten thousand aside for Emma's heirs, if Angel could find them. "That leaves us about a hundred and seventy to split."

"Whoa! Don't count your chickens yet, Lady Godiva. As far as I know, Mimi did leave her building to The Fishermen's Benevolent Society, although we won't know until her will is read. But it's an old building and they'll need money to keep it up. We should make a big donation to the Society in Mimi's name." Goldie's voice trailed off, and she wiped her eyes with the corner of her sleeve. "Lord, I miss her. We have to do something exceptional in her memory. I insist."

"Darn it, Goldie. Your perpetual kindness is sort of creepy, you know? It's no wonder you never have much money."

"To each his own, Sis. My pleasure is giving to others and yours is living extravagantly and flashing your diamonds."

"*Touché.* Okay, I feel guilty enough to yield now. How about this? In addition to the ten thousand for Emma's family we donate eighty thousand in Mimi's name to that fisherman's fund. Is that good enough for you?"

"Yeah, I'll go along with that." Goldie smiled with satisfaction. "Maybe they can even figure out what kind of a non-profit business would generate enough money to help guys like Taku when they can't fish anymore."

Godiva nodded. "That still leaves us forty-five thousand each—assuming these Russians are on the up-and-up. Guess we'll find out when they get here. So, what will you do with yours? You could build an extra bathroom in your house, or put in an elevator."

"No, I was thinking maybe I'll add twenty thousand of my share to what we give the fishermen to make it an even hundred thousand. I'm sure it won't be hard for me to find places to spend the rest."

There was a long silence. Then Godiva's face brightened. "You know, you just gave me an idea. In my tax bracket, if I give twenty or thirty thousand of it to charity, I might come out ahead in the long run. I'll check with my accountant to see how much I can give away and still make money. Donating to a women's shelter would look good for my image, anyway."

Goldie looked at her twin with a mixture of astonishment, approval and aggravation. "Well, whatever it takes, I guess."

"Hey, just make me a promise, okay?"

"Sure. What do you want?"

"Quit sprinkling me with the milk of human kindness. I've never given so much money away in such a short period of time. You're killing my survival skills."

Chapter 41

Angel answered Caesar's fifth futile phone call, and said in an apologetic voice, "Geez, I'm really sorry, but Godiva still doesn't want to talk to you. Yes, of course. I'll tell her."

She turned around, pushed her glasses up and looked straight into Godiva's eyes. "Boss, this is nuts! You're supposed to be the one who gives people good advice, but now it's my turn to wag my finger at you. You need to talk to Caesar, give him a chance to explain. And then if you aren't satisfied, tell him to get lost."

Goldie jumped in, "Yeah, stop playing this cat and mouse game. I talked to Chili before she left the house this morning, and she said Caesar is a basket case. He's putting pressure on her to get involved. You're not being fair to anyone. You need to kiss and make up or just say 'Ciao Baby'."

Godiva avoided their stares by shuffling through the letters in the "you should read" pile for the third time, she pulled one out and waved it at Goldie and Angel. "This guy has sort of the same problem that I do. His fiancé made up a pack of lies about her 'wealthy Boston family.' One day they ran into someone from her home town, which from the sound of it most definitely was not Boston, but some shanty town in the Ozarks." She put the letter down on her desk and tapped it with a vengeance. "Seems like it was quite a conversation. The friend teased her about her bad reputation with the boys, about her family's inbreeding and illiteracy. Well, it isn't much different than what Caesar did to me. Except, of course, for the lack of branches on her family tree."

Goldie prompted her. "And—"

"And so until I answer this letter, I won't know what I'm going to do. Whatever answer I give Dazed in Duluth, should be what I do myself. I wish I could just sweep it under the rug, but it doesn't look like that's going to happen."

The morning passed quickly and uneventfully. Goldie repacked Rosita Burrito's samovar, carefully attaching the certificate of authenticity she made up on her new computer. Waldo nudged her leg and whined, "*Dannnnnce.*" He had wandered around all morning trying to show off his now slightly droopy red bow. Unable to resist those big puppy dog eyes any longer, she put on the music and waltzed around the living room with him. Waldo outdid himself, proving to be a better dancer than Goldie's husband Red.

A few minutes later Flossie and Sterling came in, decked out in their spangled costumes. Flossie had put a thick coating of makeup around her black eye. Sterling fluffed Waldo's bow and said, "Okay old boy, it's Thursday, and you know what that means. It's show time! Come on. Time to go to the Home for Hollywood Has-Beens. Our audience is waiting." He gave the twins a sharp salute and the three performers did a little two-step out the door.

Early in the afternoon the DHL Courier delivered the package from Rudy. There amid the gaudy rhinestone broaches and bracelets were the two missing Stars of Siberia, exact matches to the five hidden in Godiva's safe. So far, the police had shown no interest in the smuggled gems. Either they were too absorbed in sorting out which jurisdictions should prosecute the murderers, or the tight-lipped Russians would not acknowledge they ever had the jewels.

At dinner the whole family discussed the pending visit from the antiquities officials, and Godiva brought the Seven Stars of Siberia out of her safe in the hidden room. While everyone sat around the dining room table, she carefully laid the stones out on piece of black velvet where they twinkled under the light of the chandelier. Goldie sighed, Chili gasped, Sterling harrumphed and Torch examined them silently. Flossie said a little prayer over the seven magnificent alexandrites laid out in front of her.

They discussed everything that had happened since the

samovars first arrived at the Silver Spoon. Sterling said, "The thing that still bothers me, Goldie, is how did those Dumkovskys know you had the samovars in the first place? You said they burst into your shop and demanded them. Why didn't they go to the church where the smuggling was going on?"

"It's a good question, Unk. Godiva and I talked about that last night. We both feel like there's still a missing piece right in the middle of the puzzle. But with Minsky and Pinsky gone, we may never know the whole story."

Flossie clasped her hands. "Look how these stones are such a beautiful ruby red."

Sterling mumbled, "Looks more like blood red to me."

At breakfast the following morning Goldie said, "I've really got to get back to Juneau. I never expected to be gone this long. After we finish with our Russian visitors today, you won't need me here, so I made a reservation on a flight back to Juneau for eleven o'clock tomorrow morning. Can you take me to the airport, or should I ask Uncle Sterling?"

Godiva patted Goldie's hand. "Of course I'll take you. I'm actually going to miss you, you know? As soon as you get back, you'll have to start investigating to see if you can find that missing link. I suppose Belle has been doing more snooping around than your energetic Police Chief, but I think you can only trust half of her information. Let me know right away if you unearth anything, okay?"

"I'm one step ahead of you, already." Goldie reached for her ever-present yellow pad. "I've been making a list of things to check out in Juneau. You know, Unk put his finger on it last night. How in the world did the Dumkovskys know I had the samovars? Trust me, I won't stop until I find out."

Just before noon a taxi pulled up to the estate. Ricky Thompson and his sidekick Ivan were waiting just inside the gate. They accompanied the agents—a dark haired stocky fellow in a rumpled gray suit and a younger blond man dressed all in black—to the front door. Godiva invited all four of them into the elegant foyer. The Russians smiled woodenly and flashed their credentials, "Allow us to introduce to you. We are agents Korsakov and Cherimenko. We are being excited about Seven Stars. You have all?"

"Let's not talk out here in the hall, gentlemen," Godiva said. "I hope you don't mind being accompanied by my friends here." She motioned toward Ricky and Ivan. "They will have to check you for firearms before we go any further. One cannot be too careful, you know." After establishing that her guests were unarmed, she ushered them into the huge living room.

Cherimenko swept the room with wide eyes. "Hmmmph. You live in such a mansion, Madam, surely you are not needing reward money?"

Goldie said through clenched teeth, "With all due respect, gentlemen, my sister's home is none of your business. Not only were three people killed, but an innocent man spent time in jail because of those stupid stones. That's where most of the reward money will go."

Godiva stepped in and gently pushed Goldie aside. "Would you gentlemen like a cup of tea while we work this out?" She rang for Guadalupe. "Please bring some tea for everyone, Lupe, and some pastries too."

She turned back to them and took a firm stance. "It's really quite simple, gentlemen. Your country has offered a reward for the missing Seven Stars of Siberia and we have found them. Now you must make sure they are authentic and we must make sure that you are authentic, also."

When she explained that the funds had to be received in her bank by way of an official government draft before the gems would be turned over to them, the two men looked startled. "You are questioning?" Korsakov bellowed. "Madam, it is point of honor!"

Godiva excused herself, leaving the two fuming agents in the care of her bodyguards. When she came back into the room accompanied by her son Torch, she carried the Seven Stars of Siberia in a velvet-lined box. Decked out in a tight black tee shirt and black cargo pants, the muscular young man took his place beside Ricky and Ivan. The agents shrank back into their champagne-colored chairs, eyeing the formidable trio.

Godiva placed a silver serving tray on the cocktail table and laid out the seven ruby red alexandrites. "Gentlemen, here they are, and they are truly magnificent." She asked Goldie to bring the fluorescent desk lamp from her study and performed the same lighting experiment they had done a few days before. The agents smiled with satisfaction as the gems turned a deep emerald green. "I'm only showing these to you now so you know we actually do have them and we aren't playing any games."

She allowed them to inspect the gems thoroughly while Torch hovered over their shoulders. Then she placed them back in the velvet box and handed it to her son. "Would you please put these back in the safe, Torch." He nodded, and with great ceremony carried the box out of the room while Ricky and Ivan stood by.

To the men, she said, "So it is agreed we will make the exchange only after the money from your government is in my account. Here's a copy of the receipt you will be expected to sign when I turn the gems over to you and my attorney will be here to act as a non-involved witness."

She held out the document Oscar Goldensheim had prepared for her, along with another sheet of paper. "You can read this over in the meantime, and you will find my account information on the other sheet. My banker said it shouldn't take more than a day or two for the funds to arrive. You are welcome to use my telephone to contact your agency if you wish."

Despite Godiva's earlier statement, Angel had already verified that the men were legitimate government representatives. She led Agent Korsakov to a telephone in the far corner of the immense room. The blond Cherimenko gave a wry smile. "We all happy now. My government plans big party to celebrate return of the Stars. It will be at State Hermitage Exhibitions in Constantine Palace near St. Petersburg. Town is called Strelna."

The young agent beamed with national pride. "Is perfect place to display collection. Constantine Palace and Park originally belonged to Romanov Imperial household. Government restored this fine building in 2003. Now called Palace of Congresses, official residence of President of the Russian Federation. Also houses permanent exhibition on heraldry from State Hermitage Museum collections. Very lovely."

"Mr. Cherimenko," Goldie said, "how did you and your colleagues trace the gems to Minsky and Pinsky in the first place?"

Cherimenko leaned forward and his voice took on a conspiratorial tone, "The Romanov jewels were great secret after Revolution. Someone in household smuggled out and gave to nuns in convent to keep safe. Convent has no money, no food, so old Mother Superior sells one piece to very rich man."

Goldie gasped. "The tiara!"

"*Da. Da.* Yes. Tiara. He gives enough money for keeping convent going twenty years!"

"Wow, that's a lot of rubles."

"*Da. Da*, very valuable. But this man, Sergei Kalashnikov, he must hide his treasure. Is very dangerous to possess such a thing. He puts in secret compartment in old desk. Then one day, Kalashnikov dies." Cherimenko made a slashing gesture across his throat. "Kaput! No one knows about tiara, and they push old desk off in corner."

"So how..."

"Ahhhh, now is good part. When last old nun is dying, she is telling government agent about jewels and also tiara with seven beautiful stones. It takes us four years to follow trail to Kalashnikov." He thumped his chest for emphasis. "And, what do we find? One week before, your Minsky and Pinsky are buying the old furniture from Kalashnikov's broken down dacha. We think it is when they busting up desk to use old wood to repair other antiques, they finding this treasure. Then, splut! Next thing we know, warehouse is burning like shish kabob."

Korsakov finished the long distance conversation with his superiors in Russia, and returned to his seat by the coffee table where the others were now sipping tea and nibbling raspberry scones. The two agents huddled together, and then Korsakov said, "The Chief of Antiquities Bureau will make monies transfer first thing when bank will open. Is middle of night in Moscow now. I am waking up Chief to tell good news. On one hand he is happy. On other hand, when you wake up Chief he is not so happy. How you say? He is taking bite out of my behind."

They all shook hands, and agreed that as soon as the money arrived, the gemstones would be returned. Ricky and Ivan escorted them back to the gate where their cab was still waiting.

After the men left, Goldie sat down with her nephew, and listened to all of the exciting things that were going on in his career. "Okay Torch, what kind of pyrotechnical miracles have you got coming up next?"

"Actually, Auntie, I'm about to sign a contract to work on the special effects for a new TV series called Las Vegas Blowout. It's about a team of building imploders taking down old casinos."

Godiva came back into the room and sat down on the sofa beside her son. "Well I hope they never take down the Diamond Slipper, that's where your poor father died. I'll never forget his last words as he stood beside that Megabucks wheel with the winning number— 'Made five million on a buck!' Then he keeled over and, poof, he was gone." She flapped her hand as though she was throwing dust to the wind.

"Don't worry, Mom, they're not destroying any real landmarks, the places will be fictitious and the demolition is all special effects. If this TV series works out, it could keep me in one place for a long time instead of bouncing all over the world. I'm thinking of buying one of the new high-rise condo units going up in Vegas. There's one called the High Rollers Palace under construction now. Lots of rockers and movie stars are buying them, so they're going fast. The buzz is they'll be sold out before the buildings are finished. I'm flying up to meet with the realtors tomorrow."

Godiva seemed a little disappointed that her son was

making a financial move without consulting her, but then her face brightened. "Looks like you're following in your father's footsteps, Torch. He made all his money in real estate. Just promise me you won't turn into a heartless jerk like him." She looked skyward. "He should rest in peace."

Chapter 42

Goldie waited impatiently at Gate 37B with a bunch of fidgety passengers. The scheduled departure time came and went. A crackly voice said over the speaker, "Ladies and gentlemen, Flight 75 to Seattle, Ketchikan and Juneau will be delayed approximately two hours. We appreciate your patience while we wait for a substitute crew. It seems the folks assigned to this flight must have been out partying last night and it has been determined they are unfit to fly."

At this point Goldie joined the other passengers in an aggressive protest, but it did no good whatsoever. They were still two hours late.

It was after seven that evening when her flight finally pulled up to the gate. Goldie felt bedraggled as she rode the escalator down to the terminal lobby. She brightened up, however, when she spied Belle and her whole Mad Hatters group waiting at the bottom with a warm welcome. It was impossible to keep a straight face while she scanned the ladies' hats decorated with porpoises cavorting on blue lace waves, dancing California raisins, and Belle's own creation, a top hat fashioned like a slot machine spewing coins.

They all chorused, "Welcome home, Goldie" while Belle enveloped her in a bear hug. Tourists gaped at the colorful group gathered around the baggage carousel.

Goldie's blue duffel bag was the first one down the chute, and it was in perfect condition. As she pulled it off the conveyor, she felt an affirmation of her theory that the airline only seemed to lose or damage the most expensive luggage.

The Hatters all walked with them to the parking lot, then waved goodbye and Belle hustled Goldie and her duffle into the pink Caddy.

The minute the car was in gear, Belle filled her in on the latest news. The Russian government was, indeed, pulling every string possible to extradite the Dumkovskys and, much to Ollie's relief, it looked like they might succeed.

Goldie's mother-in-law was in her glory. "The LAPD got quite an earful from the police in Vladivostok," she gushed. "Nellie called and told me all about it. I passed the information on to Ollie. Oh boy, was he surprised that I knew more than him about this case and what's going on in Russia!"

"Like what?"

"Like did you know that Vladivostok is a hotbed of all kinds of smuggling operations? There are ethnic gangs at war with each other, and the police are so understaffed they hardly solve any of the crimes committed every year." Belle inhaled deeply and executed a sharp right turn without signaling, which caused the car behind her to slam on the brakes.

She continued unruffled. "So, when the LAPD contacted the head of the regional police in Vladivostok, they were really anxious to get their hands on those two. The arson and murder at your friends' warehouse was such an awful crime, it'll make them look good if they can put the Dumkovskys behind bars. The LAPD has enough of their own criminals, and all they had on those thugs in L.A. was a little breaking and entering charge, anyway. So they'll either turn those bad boys over to Juneau, Seattle or Russia. Nellie's husband thinks they'll play the international card. Ollie didn't seem too broken up about handing them over to the Vladivostok police. He'll get credit for solving the crime, and not have to deal with all the work of prosecuting them."

Leaning forward in the plush pink leather seat, Goldie asked, "When you talked to Nellie, did she say if the LAPD got any other information out of them? Maybe how the Dumkovskys knew I had the samovars?"

"You bet, there's plenty more. Those big oafs sang like canaries. Listen, we're almost at your place. Why don't I tell you over a cup of tea?"

They chugged up Starr Hill and pulled over to the curb

214

near Goldie's house. Belle set the parking brake and opened the car door. She graciously offered to help Goldie lug her duffle up the forty-seven stairs leading to the house, but Goldie said she could handle it. For Belle, just getting her considerable bulk up the stairs would be a major accomplishment.

Goldie fixed some tea and waited for her mother-in-law to catch her breath. After a few huffs and puffs, she said, "Honey, it's just like something in the movies. Let's see, I think I've got this all straight. The Dumkovskys worked in the warehouse for your smuggler friends."

"So Uri and Vladmir really were smugglers?"

"Yup. Big time. Not all of their exports were on the up and up. Anyway, the Dumkovskys got wind something out of the ordinary was going on, and from what I understand, they realized it involved the long lost tiara with those alexandrites in it."

"I'm surprised they knew what the Seven Stars were."

"Well, Boris said he overheard Minsky arranging to ship the jewels to their contact in Alaska. He was describing the Seven Stars to a buyer in the states who brokers stolen gems. When Boris realized what kind of treasure they had in the warehouse, he and his brother decided to sabotage the ship-ment and get rich."

"Boy, that sure backfired! I'd love to know what their charts said."

"Yeah, their astrological sign is probably Bozo the Clown."

"I know you don't place much stock in the charts, Mama Belle, but I bet there was disaster written in the stars that day. You know, I'm still trying to figure out how the jewels wound up at my shop."

Belle nodded. "Well, I don't need the stars to answer your question. Boris told the police when he saw the fancy tiara in Pinsky's office, the stones had already been pried out. He hid in the storeroom that night, and watched Minsky personally pack the gems in some tobacco tins, then pull a plate aside on the bottom of each of the samovars and place a tin in the cavity. He had been wondering why their antique restorer had spent a lot of time soldering and appearing to repair several beautiful samovars. Boris is not that swift, but he managed to put two and two together and figure out something valuable was being smuggled in the cavities.

Goldie waited for Belle to take a deep breath and continue.

"Anyway, Boris saw your friend put all seven samovars in a crate addressed to Rimsky at the Russian church. That shipment and yours were both due to go to Pistov the next morning."

Goldie poured more hot tea in Belle's cup. "So they switched the shipment somehow?"

"Got that right, Babycakes. Boris and his brother actually showed amazing ingenuity. After everyone left for the night, they came back and opened your crate and the one going to the church. It only took a few minutes to switch the samovars with the tins for the ones you ordered. In the morning they sent only your crate containing the samovars with the hidden gems to Pistov. When Minsky and Pinsky came into the warehouse, they knocked their bosses out, stole their passports, locked the doors and torched the place." Belle shivered at the thought of these cold-blooded killers locking their coworkers inside.

Goldie shook her head in disbelief. "So those two weren't as bumbling as we thought they were?"

"Not by a far sight. They figured if they sent the shipment to you, by the time they arrived in Juneau, it would be easy to just buy them back for a few dollars. The contact at the church, who turned out to be Rimsky, would think that everything burned up back in Vladivostok."

"I wonder how a guy like Rimsky got the job at the church in the first place."

"Beats me," said Belle, "I guess he answered an ad in the *Juneau Fishwrapper,* or something. The thing that gets me, is now some people around town are saying Father Innocent might have known all about it, and they're even trying to figure out if he was part of the smuggling ring."

"That's crazy. I guess Father Innocent was an easy target for Rimsky to fool, though. Father Augustine was probably killed because he'd discovered what was going on."

"Yes, and that new Father Inquisitive is still combing through the records. He told Ollie he finds something new every day."

"Wow, Mama Belle, I guess the Dumkovskys were beside themselves when they got to Juneau, and the shipment didn't show up. They must have been watching my shop for a couple of weeks."

Belle took another swig of her tea. "Once it did arrive they probably thought they were home free."

"Well, they certainly were nasty when they discovered the samovars were almost all gone by the time they tried to bully me out of them. When they broke in and took the last samovar, they must have grabbed the sales slips to see who bought the rest."

Goldie tapped the side of her teacup. "There's still one piece of this puzzle missing, Mama Belle. Godiva and I have been trying to figure out who else Rimsky was working with. Someone was moving the goods once he received them at the church. Someone tore the sheet with the customer addresses out of my ledger book and gave it to him."

Belle took a hankie out of her purse and fanned herself. "Well, dearie, since Rimsky bumped off Father Augustine, Ollie is definitely going to get him back in Juneau. Maybe one of Ollie's boys can get some information out of him."

"It makes me shudder when I think of Rimsky beating up that poor old priest he was supposed to be taking care of."

"Well, getting back to some of the gossip, the folks who are accusing Father Innocent of being the mastermind think maybe he brought in Rimsky to be the leg man. I seriously doubt it though. The poor old guy can hardly remember his own name half the time, you know, but they say he's faking being senile—that he had Rimsky hit him on the head purposely to make him look like a victim. Humph!"

Chapter 43

Goldie watched Belle teeter down the wooden stairs. Then she kicked off her shoes, collapsed into an overstuffed chair facing the bay window, and gazed at the boats in the busy harbor. After all the excitement of the past few weeks, Goldie welcomed a moment of quiet and solitude. With Red's ship on an eleven-day cruise, she only had herself to worry about. She decided unpacking could wait, and reached for the phone to call Godiva instead.

Her ESP wavelength had obviously been received, because her sister answered on the second ring. "Hello, Goldie, I see you made it back, but I actually expected you to call earlier. It's almost eight o'clock already."

"Well, yeah." Goldie sighed. "Big delay at the airport. Can you believe it? The crew had a hangover, so they had to wait for a new one. And then Belle picked me up and bent my ear for the last hour. She filled me in on what's been happening around here. The most interesting part, though, is what she found out from Nellie."

As Goldie recounted Belle's story about the Dumkovskys' involvement at Minsky and Pinsky's antique warehouse, Godiva punctuated the conversation with comments like "wow" and "oh no".

At the end, she said, "I'm sorry your importer friends turned out to be big time smugglers. I know you would have felt better if they'd been innocent victims. What I'm really curious about is Rimsky. Did anyone ever suspect he wasn't on the up-and-up?"

"Well, except for the Russian Orthodox community, I don't think that many people paid any attention to him. I mean, we saw him around town, and knew he worked at St. Nicholas church, but that's about it. Maybe I'll ask Nora and Dora the next time I see them. I guess they'll be hounding me for another samovar. Truthfully, it'll be a long time before I can look at one and not think of poor Mimi." After a loud yawn, she said, "Hope you don't mind, but I've gotta turn in. I'm absolutely beat, and tomorrow will be a busy day."

Rudy came down early the next morning to make sure everything was just so for Goldie's return. When she walked through the door a few minutes before nine, there was a spring in her step and a smile on her face.

Looking up from the brass lamp he was polishing, Rudy called out, "Hey, boss, are ya through gallivantin' for a while?" He swept the shop with his skinny outstretched arm. "We got a big-ass cruise ship comin' in at eleven and three more this afternoon. Should be another busy week, so I pulled all the extra stock out of the storeroom while you was gone. Hope you like the way I set it up."

She looked around and noted the newly arranged displays, including a footstool covered in green mohair that Midnight had claimed as his own. Everything looked terrific. "You did a great job, Rudy. Thanks."

"Well, Taku helped me some. I'm gonna miss that ol' boy when he moves into Mimi's apartment. 'Course it ain't official yet, but her lawyer called yesterday an' said she did put him and the Fisherman's' Benevolent Society in her will. Taku promised me he's gonna straighten hisself up. Yessir. Gonna do it fer Mimi."

Goldie wondered what Rudy's friend would do once he had money and a nice place to live. She didn't have to wonder very long.

Rudy was beaming when he said, "Here's the plan. Him and me hatched up an idea of what to do with his money from the reward, and he already talked to the Benevolent Society, bein' as they'll own the building. He's gonna work with them to turn the teashop into a fish shop. Boy, howdy! If there's one thing that ol' boy knows, it's fish."

She gave him a thumbs up sign. "Well, Rudy, they say sometimes good comes from bad, and it looks like that's going to happen here."

"Yep. The idea is for the fishermen to donate a little of their catch to the FBS, then Taku will fillet it up and sell it. The profit will all go to the fisherman's fund after they pay his wages. Ain't that great?"

Goldie felt the tears brimming in her eyes and rubbed at them furiously. "It's not only great, Rudy, it's absolutely wonderful. Mimi would have been thrilled to see this happen." She gave him an appreciative smile and plopped down in her desk chair.

A few minutes later the little bell over the door tinkled and Dora came flying in. Goldie's first instinct was to hide in the back room, but the woman made a beeline toward the desk and cornered Goldie. She looked very agitated and instead of her usual tidy appearance, Dora's sweater was buttoned wrong and her hair was uncombed.

"Um Goldie, I hope you don't mind, but the Ladies Auxiliary decided not to give Father Innocent another samovar." Her voice sounded a bit strained, as if she was trying to control it. "Somehow, with all the terrible things that happened, we just didn't feel the same about it anymore. You know, sort of like a bad omen. So we got a beautiful icon for him from the Russian Shop instead."

Goldie felt a great sense of relief wash over her. Her whole body relaxed as she said, "I understand, Dora. You look a little frazzled today, are you okay? And how is your friend Nora? I don't think I've ever seen you without her."

That's all it took. Dora dropped her handbag on the desk and started to sob as if the world had come to an end. Between the hiccupping and gulping she managed to say, "Oh, Goldie, I ca–can't b–believe it. The police arrested her early this morning. You th–think you kn–know someone and then s–something like this happens."

Not knowing what to make of her outburst, Goldie led poor little Dora to an antique wingback chair. "Here, sit down for a minute, Dora." She patted the distraught woman on the shoulder. "Why don't you relax and I'll have Rudy fix us both a cup of tea. Then you can tell me all about it."

Dora nodded numbly and stared at her toes. By the time Rudy came in with two steaming cups of chamomile tea, she seemed to have pulled herself together.

"There ya go, Miz Dora. This'll make ya feel better." He handed her one of the cups and gave the other to his boss.

After taking a few sips, she started to calm down. Goldie said, as gently as she could, "There, there. Tell me what happened."

Dora looked at Goldie's compassionate face and her story began to pour out.

"Oh Goldie, I still can't believe it. It was Nora all along. She was running the smuggling operation here. About five years ago she recommended Rimsky for the job at the church. Said he was her cousin. We never thought anything illegal was going on. Even after weird things began to happen, everyone just thought he was a little odd, if you know what I mean..." Her voice trailed off.

Dora sighed and took another sip of the tea. Suddenly her face lit up with a broad smile. "Well, at least I get to be first for once."

Goldie didn't have a clue what she was talking about. "First?" she asked.

The woman nodded. "Yep, I'm the first one with the gossip this time. I finally trumped that busybody Belle. And this is really big, too. I'm so mad at Nora for what she did. It makes me feel better just to tell you about it. In fact I'm going to tell everyone I know before I get around to telling your mother-in-law."

Goldie felt a little thrill as she realized all the missing pieces were about to fall into place. "Well, don't stop now. Tell me the rest."

"Okay, so I went over to Nora's early this morning to have a little breakfast with her. She was just scrambling the eggs when Chief Oliver and Officer Dimwiddy pounded on the door. Nora saw them and got so upset, she dropped the pan right on the floor. Then it was just like TV. They asked her a bunch of questions, told her she was under arrest, read her the rights and everything, and took her away in handcuffs."

"Did they question you, too?"

"No, I was so quiet I don't think they even noticed me. I just sat in the corner and listened to everything. After they left, I cleaned the eggs off the floor and went home and cried!"

As Dora told the story, Goldie noticed her normal shyness seemed to fade away.

"What did the police say to Nora?"

"Well, Chief Oliver said he got a very interesting call from the Los Angeles police. They're sending Rimsky back to Juneau, you know, to charge him with Father Augustine's murder. Anyway, when he realized how much trouble he was in, he tried to strike a bargain by telling them about Nora and the whole smuggling ring."

Goldie sipped her tea and waited for Dora to continue. "It's so hard to believe Nora was involved in the smuggling. Did you find out anything else?" she prodded.

"Well, you see Nora's maiden name was Pinsky. Turns out her brother was one of the people who died in that big fire in Vladivostok."

"That's incredible! Nora was Uri's sister? She didn't even have a Russian accent."

"Oh, I knew she grew up in Minsk, that's where the Pinsky's were from, you know. But she came to Alaska years ago as a one of those young mail order brides and lost her accent pretty quick. I feel so stupid. When Belle said Minsky & Pinsky were your importers, the ones that got killed, I didn't even put two and two together." She shook her head dejectedly. "And according to the police, Rimsky really was Nora's cousin. He worked in the warehouse in Vladivostok. Her brother sent him to Alaska to help with the smuggling because he spoke perfect English."

Goldie tapped the rim of her teacup. "Nora must have been the one who stole the ledger sheet with my customer's names."

"Oh yes! When she was sitting there in the kitchen, she admitted she did it."

"But, how did she get to my ledger book?"

"It was when she told Rudy she wanted to see if there was a samovar tucked away in the back room."

Rudy, who had been silently listening to every word, let out a big whoop that made Dora spill some of her tea. "Dang it! I knew I shouldn'ta let that pushy ol' gal get past me."

Goldie gave him a sympathetic look. "Don't be too hard on yourself, Rudy, looks like she put one over on everyone!"

Rudy nodded. "C'mon, any more to the story?"

Dora hesitated, as if trying to remember everything she heard. "Well, I guess Rimsky told the police he's been receiving all kinds of valuable things since he took the job. It was Nora's idea to have the stuff shipped to the church as religious artifacts, so they could whiz past customs."

"Really? I wonder if Nora knew the samovars I was waiting for were the ones that had the gems. After all, it was the Dumkovskys who switched them."

Dora scratched her head and scrunched her brow. "You know, Goldie, I kept telling Nora we should give you a break. But she insisted on dragging me here every day to see if those samovars came in. It's funny, though, I really don't think she knew they had been switched. When we finally bought the one for dear old Father Innocent, she just left it in that pretty box you wrapped and handed it over to him."

"Well, if she did know, maybe she figured Rimsky would retrieve the stone and she would appear completely innocent. Whatever the rest of their plan was, it looks like they didn't count on the Dumkovsky brothers running their own game. That's when things really fell apart for them."

Rudy crossed his arms and leaned against a Victorian armoire. "Funny, ain't it, ladies? Sometimes things are goin' on right under yer nose an' ya haven't got a clue."

Dora nodded and gave a little sniff. "Yes, I always thought

she was my best friend. Boy, was I wrong. Now I'm just glad it's over, and we don't have to worry about who will be killed next."

"Yeah, we can finally get back to life as usual. Thanks for the information, Dora. I can't wait to tell my sister." They started to walk toward the door of the shop. "I'm glad you feel better. Sounds like your new priest will help sort out the mess and put your church back on its feet."

The woman turned in the doorway and said, "Father Inquisitive seems very efficient. Too bad he's not as handsome as poor Father Augustine. But, there is one thing that makes me happy."

"What's that, Dora?"

"With all of the rumors that started going around, I'm so glad it turned out that Father Innocent really was innocent!"

Goldie waved goodbye to Dora and realized one thing was making her happy right at that moment, too. She wouldn't have to deal with any more samovars. Ever.

Chapter 44

As the sun set on Clifton Bay, its colorful display turned the sky into a mango smoothie. A gentle Bahamian breeze kissed the broad deck of one of Lyford Cay's mini-mansions and wafted across the white sand beach. Two middle-aged men in Hawaiian shirts lounged in deck chairs beside the Jacuzzi sipping Pina Coladas.

Vladimir Minsky lifted his glass. "Uri, this is nice life, no?"

Uri Pinsky wiggled his bare toes. "*Da*, is good to be warming feet in Nassau, instead of freezing butt in Vladivostok."

Vladimir drained his drink and picked up a thick terry towel. "Karl will be here soon, so I think I go into house now. You are coming, also?"

A dreamy smile played on Uri's lips. "Not yet, Vlad. Six months we are here, and still I do not tire of watching sunset. You go, I come soon."

The short, paunchy man eased himself back into the deck chair. "You are right, I stay a little longer, too. Such a beautiful sight. Not like view Nora and Rimsky will have from jail window." He exploded in laughter.

Uri sighed and shook his head sadly. "They are so dumb, those two. Imagine my own sister and my stupid cousin thinking they will outsmart Uri and Vlad."

"Ha!" Vladimir clapped his hands loudly. "Little do they know those idiot Dumkovskys already had burned down warehouse. They try to double-cross all of us, poor fools!"

Uri sighed again. "*Chërt!* Our beautiful antiques, nothing but ashes." He slapped Minsky on the shoulder. "At first I am crying, but now, my friend, I am having last laugh."

As the sky darkened to an indigo blue, the two old friends went back into the house, arm-in-arm, to wait for Karl.

The buttons on Vladimir's flowered shirt strained across his belly, and his sandals slapped the marble floor as he traversed the entry hall to welcome their guest.

"Comrade Cherimenko, welcome to Bahamas," he said as he led the young man into a gaudy sitting room. Cherimenko's long, sun-bleached blond hair glistened under the crystal chandelier.

"Will you have a drink, Karl?" Uri rose from his chair and reached for a glass and a fresh bottle of vodka at the bar. "Tell me, have you heard anything about Alexei Korsakov?"

"Alexei? I hear he is enjoying hospitality of Russian jail. Newspapers claim he steals Seven Stars of Siberia. Chief of Antiquities thinks he killed young Cherimenko to get them. Seems they are finding body in Los Angeles airport Men's Room with my papers." Karl tapped his chest. "A toast to poor Cherimenko. So young to die!"

"To your death!" Minsky and Pinsky sang out in unison.

With all three glasses aloft, Cherimenko added, "By the way, I am now Karl Cook and have started lessons to get American accent, Dude. You like?"

Vladimir slapped him on the back. "Karl Cook, is good name. Very American, maybe we should do same."

"You are looking like lazy American surfer already," Uri added.

A deep tan highlighted Karl's sparkling teeth as his lips curved in a broad smile. "You have my money?"

"Of course. You deserve it. Without you this could not happen. Good thing you saw us escaping from burning warehouse."

Karl Cherimenko ran his fingers through his mop of hair.

"*Da. Da,* when stupid Dumkovskys set that fire, I am afraid all is lost until I see you two running from side of building."

Uri splashed more vodka in Karl's glass. "At first I am

thinking you will arrest us."

The young man smiled again. "Ah! That is what Alexei wants to do. But the minute I see you, I think this is my chance to get something for myself. I tell Alexei you must know where Seven Stars are, and we should get permission to track you so you will lead us to gems."

Vladimir laughed, his belly bobbing up and down like a huge bowl of Jell-O. "Was perfect partnership. We let those stupid *bolváns* find the gems for us. Was good you were able to convince Alexei to make government play our game, and pay reward to get gems back when we finding where they are. No one suspects you and when you turn gems over to us, already we have buyer lined up who has, how they say, big bucks. Now, all three of us are 'dead' and gone to heaven right here in Bahamas."

Uri feigned sadness. "Poor sister and cousin, not so much like heaven where they are." Then he and Vladmir had a good laugh.

Cherimenko nodded. "*Da*, and I do feel bad about stiff-necked old Alexei who is left, how you say, holding bag but not at all sad for Dumkovskys."

Vladimir Minsky opened another vodka bottle. "I will have a little more to drown sorrow."

Uri grunted as he got up, then removed a case from the hall closet containing enough money to ensure a life of luxury for the new Karl Cook. "So Karl, you didn't tell us. How you are managing to get Alexei to board plane, while you stay behind?"

The young man laughed. "He was so easy to fool. I am the one carrying gems. I tell him to go aboard first, check security. I will wait at end of line until he comes back to doorway and gives all-clear signal. I let him see me get in line and wait until he signals and goes back in plane. Then I leave. When, how you say, they button up plane and he realizes Karl and stones have disappeared, I wonder what he must think.

He touched his chest. "As for me, was easy. I go to Men's Room, where I put silencer on gun and wait. First man who comes in, he is young like me. I killing him, then shoot off his face. After I take his wallet, I put on him my identification papers!"

Uri chuckled. "And poof, you are dead. So, was good. After you are sending stones to us, we are selling to collector for big money."

He picked up the suitcase and handed it to Karl. "Here is your share, for good life—*dude*."

Karl checked the contents, nodded and closed the case. They all shook hands. Before he reached the door, Karl turned back toward Uri and Vladimir. "Was pleasure doing business with you, Comrades. Thanks to Romanoff's, we will all be rich. Is truly amazing how much seven shiny stones are worth."

Karl took two more steps, lurched forward, then clutched wildly at his stomach as the poisoned vodka took effect. After he fell face down on the marble floor, his handsome features contorted in a deathly grimace, Uri relieved him of the suitcase with the money.

"Yes, Comrade, and stones are worth even more when split only two ways."

A bonus for our loyal readers who have asked what a noodle kugel is:

The recipe for

Flossie's Fabulous Noodle Kugel

8oz. pkg. of Wide Egg Noodles
¼ lb Butter (melted) (margarine substitute optional)
1 cup Golden Raisins
3 Eggs (beaten)—(4 eggs optional)
4 heaping tablespoons Sour Cream
4 oz. Cream Cheese (softened and rolled into tiny balls)
½ cup Sugar (to taste) mix with a small amount of
 cinnamon for taste and color
1 cup Milk (a little more if you like it more moist)
Packaged cornflake crumbs (optional)

Mix all ingredients with cooked noodles that have been rinsed in cool water. Put in 8x10 (or similar size) Pyrex pan that has been greased with a little butter or margarine. Top with packaged cornflake crumbs (optional) and bake in preheated 350° oven for about an hour. Cool and cut into squares for serving. (You can double the recipe and freeze some, too.)

—Based on a recipe from the authors' mother, Rosetta.

Vanishing Act in Vegas

A Silver Sisters Mystery

Morgan St. James

Phyllice Bradner

Marina Publishing Group

Las Vegas NV 89141

www.marinapublishinggroup.com

Vanishing Act in Vegas

The Silver family gets a shock while attending Mara the Magnificent's show, when a stagehand dies during the performance. Police call it accidental, but Mara is convinced its murder. Torch told her about his family's uncanny ability to solve mysteries, so she begs them to investigate the death of her friend. They start to poke around in their clever but kooky fashion, and uncover an even bigger mystery. This time Flossie and Sterling take the lead and when they uncover a diabolical plot they come close to doing a disappearing act of their own!

For news, an interview with Flossie, and more, be sure to visit the SILVER SISTERS BLOG.
http://silversistersmysteries.wordpress.com

Read on for a sneak peak.

~Chapter 1~

A stocky woman wearing a tweed jacket, calf-length skirt and sensible shoes walked across the room, carefully avoiding the pool of blood. She craned her neck to get a better look at the crumpled body lying face down on an Oriental carpet. Lights flickered ominously, then went out, plunging the drawing room into complete darkness. All five guests froze, afraid to upset the crime scene.

The woman rummaged around in her plain black handbag, and produced a flashlight. As soon as she clicked it on, everyone gasped. The body was gone!

Flossie Silver snorted. "Looks like this one's going to be a load of hogwash, Godiva. Who thinks up such goofy plots?"

Godiva Olivia DuBois threw her hands in the air and said, "Oh calm down, Mom, give her a chance. You know they always open with something dramatic. They need a real zinger, so they can wind up to that 'aha' moment when Mabel figures it all out. That's what makes it so much fun."

Flossie clicked her tongue. "Fun, schmun, I don't buy it. The lights were out for less than a minute. Are we supposed to believe someone got in there and hauled the body away that quick?"

"Making that body disappear in a minute isn't such a big deal," Uncle Sterling grumbled. Didn't my brother Harry make you disappear every night when we did our vaudeville act?"

"Yeah, but I was alive! Dead people don't cooperate that well, Smartie Pants."

Sterling grabbed the remote and turned up the volume. "Pipe down, old girl. How are we supposed to see if this thing is worth watching, if you keep yapping? Isn't that right, Godiva?"

Whenever they watched *Mabel McBride's Murder and Mayhem* it triggered lively discussions between Godiva's eighty-one-year-old mother and uncle. The oldsters tried to analyze the plots

1

and devices, but usually wound up bickering and badgering each other. Even Godiva, who wrote a syndicated advice column, couldn't come up with a good suggestion for harmony in her own family.

While Mabel McBride poked around the drawing room looking for clues, Flossie, Sterling and Godiva settled back in their cushy leather armchairs, eyes focused on the big screen TV in the corner of the mansion's massive family room. Just as the British detective located a scrap of torn fabric, Godiva's son Torch blasted in.

"Whoa! Are you three still watching that show? I thought it was only on for an hour. I swear, you guys are addicted to those stuffy British mysteries."

Godiva gave him a hug. "It's a *Murder Marathon*, honey. Four in a row. This is the last one. Grandma and Uncle Sterling are having a hot debate about whether this one has any merit."

Torch shrugged. "I know the answer to that one."

The commercial came on, and Sterling turned off the sound. "Torch, you have no appreciation for good old-fashioned acting. If things don't crash or burn or blow up, then they're just not worth anything to you."

"You got that right, Unk. Face it, I'm an FX man. That's how I make my living. You, of all people, should appreciate that. After all, you gave me my nickname."

"Damn near burned the garage down when you were a kid. It's hard to believe they pay you to do that now."

"Yeah, I can't believe I've made enough money to actually buy my own place in Las Vegas. I'm gonna miss living here on the 'old homestead' with you guys, but that's where the job is. You know I'll come back here to visit when I can."

Torch had landed a contract as Special Effects Director with the hit show *Las Vegas Blowout*. Like so many of the hip Hollywood crowd, he immediately bought a condo in a new luxury high rise with fantastic views of the Strip.

Before heading out, he looked around at the Beverly Hills mansion built by his late father, self-made millionaire Max DuBois.

He winked at Godiva. "Well, Mom, I'm about to become a swinging bachelor. Great gig, great job and things happening twenty-four-seven. The last of my stuff is loaded and I just wanted to say goodbye before I take off."

She kissed him on the cheek, sensing that her son couldn't wait to leave the nest and spread his wings.

Sterling turned the sound back on, but Flossie grabbed the remote and turned it off again. She looked at her grandson and smiled sweetly. "So, *tottelah*, your Uncle Sterling and I will be there in two, maybe three days. You know your uncle is afraid to fly, so we'll just tune up the Caddy tomorrow and be on our way."

"Whaa–?" Torch stared at her blankly.

"Torch, honey, you'll need help getting things in order, and no one does that better than your Uncle Sterling and me. I'll set up your closets and kitchen, and cook some good Jewish meals for your freezer. Uncle Sterling can putter around and help you hang pictures and do little odd jobs."

Torch looked to his mother in desperation.

Flossie jumped up and tweaked him on the cheek. "Look, Sterling, he's so happy we're coming he's speechless. Good thing you bought a three bedroom. I guess we'll stay for three or four days. Who knows, maybe longer if we get lucky. Magic acts are big in Vegas again."

Sterling punched the remote and turned up the sound on *Mabel McBride*.

Torch choked out, "Mom-m-m—"

Excerpt from Vanishing Act in Vegas

About The Authors

Sisters MORGAN ST. JAMES and PHYLLICE BRADNER teamed up to write the Silver Sisters Mystery series, featuring identical twins somewhat based upon their own personalities. The cast of regular characters was inspired by zany family members and friends. Each book in this series stands on its own. *A Corpse in the Soup,* the debut book in the series, was named Best Mystery Audio Book by USA Book News.

Both sisters have marketing backgrounds and are vigorous self-promoters. They have become best friends through writing the Silver Sisters Mysteries series. Watch for many more Silver Sisters escapades in the future.

Morgan St. James

Former interior designer, MORGAN ST. JAMES lives in Las Vegas with her rescue dog Dylan, She is on the board of Writers of Southern Nevada and belongs to multiple writers' groups. In addition to the Silver Sisters series, she collaborates with other writers in addition to writing her own novels and short stories. Morgan frequently appears on the radio, author's panels and is an entertaining speaker. She even co-narrated an episode of A Crime to Remember on Discovery ID Channel. Published short stories include contributions to three Chicken Soup for the Soul books, many anthologies including the single author anthology *The Mafia Funeral and Other Short Stories. S*he gives workshops at writers' conferences and has written 16 books and over 600 published articles on diverse subjects.

Visit www.morganstjames-author.com

http://writerstricksofthetrade.blogspot.com

Phyllice Bradner

After living in Alaska for many years, PHYLLICE, an award-winning graphic designer, fine artist, and published writer, who formerly owned an antique shop in Juneau, moved to a quaint 100 year old house in McMinnville, Oregon.

She has been a political print consultant for campaigns including four gubernatorial races and five candidates for U.S. Senate.

Over the years Phyllice has won four Alaska Press Club awards and two National awards for newsletter publications. She is the co-author of *Juneau Centennial Cookbook* and *Touring Juneau.*

Phyllice works out of her own art studio, and is a co-owner of the Currents Art Gallery in McMinnville, Oregon.

Visit www.bradnerartstudio.com

Silver Sisters Mysteries

A FAST-PACED, FUNNY MYSTERY SERIES
By Morgan St. James and Phyllice Bradner

If you would like to be included on the master email list to receive updates and announcements regarding the series, including release notices of upcoming books, purchase specials and more, please

Subscribe to eMail List

http://eepurl.com/cG3sfj

Made in the USA
San Bernardino, CA
18 January 2020